THE
DARLING
KILLERS

THE
DARLING
KILLERS

*Sarah
McCarry*

This paperback edition first published by
Macaulay, Abernathy, & Winter 2022

ISBN 979-8-218-06268-2

for meg p. clark, who gets all my donna jokes

Tell me about a complicated man.

—*The Odyssey, tr. Emily Wilson*

art is nice but the question is how are you
making money

—*Morgan Parker*

It all seems ridiculous now, but I was
younger then.

—*Mikhail Bulgakov*

The Door to the Garden

The story I am about to tell you happened a long time ago, but Alison's memory remains written into my everyday. The tea she taught me to drink in the yellow mug that once hung from a hook over her kitchen counter; her clothes, silk and leather and soft cashmere, hanging in my closet; her books intermingled on the shelf with my own. I find her notes in the margins, peacock-blue ink in her straggling, crabbed hand; the lines she marked and the pages she dog-eared to return to later.

It's Alison's eye that picked out the paintings in my apartment, the creamy walls and jewel-colored carpets; her hand that arranged the sprawling jungle of greenery that tumbles from end tables and windowsills; her touch that revels in my soft linen sheets and thick-piled rugs, the leather spines of the antique editions of my beloved classics.

My life, patterned ever after hers, because she was the first person to show me what her kind of life could be.

I was there the night she died. I was there for Jaxson's party and its aftermath, the clamor of guests gone bacchanal from such delirious proximity to a sudden death; the flashing lights; the sirens; the police. I remember a lone EMT standing in front of Jaxson's bookshelves, reaching to touch the spines with one finger, her purpose there momentarily forgotten. I remember the blood pooling around Alison's dark hair, her mouth parted, her dulled eyes open and looking past me at whatever it is the dead see first and are unwilling or unable to report to the living.

What flashes would have sparked in the final seconds of her swan dive, if that tired old saw is true? Alison behind the wheel of her car, hair twisting in the wind. Alison as a girl in the desert, white sun burning its radiant signature into her skin. Alison trying on perfume in a tiny store full of glass bottles, lifting the pale inside of her wrist to her nose. Alison peeling an orange in her kitchen, the late-morning light falling around her in radiant sheets and gilding the curve of her lower lip.

Alison, Alison, Alison. I loved her then, you know. Despite what I'm about to tell you, I love her still.

I wrote it all down, Alison, I say when I find her in my dreams. *That's what makes it real.*

She is a few steps ahead of me in her white dress, one hand on the knob, halfway out the door already.

Maybe, she says. *But that doesn't make it true.*

PART ONE

Before the Fall

1.

Muse, let the memories spill through me, as Jaxson liked to say before he told us a story. I loved Jaxson, too, back then; I loved him first, and most of all, and nearly up until the end. Jaxson—Jaxson!

Even now I cannot entirely unsee the man he was when first I met him: that great golden bell of a voice; that low, easy laugh; that careless grace. That hair, those eyes, those hands. It was almost too much gift for one person, that ruinous, reason-crushing charm. I defy the strongest among you to withstand the twinkling arrow of his gaze, the wry quirk of his mouth. O reader! our Jaxson, hero out of yesteryear's fables, noble warrior on the battlefield of love and language—you think I exaggerate, but I was not the first or least to fall, and my heart is harder than most.

To be a writer, he told us, *is to name the truth at the heart of every fable*. Everything he said fell upon us with the weight of his seasoned wisdom, his noble bearing, the strength of his *book*—god, that book—and though his writerly peers also knew among them great success—bestseller lists and speaking engagements and diversity panels and keynote lectures at conferences attended by thousands of housewives and librarians and enthrallèd teens, serial television deals and film options, the numbers of producers and media moguls in their contacts—none of them had written a book like Jaxson's, and all of them knew it.

If you'd read that book, Jaxson's book, you'd have loved him too. But now I am getting ahead of my story.

First, then, dear reader: how Alison and I came to be. *Idle youth, enslaved to everything; by being too sensitive I have wasted my life.*

I was born in the high blue-green hills that ring the shores of Lake Lucerne, a destination resort for wealthy Europeans who zip up and down ski slopes and portly, ruddy-faced New Jersey retirees booking boozy cruise tours of the turquoise-chip lake. My father was a lesser secretary at the American embassy in Basel, my mother an Italian ex-model who entranced him in one of the nightclubs into which he had stumbled one evening, dazed by Swiss wealth and Swiss women, soon after moving to the city. My unexpected—and most likely unwanted—arrival provoked an unwelcome entrée into an adulthood both of my parents had managed successfully to avoid until that point, and as soon as I was old enough to tie my own shoes, they shuttled me off to a succession of second-rate and fungible boarding schools on the East Coast. Squash matches, green fields in summer, Latin (long since forgotten), ponytailed girls chasing a soccer ball, their woolen skirts rolled up to expose a forbidden extra inch of knee.

My parents were killed in a car crash when I was thirteen years old. By then I had seen almost nothing of them for a long time outside of the occasional winter

holiday. They had not been wealthy, but they were a little better at money than they were at child-rearing, and
there was enough left tucked away in a trust to see me
through one last shabby old school before I was left to
my own devices.

I had no family and only one friend, but it did not
occur to me to be lonely, because I had Wendy, and I
had books. I was partial, for obvious reasons, to stories
of impoverished orphans miraculously revealed as heirs to
fortune and love, self-made tycoons magicking over their
sordid histories, self-reliant loners who lived by their wits:
neglected and noble Sara Crewe in her garret; Gatsby
and his façade managed out of ice and water; the Artful
Dodger and his nimble fingers; Peter Pan, *gay and innocent
and heartless.* And I could imagine no fate more wondrous
than that of Bastian Balthazar Bux, tumbled into the
many-splendored world of Fantastica, traveler inside the
ouroboros of a story without beginning and, more marvelous, without end.

(And Wendy—

I think I'll tell you about her later.)

I left school with nothing other than a head full of
books, a knack for forging teachers' signatures, and a
beautiful copperplate hand—an utterly useless skill set in
an online world. I had not bothered to apply to college,
having no idea what line of study I might pursue, and my
parents' money was nearly gone. I dreamed of becoming a
librarian, a job that seemed to me a placid continuation of
my life thus far: a quiet, solitary profession in some ma-
jestic, gabled building of crumbling, ivy-wreathed stone,

reading the classics (the *Classics*) at an old oak desk. Cellos, dark windowpanes, snow.

Instead:

I didn't know a thing about Los Angeles, but I'd read about it in books. Pale slabs of light moving across the heaving sea; hot sun-whitened streets; the chlorinated blue of swimming pools; long strips of exhaust-soaked asphalt ribboning under the wheels of a convertible with the top rolled down. Pretty girls in pretty dresses, poolside parties, washed-up actors and weary-eyed dames who carried pistols in their handbags and secrets in their hearts. I had spent most of my life in cold places and had never seen the Pacific—the Pacific, not that ancient, sullen grey monster, the Atlantic of whaling ships and Nantucket and sou'westers, but a great aquamarine wonderland, home of surfers and rum cocktails and baby-oiled skin baking on white-sand beaches. California was as real to me as the surface of Venus.

I used the cash I had left to buy a battered old Toyota, packed the trunk with books, said goodbye to Wendy, and headed south and west. I had never felt so free or so alone as in the days it took me to find my new city. Truck-stop coffee and night skies bottomless with stars, the white salt flats of Nevada, a fever dream of cacti and canyons and the unending freeway. The days blending into a blur of sweat and sunlight until I crossed over into California, where palm trees sprouted out of the dull earth like beacons and the yellow rise of the mountains swallowed the horizon. I drove straight through the skyscrapers of downtown Los Angeles until I could drive no farther west, because I had come to the ocean. The sky was pale as the white of an eye that day, the light hard on the water, but I didn't care. I had come home.

I slept in my car until I found a studio apartment for sublet in Hollywood whose legitimate tenant was willing to take payment each month in cash and did not ask questions. Hollywood! the name alone, at first, offset the apartment's decrepitude, the sad, shambling drunks that pushed shopping carts full of cans and garbage bags down the boulevard, the shuttered theaters, but I soon realized the magic was cheap gilt on a rotten frame. The apartment was close-walled and sordid, the dirt of tenants long gone tracked permanently into the decaying grout of the bathroom tiles and the seam around the tiny metal sink in the kitchenette. I did not meet any handsome and generous celebrities. I was not invited to the cocktail parties I'd imagined while hurtling westward. I did not stumble upon debauched nights in downtown hotels haunted by movie stars lingering over martinis decades after their deaths. For a long time, I did not speak to anyone at all other than the woman who resided with her junk-stuffed, environmentally friendly plastic tote in the parking lot of the liquor store down the street.

It took a while to find a job that suited my plan, and it was only thanks to a delicious trick of fate—a castaway line in an online post—that I ended up at the Blissfulle Beane, a coffee shop in Echo Park. I did not mind the work, although it was the kind of employment charming only to a bright-eyed girl with a dithery temperament, one-word mantras (BREATHE) tattooed in delicate script on her rib cage, and ambitions of acting. It was not the kind of place one would ordinarily want to wash up for longer than a scatter of months until one's ship came in.

Everyone who worked at the Beane was nearly as young as me, except for the owner, Rob, a balding old hippie who scraped his straggling hair into a thin ponytail and who wore tropical-print shirts and hemp necklaces dangling blown-glass mushroom pendants. I was the only one of his nubile fledglings who showed up on time nine mornings out of ten, who bothered to run the espresso machine with the toxic white powder that cleaned out coffee residue, who split the tips fairly and made the bank drop instead of forgetting the cash bag on the counter next to the warming milk delivery, and so Rob grudgingly paid me in cash every week and kept his complaints, for the most part, to himself. In return I palmed fives and tens out of the cash drawer on nights I counted the till and waited patiently for the life I'd come out west for to begin.

Which it did, exactly as I'd hoped, if not at all in the way I'd planned.

2.

It was an ordinary morning in late September, cool and clear, when I first saw Jaxson in the flesh. I could've sworn the breeze smelled of salt and sunlight, no matter how far off the ocean lay, and as I unlocked the Beane's door for the morning and set out the milk pitchers and warmed up the espresso machine, I felt for the first time on the verge of making a life for myself. The morning rush was steady but manageable, the regulars friendly. Some of them already knew my name.

And then I looked up from my work, and my heart lurched in my chest like a drunk.

Jaxson was—is—as beautiful in person as in press photographs, as unlikely as that sounds. He has always had about him that ineffable combination of innate charisma and inhuman good looks that charges an entire room with the certainty of his importance, a quality that is not so much an aspect of appearance as a tangible physical force. His eyes blue as glass chips on a beach, his mane a golden tangle spilling to his shoulders, his surfer's lean and muscled build evident even under the butter-soft biker jacket he went around in regardless of the weather. He had on black jeans, fitted but not effete, and he wore a pair of beautiful

Italian motorcycle boots with carefully applied wear at the toes and along the lines where the leather rippled at the ankle joint. His sinewy forearms were snaked with intricate tattoos; his voice had a gravelly note in it that suggested women known and whiskey drunk. He wore mirrored aviator glasses, which he pushed up now in order to look at me. His eyes were kind and laughing.

"You're new," he said.

I could only nod.

"Just an Americano, please. To stay."

I nodded again and turned to the machine. My hands were shaking. His face had hit me like a sucker punch. The door jangled again, and he looked up with a smile that only worsened the carnage.

"Hey, Als," he said.

The woman he'd greeted was small-boned, radiantly pretty, in a loose black dress and sweater and stylish black ankle boots, her glossy dark hair pulled into a messy topknot. She stood on tiptoe to greet him, but he still had to bow his head for her kiss to reach his cheek.

I gave him his coffee, and he turned that smile on me. I still couldn't speak, counting out his change in silence, my fingers brushing his broad palm with the coins. He put them in the tip jar and took his coffee to a table by the window, and the woman he'd called Als smiled at me, too. A third woman came in, older than the first; more cheeks were kissed, more coffee was ordered, bags were unpacked at the table Jaxson had chosen, and they settled into their labors.

I didn't know it yet, but their habits—Judith, the older woman; Alison, the younger; Jaxson, the lion attended to by his doting pride—were as metronomic as those of elderly people. They met almost every Tuesday and Thursday morning at eleven, after the early morning rush had dissipated. Judith and Alison carried identical laptops in a series of nearly identical tote bags screened with the logos of publishers and bookstores. Unlike Alison and Judith, Jaxson wrote longhand, with a nib pen and a bottle of ink, in a series of dog-eared old notebooks with the covers half-worn.

I would have noticed Alison and Judith even if they had been perfectly ordinary, because they were with him, but they were no such thing. Judith was magnificently fit and smooth-skinned, her long, straight hair of a rich, burnished gold-brown that was so expensive, it looked natural. She preferred leisurewear, the sorts of vacuum-sealed, vented yoga tights and sloganed tanks that signaled someone who'd just come from an upscale boutique rather than an exercise class. She was not beautiful, but she had an excellent dermatologist.

Alison had dark hair and sharp, angular features (her mother, I learned much later, had died shortly after she was born under suspicious circumstances, her father a violent and alcoholic Mormon; she'd run away to New York on her sixteenth birthday and never spoken to him again). She often wore the same sorts of clothes as Judith but was just as likely to show up in some shapeless, complicated mass of black fabric folded in on itself or draped in elaborate pleats like a television-show toga. Somehow these garments resolved themselves around her delicate limbs in a manner cloudlike rather than ridiculous. But despite her smiles and warmth and what I think was genuine kindness, there was something absent about her. Her manner was not artificial but neither was it artless. And behind the proscenium of her affect there was, I sensed, another play unfolding, unknowable in its complexities and mysterious in its action.

They were as exotic to me then as the luminous figures who populated the dreamscapes of my childhood: Raymond Chandler gnawing at his pipestem, Hemingway and his rifle, Edward Gorey asleep amid a luxury of cats. Once I learned their routine, my weeks orbited the twin stars of their morning dates. I was careful with my hair and makeup, wore only my favorite shirts. I couldn't afford new clothes, but I did my best. I memorized their coffee orders and their mannerisms. They liked to sit at the same table by the window whenever they came in, and I took to shooing people away from it around a quarter to eleven, to ensure it would be available. I showered and shaved my legs on Tuesday and Thursday mornings even though the opening shift began at five a.m. I was cautious with them, friendly but not too friendly—although looking at Jaxson over the counter felt like walking into a brick wall; when he placed his coffee order, I wanted to chew through his clothes—cheerful but not bubbly, polite but not obsequious. I was desperate for them to like me, certain it didn't show.

I was, as I think I've mentioned, very, very young.

Oddly enough, out of the three of them, Alison soon became my favorite. Judith ordered her nonfat-half-caf-sugar-free-extra-foam-vanilla latte week after week with a dead-eyed stare that suggested she had never seen me before in her life; Jaxson made me so nervous, I dropped his change half the time, even though he always told me with a wink just to put it in the tip jar; but Alison was human. She had a habit of greeting me in a soft purr with her head cocked that made me feel as though her hello contained other multitudes—*it's good to see you* and *how are you* really *though* and *don't you look pretty this morning* and *thank you for always remembering* extra *ice*. She was the first of them to learn my name and use it.

And though both Judith and Jaxson wrote with a concentration that could be unnerving, it was Alison whose ferocity of attention gathered a palpable charge around her as she worked. She could peck away furiously at her laptop for hours without pausing. When she was done, she would slap the computer shut, sit up straight, and blink at the real and breathing world as though she were only just returned from a stranger and far more elegant country.

I did not know her last name or anything else about her, and so her work remained an enigma to me, but the way she wrote seemed to me, in my limited experience, the *correct* manner, as if her tablet were only a portal and she a traveler who moved about in a land brighter in its colors and more vivid in its passions.

Ironic, of course, since out of the three of them, she was by far the least successful.

Jaxson said, when I knew him better, that he'd chosen the Beane because of its anonymity. He was famous enough after the movie came out that he could not frequent a popular or hip café in some more mediagenic neighborhood without being besieged by a heckle of his public demanding selfies snapped at his side—though really, a dedicated fan could have found him even at my humble place of employ.

He was not so discreet as he thought about where he liked to work, and I think his impulse to divulge was rooted in an unspoken desire to be sought out by someone who loved him enough to sift through his chatter for the trail of bread crumbs it concealed.

I believed then—and believe still, all these years later—that what drives writers like Jaxson is a fundamental longing to be seen. I have watched him field countless queries about his books with the professional veneer of an actor—on his craft, on the source of his ideas, on his process, on whether he can help with homework assignments—enquiries for which he has ready-made answers smooth and well-worn as a stone at the bottom of a river.

But, every now and then, at a party or in the melee after an event, some enterprising interlocutor will find a question—intimate, personal, wise—that Jaxson has never heard before, a question that shows both a deep under-standing of and a profound respect for the work, a question that manages to be both subtly flattering and genuinely insightful, and I will watch, from across the room, as Jaxson comes alive, his face radiant with pleasure.

What greater magic is there than to name the thing within you that finds an echoed home in another heart? What greater gift than to have that matched desire acknowledged?

A writer is a person who hides out of a longing to be found.

3.

It took me a long time to work up the nerve to say anything to the writers beyond facile commentary on the weather, the books they were reading, their coffee. I was dazzled by Jaxson, intimidated by Judith and Alison. I'd spent most of my life in books, not trying to get at the people who made them; it had not occurred to me until relatively recently that a writer was a sort of person one might encounter in the real world.

I found my way in one rainy Thursday afternoon. The café was almost empty, the sky outside glowering and ominous. They were at their usual table by the window. I knew their moods well by then and could tell they were having trouble working. Judith checked her phone every five minutes; Jaxson's hand was splayed on the page before him, his fingers tapping restlessly; even Alison stared listlessly out the window, chewing on her straw as though she would have preferred a cigarette. I wiped tables that were already clean, drifting into orbit until I could overhear their low conversation.

"Now you're thinking of falling back on a retelling?" That was Judith, her voice skeptical.

"I don't know," Jaxson said. "Celia liked what I sent her, but it's still rough. Needs a skeleton to hang the flesh on."

"I'm always happy to help you put together something—"

"I like the one with the locked-up wife," Jaxson said, ignoring her.

"*Jane Eyre*?" Judith said. "That's been done a million times."

"It's been done because it's good," Jaxson said. "Celia thinks there's still a big market for retellings."

"Celia knows you can do whatever you want," Judith said. "Some of us have to find more *commercial* plots."

"There are plenty of classics that haven't been done, though," Alison interrupted. "There's all of Dickens. Or *Northanger Abbey*. That would make a funny send-up of supernatural romance. You could do a girl who thinks she's headed into a high school full of vampires, but really it's all in her head—"

"Vampires are dead," Judith said. "Even for Jaxson."

Alison continued as if she hadn't heard. "Or that one with the orphan girl who passes herself off as an English teacher in France and falls in love with a professor—"

"I love *Villette*," I said. They turned as one to look at me. There was a long, pained silence.

"So," Judith said. "It speaks."

I blushed. "Sorry, I didn't mean to eavesdrop, I just..." I dunked my bleach rag in its bucket, resisting the impulse to crawl under a table.

"Don't be sorry," Alison said. "It's Sofia, isn't it?"

"Yeah," I said bashfully.

"There won't be much of a market for a retelling if nobody's heard of the book," Judith said.

Alison gave her a look. "It's *Brontë*, Judith."

"We read it in school," I said. "You're all—you're—writers?"

"That's what they tell me," Jaxson said with a wry, winning smile.

"Me too," I blurted.

Even now, after all this time, I don't know what prompted me to say it. I'd written things—silly papers for school, tearstained adolescent journals, reams of poetry long since lost, thank god, to the ravages of time. As a child, I'd filled a notebook with a long, convoluted narrative about a team of cat detectives that I proudly referred to as my "novel."

But a *writer*—a writer was something else entirely, some unattainable, otherworldly mix of alchemist and seer and sage; I would have sooner called myself a sea-captain or billionaire or the president of the United States, for those callings I understood as belonging to mortal beings and thus at least in theory accessible to me as career paths. It was a statement uttered out of impulse, not design.

As you will see, it proved quite fateful.

"Everyone thinks they're a writer," Judith said, rolling her eyes, and turned back to her computer. Certain I had committed some inexcusable offense, I retreated, bleach bucket in hand, to the counter. A few seconds later, the murmur of their voices resumed.

Shortly after that, Judith and Jaxson clanged out the door, leaving Alison to collect her things from their table with a thoughtful look on her face.

"Sorry about that," she said. It was a moment before I understood that she was speaking to me.

"About what?"

"Judith." She gestured at the chair the older woman had occupied. "She can be prickly."

"I hadn't noticed," I said untruthfully.

"She doesn't mean it, she just…" She trailed off. Judith had clearly meant it. "I'll have one more latte. To go this time. Iced with—"

"I know what you drink," I said, more sharply than I had intended.

I poured almond milk over ice and espresso for her. She pulled the elastic band from her hair, shaking loose the dark waves, and gave me a hesitant smile as I handed the cup to her.

"You have a good memory."

"Most people always get the same thing."

She nodded as though I had said something profound about human nature. Outside, a sudden crack of thunder boomed across the darkening sky, and the rain increased to a downpour. "Goodness," she said, peering out the window. "It's like New York out there."

I did not know how to respond to this. "It doesn't usually rain like that here," I said, unsure if I was agreeing with her.

She looked over her shoulder at me. "You seem like someone who belongs somewhere else, Sofia."

"It's slower going than I thought it would be."

That won a smile. "I'm Alison, by the way. Alison Keene." She put out her hand, and I shook it as gravely as a banker.

"The three of you come here a lot."

"Jaxson and Judith live in Pacific Palisades, but I make them come to civilization for writing group. And I like the light."

I knew what she meant. Slow mornings at the coffee shop were the only moments I could tolerate my job: thick, buttery light falling through the windows and pooling on the terracotta-tiled floor, softening the garish coral walls to the color of weather-beaten adobe.

"You live out there, too?"

"Oh, god, no. I live in Silver Lake. But Jaxson likes being anonymous, so he doesn't mind the drive."

I hesitated, deciding what to say I knew. "He's famous?"

She gave me an odd look. "Extremely. *The Bone Girl*?"

"I don't know it."

"Really," she said, looking at me with new interest; my instinct had been correct. "That's refreshing. What do you read, then, besides *Villette*? And how did you end up in Los Angeles?"

I had a line or two, dry as dust mites, that I offered up to strangers who queried my origins in an effort to solicit companionship or sex. But, for Alison, I cocked one hip against the counter and bypassed my usual pat summary for the longer version. Not the whole story, just the more luscious bits: dissolute childhood, poshly distant mother, tragic orphancy, and lonely boarding-school adolescence.

Alison's eyes were wide by the time I'd finished. "Wow," she said. "It's like something out of Fitzgerald."

"Yes," I said, pleased. "It is, isn't it?"

"And now? What do you write? Anything published?"

I looked down at my hands reflexively: skin cracked and dried from the bleach bucket, coffee grounds under my stubby nails and staining the faint webbing across the backs of my fingers. "No," I said, embarrassed.

"That's all right, you're young," she said. "You've got ages ahead of you to worry about that."

"I'm working on a novel," I said.

"Are you really? How brave of you." It would have been bitchy coming from anyone else.

"Anyway," I said, self-conscious now. "I think the rain is stopping."

She looked out the window again and took a long sip of her drink. "I'd better be going. It was lovely talking to you." I was overcome by a terrible desire to detain her somehow. "I don't get to meet people who don't know who Jaxson is very often," she said. "It's a bit of a treat, to be honest."

"Serendipitous," I blurted. She paused, half-turned from me already. I wanted to reach out and grab her shoulder. "The rainstorm, I mean. It was serendipitous."

She smiled at me. "Wasn't it? You know, if you wanted to get coffee sometime…"

"Oh," I said, hardly able to believe my luck. "Really? I *do*. I mean—that would be great. Super great." *Super great.* I wanted to kick myself in the teeth.

"Then it's settled. Why don't you give me your number?"

"All right," I said, hiding my elation with difficulty as I scribbled my number on the back of a guest check and handed it to her. She tucked the paper into her purse and smiled at me again.

"See you soon, Sofia."

"See you soon." I watched the lovely muscles of her back move as she opened the glass door and went out of the Blissfulle Beane into the petrichor-scented streets, half-certain I would never see any of them again.

But I did. And that was how everything else began.

4.

I was as nervous and elated that rain-damped night as if I'd given my number to a crush at school. I hovered over my phone, checking every ten seconds to be certain it was charged and on. Alison didn't call, not that night or the night after and not the night after that; she didn't come into the café, either (not that she ever had without Jaxson and Judith, but still I took it as a sign that I had done or said something unforgivably banal, frightened her off; she'd come to regret the offer, the exchange, my entire existence; I'd well and truly blown it, I'd never see her again, I'd have to start over—a great many other thoughts in this vein).

On Tuesday I shooed loiterers away from the writers' usual table and checked my hair in the Beane's tiny bathroom, my heart racing. But eleven came and went, and then eleven fifteen, and eleven thirty, and hope sagged forlornly in my chest when I finally admitted around noon that they weren't coming in. They had missed the occasional day before, but this seemed particularly ill-omened.

I carefully went over everything I'd said to Alison, scrutinizing the conversation for clues as to my offense. I was certain I had done or said something so off-putting or humiliating that I did not even recognize it as the gesture that had decided them against me. I remembered Judith's eye roll, a time I'd been overly enthusiastic when handing Jaxson his coffee, a compliment I'd given Alison that might have come across as insincere or obsequious. Somehow, they had seen me as a phony, a sycophantic toady, a *fan*. The corners of my eyes stung hotly with tears, and I dashed them away with a furious hand, refusing to look toward the door. I could quit. I'd quit. I'd find another job somewhere else in a cheaper city. I'd forget all about him. I'd disappear again.

It doesn't matter, I told myself. I'd landed on my feet before, hadn't I? *It doesn't matter.*

But it did.

And so, I went looking for them the only way I knew how.

5.

I'd spent much of my early life in the reading rooms of libraries or curled in an inconspicuous corner with a battered paperback—whatever I could scrounge up from donation boxes or pocket in the checkout lines at the supermarket, books I found in Laundromats and bus stops and yard sales. I'd read with a voracity that undergirded my appetites in all other things: first food and freedom, later for sex, drugs, and shucking my pasts like dead skin. When I was young, I believed you could stockpile experience. But, of course, you can't hoard anything that really matters, which is why it's so easy to always want more.

I never told Alison, but it wasn't just literary orphans who snared me. I'd loved, too, Danielle Steele and Jackie Collins, Anne Rice and Daphne du Maurier: a wondrous mélange of monsters and ambition, dashing businessmen and dapper vampires, cocktails and starry nights, sad rich girls and fast cars and mean-eyed men gentled by a heroine's charms.

I'd learned early through books, too, that a different sort of sorrow plagued the wealthy. Boredom, indolence, lost romantic opportunities, too much drink—a set of weights upon the soul that struck me as far lovelier than my own humdrum woes. I didn't know anything about rich people then; I thought people who had money had earned it through difference, some remarkable set of qualities that set them magically apart from those of us who took out other people's garbage and smiled for a living.

This illusion, of course, is only material from a distance. It takes little time in proximity to understand that no one is stupider or less deserving than the very rich. Worse, no one puts money to less interesting use.

The local branch of the public library was only a few blocks' walk from the studio. When my turn at the computer came, I entered Alison's name into a search engine. Alison Keene brought up a few short stories published years ago and a forlorn, single-page website with a younger Alison staring broodily out of a black-and-white photograph. There was no biography, only an all-caps COMING SOON where text should be and a Hotmail address. She had published one novel a decade earlier, a modernized retelling of Medea's story, which had received several glowing reviews and then vanished completely into the ether. I tried other spellings of her name and found only an Allison Kiehn, personal chef and nutrition counselor, with blinding white teeth.

Judith, by contrast, yielded reams of information: interviews, tour dates, television deal announcements, press photos, charity fundraisers, book festivals. Her young adult novels focused on the adventures of a rogue princess engaged in a desperate—and, I thought, distinctly Oedipal—battle with her despot father. The princess had been radicalized when she fell for a household servant who belonged to a caste her father wished to exterminate; dramatics ensued. The princess must have had rather a lot of problems to make them stretch out over six books and an attendant suite of electronic novellas written from the perspectives of various minor characters in the series. Judith's author photo was professionally taken but nevertheless had a vacant, Xanaxed look about the eyes.

Lastly, I pulled up an article about Jaxson, a *New York Times* profile from a year ago: "The World Waits, Breathless, for a Second Masterpiece." The photograph was of Jaxson at home, reclining in a leather armchair next to a massive mahogany desk piled high with volumes, his hair spilling over his toned shoulders, his black Henley unbuttoned just enough to hint at the generous musculature of his cleavage, his blue eyes piercing and grave. Behind him a set of French doors revealed an azure chunk of sea. A hint of a smile played at the corner of his mouth.

PACIFIC PALISADES, Calif. —Growing up on Long Island, Jaxson Dace took to water before he took to books. "I learned to swim before I learned to walk," Mr. Dace, 42, says in his distinctive baritone. "The writing thing came much later."

We should all acquire our gifts so late in life. Mr. Dace's first novel, *The Bone Girl*, is an international bestseller and remained at #1 on the *New York Times* bestseller list for an unheard-of 131 consecutive weeks. The film version of the novel, starring model Minna Perkonnen and up-

and-coming ingenue Laila Berkowski, grossed nearly $2 billion worldwide, beating out even the Harry Potter franchise juggernaut at the box office. A cerebral and gothic story of love and death with references ranging from Norse mythology to Grimms' fairy tales, the novel is something of an outlier when it comes to young adult blockbusters. *The Bone Girl* focuses not on the improbable vampire romances or bleak dystopias of most bestselling teen fiction but the close bond between two sisters born to bitter parents in an imaginary kingdom. Though the siblings encounter such archetypal set pieces as a dashing, evil sorcerer, an enchanted wood, and a glass mountain, their relationship is depicted in language that is startlingly fresh and inventive.

"No one was more surprised by the book's success than I was," laughs Mr. Dace warmly. In person, he is tall and fit, with a manner both courteous and unpretentious. "I was just some surfer sitting in a room by myself with a pile of notebooks for years. I never thought anybody would read it but me."

Luckily for Mr. Dace, the legendary editor Celia van der Waals, whose stable of writers includes a roster of household names, disagreed. "The talent just leaps off the page," she said over the phone in a recent interview. "He's extraordinary. I've never worked with a writer like him." Ms. van der Waals, profiled in this newspaper earlier this year, has an uncanny knack for picking out fresh talent, and her editorial oversight is a virtual guarantee of a book's critical and commercial success. As publisher and editorial director of a children's imprint at Forsyth and Montpelier, she has overseen dozens of rags-to-riches stories among young adult authors, including Barry Koople, Judith St. Clair Montserrat, and breakout star Brendan Faylor, whose debut novel *She, Her, and Me* Ms. van der Waals acquired for a rumored seven-figure advance. Mr. Dace notes that several of Ms. van der Waals's more established authors have become his good friends. "Their whole world was totally unfamiliar to me," he says. "But they just, like, adopted me as one of their own. It's been an amazing journey, and I'm very grateful."

Unlike Ms. van der Waals's other titles, *The Bone Girl* was not written with a young adult audience in mind, Mr. Dace says, although he has been gratified to see its success with younger female fans. "I hope [sisters] Calliope and Clio inspire young women to be true to themselves," he explains. Not all parents support his vision: the book has been banned in schools in almost every state. "The ending is a little dark," he says with a chuckle. "But kids are smart. They can handle the difficult stuff."

Readers will have to wait for Mr. Dace's sophomore effort, however. "I'm hard at work, I promise," he says, gesturing to a stack of legal pads in one corner. "But I draft longhand. And I'm a firm believer in taking as long as the book needs. It would kill me to publish something that wasn't perfect just because I was in a hurry to get it out there."

The library didn't have Alison's Medea novel, but the children's section sported multiple copies of Judith's princess books. I checked out *Crown of Thorns and Daggers*, the first in the series, its cover decorated with a blood-dripping crown and a bosomy young white lady evidently meant to depict the princess. Homework in hand, I headed for the apartment.

6.

Poor princess Melisande, to endure such trials! Judith's book opened with an attempted coup and a threat to her life, after which her father spirited her away to a secret fortress, after which she learned via a series of conveniently placed messages that her father had in fact been the traitorous coup-stager and aspiring assassin, for reasons that were myriad but a bit difficult to follow. Melisande's only hope lay in allying herself with the rebellious young people upon whom her father had blamed the purported coup attempt, in particular, a handsome young fellow, formerly her stable-boy, who was always getting wounded in the chest and having to take his shirt off. Melisande was prone to lip-biting, fainting spells, and adverbs.

I gave up after a hundred or so pages. For a person raised in no small part on bodice-rippers in which quivering manhoods conducted explicit plumbing of flowery depths, Judith's coy insistence on interrupting every nascent sex scene with a surprise enemy attack grew irritating quickly.

I tossed Judith's book aside and picked up *The Bone Girl.* Wendy's copy, battered and stained, its pages worn soft as napped leather. She'd put it in my bag the night I left; I didn't find it until I got to California. When I held it close to my face and closed my eyes, I could almost believe it still smelled of her, cigarettes and vanilla and the smoky burnt-grease scent of her house. Its epigraph, from Anne Sexton, greeted me like an old friend: *Don't bite till you know if it's bread or stone.*

(You thought I hadn't read it. I lied.)

Once upon a time, a girl lost her sister in the enchanted forest on the far side of the lake of blood, the novel begins. *That place, the people said, was a place that swallowed girls. The sisters were so close, they spoke with one mouth, breathed with one set of lungs. When the girl realized she was alone, she thought first of death, that old termagant, that spinster, that ruse.*

It was only later that she thought about maps.

I reread the whole thing without stopping: the story of Calliope and Clio, sister bright and sister dark. Calliope the golden one, radiant and joyful. When she smiled, leaves budded and flowers blossomed; when she laughed, the birds came out of the trees singing. Clio storm-clouded, fierce warrior, her hair a brambly tangle, her footsteps thunder.

Never in all the histories of all the worlds had two girls loved each other so; never would they again. Their mother, the queen, burned with jealousy, shut out by the secret language of their twin souls. Their father was a sorcerer, cold and cruel and heartless. Their castle in the woods had no neighbors. In darkness the sisters grew, telling each other stories about mountains and oceans, the far plains, the places beyond the forest. When the time came for them to make their way in the world, their father turned them out into the woods like orphans and shut the door of his palace to them forever. From the window their mother watched them, weeping, but when they begged her to let them back in, she turned her face away from the glass. And so, the sisters were on their own. But they were never alone, because they had each other.

And then, another sorcerer, a protégé of their father's, enchanted the path they tread through the forest. Without their knowing, his road carried them to Faerie, a world where magic was real and reality an illusion, a world where rivers ran with mortal blood, and birds were once human brothers, and bones bloomed from the cold earth like flowers.

Unseen by the sisters, the sorcerer stalked them through the enchanted woods until he saw his chance: Clio, brooding on circles, turned away from her sister to look for landmarks. The sorcerer stole Calliope and sealed her in the icy dirt. Clio turned around again and found herself alone in the haunted wood, her sister taken from her, the light of her days snuffed like a candle. She wandered the forest, led by a guide who might've been a trickster and might've been her sister's ghost. Along the way she met maidens and monsters, witches and crones, caught magicked apples from trees with leaves like knives, and split open coffins of glass and ice to set free all the other girls the sorcerer imprisoned— all except her sister.

Finally, her body worn down to bones, she confronted the sorcerer in his glass mountain. He served her food made of dust and ghosts and said her sister was never real, had only ever been the better part of her own nature, and his meal took away her memory, and he raped her and made her his bride under the mountain.

Calliope watched them from behind the mirrors, jailed by glass and silence, unable to reach the sister who no longer remembered she was ever alive.

When I turned the last page, my cheeks were tear-soaked.

Calliope and Clio, me and Wendy—how had Jaxson seen so clearly what it was like to love a girl with the kind of power that could cover the earth in blood? I wanted to see inside his brain. I wanted to be with him, until we came to the end. The thought that he might be lost to me—to *us*, me and Wendy—now was unbearable.

I'd find him again. I didn't have a choice.

It was long past midnight, and I had work the next morning, but my head wouldn't settle. I left Jaxson's book on the floorboards by my pillow, though really all I wanted was to read it again that minute, and dug up my old half-full notebook from under the mattress.

Medea, I thought. *Alison wrote about Medea.* That witch with her own fairy tale, swimming in a lake of blood. With Jaxson's language still rich in my head, I scribbled out something neither fact nor fiction, a story that belonged someplace in between. I did not remember falling asleep on the hard mattress in a tangle of dirty T-shirt and unbrushed hair.

In the morning I woke to the buzz of an incoming text.

hi it's Als! Why don't u come to a reading at Judith's house tonight? 7pm.

Judith's address, in a second message.

They hadn't forgotten me.

Or, at least, Alison hadn't. At any rate, I took it as a sign.

7.

The night was cool, the stars coming out one by one. Once I was on the Pacific Coast Highway, the congestion thinned, and the air coming off the ocean smelled like all the places I had never been. I'd barely seen the water since I'd first come to Los Angeles. I often forgot I lived in a city bordered by an ocean, that just past the smog and dust and hot sidewalks lay the heaving aquamarine mass of the Pacific.

Judith's house was a vast modern thing in the hills, self-consciously architectural, stone layers and glass vistas of moon-silvered crashing waves. A jacketed caterer let me in.

Beyond the monstrous front door came the animated chatter of a cocktail party in full swing. There was an assortment of canapés, and everyone in attendance carried with them the cultivated glow of success. They were casually dressed and white, all of them, save for a stunning, familiar Black woman in a pale slip dress who was easily six feet tall and leaned angularly against a white marble bar with a supermodel's carelessly elegant grace, surveying the room with an air of faint disdain.

I hadn't known what to wear; I hadn't anything sophisticated, and neither time nor money to go shopping with Alison's short notice. I'd put on my only clean pair of jeans, a black T-shirt—writers wore black, didn't they? Jaxson and Alison did—and my ratty old sneakers. There was nothing I could do about my clothes. At least I was pretty. I ran my hands down my jeans self-consciously, looking around the huge room for a familiar face, or at least a friendly one.

"What are *you* doing here?" Judith had come up behind me.

"Alison invited me," I said.

Judith's nostrils flared. "Mmm," she said. "Alison." Her features snapped to attention like a sail ballooning with wind, an expression that did not match her tone in the slightest. "In that case, why don't I introduce you to a few people?"

She did not wait for my answer, seizing me in one skeletal red-taloned hand and towing me across the cathedral-like living room toward the only other person in the room who looked as awkward as I felt. I had never been to a reading before; I hoped they were not all like this.

"Barry, this is Sofia," Judith said lethally. "Why don't you make her feel at *home*."

She dropped my arm as if it had burned her and clacked off into her party.

Barry proved to be a middle-aged white man in a black collared button-down tucked into conspicuously new black jeans. He beamed jovially in no particular direction, his pasty forehead sheened with a thin layer of sweat. His black horn-rimmed glasses slid down a prominent nose, and his thinning yellow-grey hair, in an act of hubris that was obviously intended to convey a youthful effect, had been gelled into an array of spikes through which his scalp glistened palely.

"Barry Koople," he brayed, pumping my hand with enthusiasm.

I remembered his name from Jaxson's profile. "Sofia," I murmured, extricating my hand from his clammy grasp.

"Very nice!" he shouted. "You a writer?"

"Oh yes," I said.

"Young adult?"

"I'm working on something just now. It hasn't really got a shape yet."

He nodded again, sagacity stealing across his face like a tiptoe of sprites. "Most difficult part," he said. "The thing is breathing in you, an animal waiting to spring free—only you can give it form in the world outside your mind! Set it loose!" He was listing slightly; I wondered how much he'd already drunk. "When I was working on *The Girl From Outerwhere, and How I Brought Her In*—you know it? No? Really? Best-seller, several awards, the Printz—no? Well, ha ha. There's no accounting for taste, is there. But the first book, I find, is the most difficult, the threshold hovering before you like a clock ticking doom"—he paused as if to consider the success of this metaphor, seemed to find it satisfactory, and continued his soliloquy with a reeking, high-proof exhale— "tick, tock, tick, tock! But wait, my girl, just wait until you've really *completed* something, the way it keeps you up at night, the demons— everyone around you singing its praises to the skies, all the re-views piling up—'Innovative!' 'Brilliant!' 'Like nothing we've ever seen!'—and it won't matter to you, not a word, it'll all be just babble. The only thing, honey, that matters, the only thing the page in front of you—" He thumped a sideboard next to him with lusty vigor, sending his champagne glass flying into the waiting hand of a sharp-eyed caterer who lunged for it and miraculously snatched it out of the air seconds before it exploded into glassine fireworks on the marble floor.

Barry, undeterred, plucked another off a passing tray and downed half of it in one gulp. "You're a pretty little thing, aren't you, shweetheart? They can pay you all the money in the world, but it doesn't make a difference." He regarded me with some satisfaction.

"Me?" I ventured.

"Me," he agreed vehemently. "All the money in the world, and believe me, it was a fine advance, can't complain there, although they fucked me on the option, and my publicist is an idiot, where they get these girls I can't even imagine, some airhead factory at fucking Vassar, can't even manage to find one with perky tits—" He brazenly inspected my own modest bosom.

"How difficult that must be," I said.

"*My Martian Girlfriend*, that's the new one! A boys' book!" he said. "No girls, really! Just one! She's the queen of Mars. But human. Sexy! The kids like that, you know. Teenage boy goes to Mars, falls in love with this kooky chick—she's got silver hair, the reviewers went nuts for her, 'dodges the manic pixie stereotype neatly to render a fully crafted and exquisite creature in all her flawed glory'—that's the *Times*—anyway he falls in love with this chick and has to convince her to leave Mars, only they don't want to lose their queen, she's the only girl on the damn planet! He has to find his way home while battling Martians! Great hook, am I right! I am!" He barked out a laugh.

"What happens to the queen?"

"Slits her wrists," he said dismissively. "Homesick! Can't go back to Mars, his love isn't enough to save her! The kiddies love that stuff. Ghoulish little fuckers. There was a lot of backlash online—you're online?"

"Not actively," I said.

He lowered his voice, looking around the room as if enemies might spring forth from the corners. "You see that chick over there with the blue hair?"

"Mmmm."

"Book blogger? 'Alexandra's Basket of Books'? She's the worst of 'em. *She* never tried to write a book. Wouldn't know how to do it if her life depended on it. Always going after perfectly decent people for telling stories that rn't *theirs*. She'sh fucking *after* me. Censorsh—sh—ship!"

"Stories that aren't theirs?" I echoed, lost.

"Y'nno." He waved his glass and lowered his voice to a conspiratorial whisper. "White guys aren't allowed to write about women and the *blacks*."

The blue-haired woman he had indicated was in animated conversation with another white woman who was overly hectic in her movements and kept rubbing her nose. She did not look like a censor; she looked like one of those teenagers you saw moping around downtown in oversize black sweatshirts with safety pins stuck through their earlobes.

"What about Jaxson?" I asked.

"What?"

"What does she have to say about Jaxson's book?"

"Oh, *him*," Barry said sourly. "They all love *him*. He c'n do whatever he wants, he's got the bish—bish—*bitches* eating out of the palm of his hand."

"Really?"

"You haven't noticed?" He shook his head. "Shameless. Embarrashing, if you ask me. He's got everybody fooled. But not me, little missy. Not. Me." He laid a stubby finger alongside his nose.

"I like Jaxson," I said.

"He's empty inside," Barry hissed. "Fucking... empty."

"The book is good," I offered, curious to see what would happen.

He scoffed through his nose. "You know why he wrote that book?"

I shook my head, and he leaned in close. I recoiled slightly from the hot onslaught of his breath.

"*Pussy*," Barry said. "He wrote it to get *pussy*. 'N it *worked*." He got hold of my arm without my realizing; his forefinger moved with deliberate intent across my skin.

Mercifully, Alison chose that moment to appear.

"Sofia, you made it! I'm so happy to see you!" she trilled, bearing me aloft toward a white-draped table where a bartender in suspenders was mixing drinks. "He's awful," she sotto-vocèd in my ear. "Felt up one of Judith's friends at a book panel. Like, in front of the audience."

"Judith knows he's like that?"

"Everyone knows he's like that. He's a monster. Are you having a good time?"

"Yes," I said hopefully.

"I'm so glad! They'll settle down in a minute, and then we'll get to the reading. It's all young adult writers tonight; sometimes there's a little more variety."

"Princesses," I said.

She smiled. "I'm afraid so."

"Alison." Judith had spotted us. "May I speak with you for a moment?" She pulled Alison away from me, hissing something in her ear.

"Oh, don't be such a snob, Jude," Alison said, loud enough for me to hear. My cheeks burned. A second later they were back.

"How did you like Barry, Sofia?" Judith said, baring her teeth. "Isn't he just a *card*? You know, usually these readings are by invitation only, but since you're a *writer*, perhaps you'd like to share something with us tonight?"

I was momentarily speechless. "Oh—I couldn't," I said.

Alison looked back and forth between us anxiously. "Jude, come on."

Judith was grinning at me like a basilisk. "I insist," she said. "The series is meant to be an *incubator* for new blood, after all." I had a sudden image of Judith looming over the corpse of some hapless writer, gore-strung fangs bared in a feral grimace. "Sometimes it can be so helpful to share our work in a supportive environment, get some *constructive* feedback?"

"Judith…" Alison said.

Why not? I thought. I had my journal in my bag. Nothing ventured, nothing gained. Anyway, my writing couldn't possibly be worse than Barry Koople's.

"I'd be honored," I said. Her smile widened.

"How wonderful for us," she said. "Why don't you read last?"

"Sofia, you don't have to—" Alison began, as Judith plunged back into the crowd.

"It's all right, really," I said.

"If you're not prepared—"

I smiled at her. "I'll wing it."

The noise level surged, and I looked up. Jaxson had sauntered into the room, kissing cheeks and shaking hands. The supermodel moved gracefully from her place at the bar to drape a beautifully shaped hand carelessly over his muscular shoulder. A band of diamonds flashed brilliantly against her ring finger, and I realized with a start she must be his wife—though he did not himself wear a ring and had never mentioned her existence, nor had Judith or Alison. She said nothing as he talked; she was not looking at him but at something only she could see a few feet over his head.

"I didn't know Jaxson had a wife," I said. I felt Alison tense slightly next to me.

"Minna? He's discreet about her. Doesn't want to disappoint the fans."

I thought of what Barry had said about pussy. "She looks familiar."

"She's a model. Quite a successful one. You must've seen her in magazines. She was in the movie version of *The Bone Girl.*"

"She played Clio," I said.

"You saw the movie?" Alison asked sharply.

"Just the posters."

(Wendy and I had driven an hour each way to the theater three times a week for its entire run.)

Alison laughed. "Right. It would've been hard to miss those. Anyway, he says it was love at first sight. She's Finnish, moved here for him—he likes to tell people he married her so she could get a green card, otherwise he's against the institutionalization of romance. She barely speaks English, just stands around and looks like that."

"She doesn't seem friendly."

"Would you be?"

"Not if I had that face," I admitted.

"Not to these people, that's for sure," Alison said.

Aren't these your friends? I thought.

We both looked out at the hectic, raucous glee of Judith's party, the high, sharp chatter, the whispers circulating in the room like a damp fog.

"He's so good with women," Alison said, watching Jaxson. His arm was around Judith's shoulders, his head thrown back in laughter like someone in an ad for chewing gum. Minna stared into the abyss beside him, expressionless. "'You can be writers if you want,' he tells them. 'But you could be scientists, too. You could be doctors or lawyers or the president. Wherever your dreams take you.'"

"Are you and Jaxson—"

It was a shot in the dark and a mistake; she glanced sharply at me, her mouth twisting in displeasure. "Sorry," I said. "None of my business."

"What about you?" she asked, her voice abruptly brassy with cheer. "You dating anyone?"

"No." She had startled me into the truth, but the beautiful Sofia Bencivenga, glamorous orphan, would not often spend her nights alone. "Not seriously," I amended.

"That's smart," Alison said. "You're so young. Have you ever been in love?"

I should have said no. But the way she was looking at me, as if she wanted to know, truly, what my life had been like before her, picked at the seams of my story until some of the artifice fell away. "Once," I said. "It didn't work out."

"In Europe?"

Earl had never left Iowa, had, as far as I knew, never even set foot outside Pottawattamie County. "At school," I said, which was not untrue. "Earl."

"Peer of the realm broke your heart? You *do* play your cards close to your chest," she said, arching an eyebrow. I didn't understand what she meant for a moment, and then it was too funny to correct her.

"I don't know how that stuff works, really. He was the son of somebody important." That part, also true. What was a sheriff, if not a little lord? "Good-looking, rich" —a slight fib, though Earl and I had come into some money for a while there, before it all went to shit— "charismatic, you know. The whole thing."

"Oh, I know," Alison said. Across the room, Jaxson leaned over to murmur something in the flawless whorl of Minna's ear.

"When does the reading start?" I asked.

"When everybody's fucking trashed," she said.

As if on cue, Judith clanged a spoon loudly against a glass.

"Take your seats! It's time to begin!"

Murmuring, the assembled crowd of writers took their seats on Judith's oversize furniture. Alison sat next to me. Jaxson gave her a little wave, and me a surprised smile, as he seated himself regally next to Minna.

"Anna, why don't you start us off?" Judith asked. The woman I'd seen earlier in conversation with the blue-haired book lady stood up, still rubbing her nose, and shuffled a sheaf of papers.

"Thanks, Judith!" Her voice was too perky, her eyes overbright. She was, I thought, coked to the gills. These children's book writers certainly contained surprising multitudes. "It's always such a pleasure to be here! I'm going to read from something new!"

"Wonderful," Judith said loudly.

Anna looked down at her papers. I sat up straighter. Her voice wobbled slightly; she was obviously nervous, although her speech smoothed out after the first page. I liked what she read; her princess had a good deal more spunk than Judith's and did no fainting. After she finished and took a seat to enthusiastic applause, Judith called up the next reader, who turned out to be Barry.

I will not deliver too extensive an account of his reading. The Martian queen, buxom and big-eyed, beloved by her countrymen, proved to be the sort of girl who thought mostly about the weighty heft of her own breasts and the flawed ratio of her generous hips to her tiny waist. The passage, delivered in his stentorian bellow, seemed to dull the spirits of the other audience members as much as mine.

I looked over at Alison. Her face was absolutely expressionless.

"Thank you, Barry," Judith said, her smile tight, when he had finished. "Mars! How charming. And now, a special surprise—Alison's *dear* friend, Sofia..." She paused, savoring her moment. "I'm afraid I don't remember your last name, darling."

The book blogger tittered appreciatively.

"Bencivenga," I said. My palms were sweaty, and I felt as though I might vomit prodigiously upon her immaculate floor, but I was not going to let this dreadful woman see me afraid. "Thank you for the chance to share my work with you," I added. I dug my notebook out of my bag and stood, straightening my spine and throwing my shoulders back and doing my best to appear before them a composed and talented and experienced and confident authoress for whom reading aloud something she had scribbled in a heightened state the night before to a room full of strangers was all in a day's work. I was beginning to regret my confident words to Alison moments earlier; I should've taken the out she'd offered.

But in the flattering light of Judith's living room, the assembled writers looked more confused than hostile; reasonable, considering none of them had any idea who I was or of Judith's underhanded attempt to engineer my ruin. Jaxson gave me a slow, deliberate wink.

And, as I read, I could feel the energy in the room change, the air itself charging, the attention of the guests sharpening with me as its focus. I felt rather than saw their expressions shift from bewildered boredom to alert interest. I had them, I had nearly all of them. I had Jaxson, certainly, could sense the blue weight of his gaze, his admiration, and the power of it ran through me like an unfamiliar and marvelous drug. I had never felt like this before, never felt this intense and delicious pleasure; I could do anything I wanted

with them, transport them to a place of my own making—
no wonder, I thought, no wonder Jaxson moved with such
confidence in the world, if this was what his life was like, if
he could command this magic at will.

The room was silent for a long moment when I stopped.
Barry, his head slumped to one side, emitted a low snore,
bringing me back to myself. Perhaps what I'd felt as I read
was pure illusion. But the rest of them still looked at me,
and I would have sworn it was delight I saw in their faces.

Slowly, regally, Jaxson stood and brought his hands together in a slow clap, and I could have wept with relief. The
smile on his face was authentic, I was sure of it. He was
the kind of man who would've commanded the room to
congratulate me even if I'd failed, but this was no pretense.

"Bravissima, Sofia," he said. "Wow. Absolutely fantastic." All at once the rest of the audience joined him in enthusiastic applause. My eyes met Judith's. The look of pure,
unfiltered rage on her face was like a heavenly balm.

That'll teach you, I thought.

"Thank you, Sofia, that was very unique," she said
coldly. "That's all for tonight, but there's still plenty of
champagne."

The cocktail party chatter rose as the guests descended
anon upon the restocked champagne trays.

"Sofia," Jaxson said, cutting through the crowd. "What
a beautiful piece of writing. From something you're working on?"

"Oh, it's nothing, really," I said.

"Alison's a huge fan of Medea, too—Als, come over
here, congratulate your protégé."

"Sofia, that was great," Alison said. "I had no idea."

"What amazing use of language," Jaxson said. "So modern and punchy. Don't you think, Als?"

"Yes," Alison said. "That's exactly right." She was looking at me with an expression I couldn't decipher. Her eyes moved between Jaxson's face and mine, reading his delight reflected in my own, her body canted unconsciously toward his. There was something there I couldn't parse, something more than just attraction.

"You have to read for us again sometime," Jaxson said. "I can't get over how good that was. In fact—" He turned to Alison.

She understood his meaning before I did. "That's a great idea, Jax," she said. She was unhappy, I thought, but she hid it well. "Sofia, why don't you come work with us sometime?"

I was as surprised as if she'd asked me to marry her. "You mean—come to writing group with you?"

"We could use a new face," Jaxson said, taking my hand. Alison's eyes flicked toward the gesture and away. "What does Judith always say? Fresh blood."

"But I'm not—I'm only—" I bit down on the words, collected myself. I wanted to be what they thought I already was.

That Sofia starts now.

"That would be divine," I said. "I'd absolutely love to."

"Then it's settled," Jaxson said. He winked at me again and gave my hand a squeeze before dropping it.

"I'll text you next time we meet," Alison said, her voice flat. "Can't wait."

Jaxson bent to kiss my cheek. His smell—salt water, sunlight, clean skin—knocked through me like a bullet. "That really was fantastic, Sofia. See you soon."

Two days later my phone buzzed with another text from Alison: *Writing grp tomorrow—u should come! at dharma house, 11am.* I knew the place by reputation. It was another coffee shop in a trendy part of Silver Lake where the dishes were named things like *I Celebrate Wonder,* and the counterpersons were not allowed to serve you unless you recited each mantra-themed sandwich name in its entirety. It was not the sort of place I was likely to frequent in my off hours, but I did not care, would have gone with them to Burning Man if Jaxson had asked, or Monte Carlo, or any other hellish landscape at which he had demanded a rendezvous. I found, to my surprise, that I was crying.

Oh, Wendy, I thought. *Wendy. We did it.*

I'd done it. I'd found my way in.

8.

I called in sick to the Beane the next morning, something I'd never done before. Rob would be furious, but I didn't care. I had a new incarnation of Sofia to conjure, a Sofia who soon wouldn't need the café at all.

The traffic was manageable, and I lucked into a parking spot. I straightened my skirt, fixed my hair, checked my mascara for smears. It was a few minutes past eleven when I walked into the Dharma House.

They weren't there.

I stood for a moment inside the door, crushed by disappointment. She'd forgotten, she'd gone somewhere else, she was sick, she'd told them she invited me and they had insisted on going somewhere else, all three of them had been killed in a traffic accident.

And then someone discreetly cleared his throat behind me, and I remembered myself and stepped out of the way. Jaxson swept past me, his gold hair caught up in a careless knot, his jacket slung over one shoulder.

"Jaxson," I said. He stopped short, turning slowly, his features resolving themselves into the coolly reserved mask—neither unfriendly nor approachable—that he used for his many paparazzi, until he saw who'd said his name and a genuine smile spread across his face.

"Sofia! Welcome, so glad you could make it. Can I get you a coffee? Sandwich? I suppose one oughtn't to call them sandwiches here, the staff gets so upset."

"Coffee," I said. "Would be great. Just black."

"How all the true aficionados drink it, eh? I'm not nearly so tough as you, can't stand the stuff without a little sugar—" His patter was low and soothing, as though he were a jockey gentling a spooked racehorse; his hand, at the small of my back now, burned a hole through my clothes as he steered me up to the counter, placed my order and his, waved away my feeble attempt to reach for my wallet, and guided me toward a table in the corner, where he pulled out a chair for me with an ironic bow and a wink. I sat, almost panting with terror and elation, and realized with a stunning crash of dismay that I had completely forgotten something to pretend to write. The tattered journal was stuffed under my pillow, replete with the details of my triumph at Judith's. Jaxson glanced over my shoulder and brightened, the crushing force of his attention mercifully deflected for the moment.

"Jude! You brought Princess Snowflake!"

Judith sauntered toward our table carrying an enormous leather handbag, out from which peered a tiny white dog in a ludicrous bejeweled collar and massive rhinestone pendant. *Look what we've done to wolves*, I thought wildly. Jaxson lifted the dog from its sack and bestowed several kisses upon its pinched little nose; a look of terrible resignation crossed its features as he restored its inert body to Judith's bag. "Hi, babe," he said.

Judith gave me an incredulous look. "Don't tell me," she said. "Alison invited her."

"I did, actually," Jaxson said genially. "Time for a fresh young face around, don't you think? Sofia'll give us old birds a run for our money, I bet."

Judith had gone a little white around the nostrils. "Mmmm," she said. Jaxson had won me the round, but I had a feeling Judith was a holy terror in the trenches.

"I'm going to get one of those awful roll-ups, want anything?" This was pointedly directed at Jaxson, not me. He shook his head, and she went up to the counter, radiating disdain.

Jaxson smiled at me. "She's not great with new people," he said, as if we were discussing an errant house pet. "What are you working on, Sofia? That Medea piece?"

I cast my eyes about the café, looking for a way out, and saw a dirty napkin scribbled with doodles. Inspiration struck.

"Poetry," I said. "For the moment, anyway." I dug around in my bag for a pen, issuing a silent prayer of thanks to whatever benevolent deity had prompted me to tuck a cracked and leaking ballpoint in with my slender wallet, and emerged triumphant with my fingers stained blue. Jaxson cocked his head.

"You write longhand?" he asked.

"Just for drafting," I said. "It feels more real, you know?"

His smile was even warmer this time. "I do," he said.

I seized a wad of paper napkins from the dispenser. "Usually I use a notebook," I offered. "But for poetry I like loose-leaf."

Judith returned from the counter, eyeing my inky fingertips and pile of napkins in silent disbelief, and sank into

a chair next to Jaxson, pulling out her laptop as Jaxson unearthed a stack of tattered notebooks, pens, and bottles of
ink and spread this detritus across half the table in lavish
disarray.

Alison came in, sweet-voiced and giggling, smelling
of sandalwood and cardamom—"So sorry I'm late—Sofia,
you made it!—poetry! Is there anything you *can't* do?"—and
settled into her own chair in a flurry of cheek-kissing and
hair-tossing.

And then, with the suddenness of a cleaver descending,
they set to work.

That first day I was excruciatingly self-conscious, but I
needn't have worried; they paid me no more mind than they
did the furniture. I scratched away at my napkins, looking
up as often as I dared to steal a glance at Jaxson. I've read
any number of books by men with female protagonists; there
is almost always something off-putting about the women
these authors imagine, as though they are only simulacra
of the real thing, drawn by a bewildered naturalist looking
through a telescope with a faulty lens. But the women in
The Bone Girl were as real and raw as any flesh-and-blood
human being, funny and flawed and wise. Jaxson's eyes met
mine, unblinking, and I stared into their fathomless azure
depths. One eyelid flickered in an unmistakable wink.

He's discreet about her. Doesn't want to disappoint the fans.

I blushed and grinned at him before dropping my own
gaze. Underneath the affable surfer's veneer was something
almost feral.

Find out how he does it, I wrote. *Figure out what's in there.*
Figure out what makes him tick.

Judith and Alison, heedless, banged away at their laptops, stopping on occasion to get up and order some wildly
expensive comestible or other, which they would leave
half-eaten until a waiter cleared it away and they rose once
more to repeat the cycle. I was so hungry, I almost asked
if I could finish their leavings. Months later, Alison would
tell me how much she admired my economy in that initial
meeting. "No wonder you're so thin," she said, regret tint-
ing her voice as if she were not in fact thinner and rippling
with Pilates-hewn muscle besides. "You didn't care about
anything," she'd added. "Writing poetry—I was practically
obsessed with how cool you were, Sofia."

It is an inescapable quality of self-construction that one
can never be entirely certain how one's presentation is per-
ceived; I had had so little time to prepare a persona both
effortless and seemingly long inhabited that I assumed the
three of them saw me immediately as the fumbling and fal-
sified creature I so essentially was. But I had inadvertently
stumbled on the perfect guise with which to cloak myself;
by putting forward the idea that I had no idea who they
were, I had set myself apart from the parade of Jaxson's
sycophants. My napkin-scribbling naïf had assured him I
would not pester him for assistance, referrals to his agent,
glowing endorsements for my then-fictitious literary efforts,
high-profile slots at well-attended book festivals—a kind of
patronage, in short, that was relentlessly demanded of him
by his savvier peers.

I am certain now if I had come to them with flattery
and admiration, they would have sent me packing at once,
and so, as you will see, what I thought then a terrible mis-

step in fact proved a rather fortunate gambit. Judith would certainly have poisoned me if she thought she could get away with it, but Jaxson's favor secured my place among them, a favor that, I understood implicitly, could be revoked at any time, but, so long as it lasted, extended to me considerable protections.

I was, at the time, utterly starstruck. For all Judith's bitchiness and bosom-heaving palace runaways, I was among *writers*, real writers, people who had written and published real books—in all my life, I had never imagined myself seated so casually at such a table, in proximity to persons of their stature. What was it like, I wondered, to be a novelist? Did one's very thoughts move differently? Did it require a particular education, or quality of habit, or diet? Did they rise early each morning like monks and ponder their work in silence before coming together as they did to bring it into being?

I stole looks at them when their attention was elsewhere, memorizing the furrows of their brows, the way Jaxson mouthed something to himself as if testing the weight of the words on his tongue, the intervals at which Judith huffed and flipped her ponytail over alternating shoulders, the expression on Alison's face when she paused, sometimes for as long as five or ten minutes, and stared fixedly over my shoulder at some point visible only to her.

I felt like a magician's assistant backstage, caught by the wonder of the prestige but with the hope, too, of someday revealing its workings. And I understood something I had not previously realized about myself: I did not only worship writers, the worlds they created and the characters with which they peopled them, the magic at their disposal and the beauty rattling round their skulls. I wanted to *be* one, to make real the lie I'd tossed off in the Blissfulle Beane. I wanted to understand what Jaxson had and to procure it for myself. I wanted him, sure, but as much I wanted his self-assurance and his easy way in the world and the power with which he called into being stories that changed the course of people's lives. I wanted not to be like him or even only favored by him but to truly belong at the table to which he had so casually invited me, to know what he knew.

I set my pen down and gave up pretending, stunned by the obvious: I'd said I was a writer not because it was an ingratiating fiction but because I wanted it to be true. I wanted it more than I'd ever wanted anything in my short life.

And if anyone could show me how to do it, it was Jaxson.

They wrote for hours, the ebb and flow of the café's patronage passing without interfering with their concentration. I had built a mountain of shredded paper napkins— long since run out of poetry ideas, I'd taken to fantastical and elaborate grocery lists for delicacies I could not afford, tallied luxury destinations I would never see, invented titles for songs I had no idea how to write—when Judith shut her laptop with a firm click and sat back, cracking her knuckles.

"Time for something stronger than coffee," she said.

Jaxson looked up from his notebook. His handwriting, I noticed, was surprisingly ungainly. "Bit early, isn't it?"

"It's always happy hour somewhere," Judith said.

I was grateful for the excuse to abandon my sham poetics, and Alison, too, seemed relieved to push her computer aside.

"A drink sounds nice," I said, although I hadn't touched alcohol, or anything stronger, since I'd landed in Los Angeles.

"Are you going to Brendan's drinks thing?" Judith asked Jaxson, ignoring me.

He gave her a bemused, exasperated look. "Don't think so," he said. "Our friend," he explained to me.

"Your friend, maybe," Judith said. "I can't believe Celia gave him *my* publicist and passed me off on some troglodytic infant who wants me on fucking *TikTok* and doing *blog* tours like it's fucking twenty-*twelve*. 'Celia,' I said, 'for fuck's sake, I spent fifteen weeks on the *Times* list, I'm not doing an interview with fucking Alexandra. Get me a fucking full-page spread in *Entertainment Weekly*.'"

"Hmmm," Jaxson said. "Sounds tough."

"Oh, don't patronize me, you ass. Just because Celia thinks *you* shit gold." Judith pulled out her phone, scrolled through messages, and made a disgusted noise. "Did you see this?" she asked, thrusting the screen at Jaxson. He shook his head, not even bothering to feign interest, so she showed Alison.

"Poor Anna," Alison said, tilting the phone toward her.

"I think the word you're looking for is *pathetic*," Judith said. "This is worse than her charity auction for chimney sweeps."

"That was for refugees, Jude," Alison said.

"Refugees," Judith spat. "How could I forget what a standard-bearer Anna is for the disenfranchised."

"Your friend who read at Judith's," I said.

"Yes, exactly," Alison said. "Her cat's sick."

"*Edward Catten*," Judith said in a lethal tone, snatching the phone back. "And *she's* not my friend, either. Listen to this shit, Jax. 'As you all know, our community means more to me than family. For many years I have used my platform'—as if she has one—'to support diversity and good representation in books and in our precious world. Now I am hoping you can come together for a cat in need in time for the holiday season. My precious'—god, she didn't even edit this garbage—'Edward Catten requires back surgery to live out the rest of his kitty years in—'"

"Why Edward?" I asked. Judith, displeased by the interruption, made a huffing noise.

"Edward Catten?" Alison was laughing. "You don't know *Twilight*, Sofia? What a wonderful life you must lead."

"Vampires," I said.

"Yes, that's right. Edward Cullen is the main vampire. Anna's a fan."

"Anna's a star-fucking, talentless attention whore," Judith said, still not looking at me.

"Jude, that's a bit harsh," Jaxson rumbled.

"That's the kind version," Judith said.

"But she read at your party," I said.

"We have the same agent," Judith said, as if this explained something.

"Anyway," Alison interrupted hastily, "our friend—colleague"—Judith snorted—"Anna's cat needs some kind of medical attention, I guess—five thousand dollars, good lord, *I* don't spend that much at the doctor—and Anna's trying to raise money for the poor thing."

"She wouldn't need fundraisers if she hadn't blown her entire advance on a pony," Judith said.

"A what?" I asked, certain I had misheard.

"She did always say she wanted a pony," Alison said.

"Who spends a hundred thousand dollars on a pony?"

"A hundred thousand dollars?" I echoed in disbelief.

"That's nothing," Judith said without looking at me, scrolling frenetically through her phone. "That's not even good for a foreign sale. But if it's all the money you're ever going to make, I wouldn't blow it on *livestock*. Look, Jax, Celia gave her a hundred dollars."

"Celia did? Really?" Jaxson looked up from his notebook, exhibiting interest in the tribulations of Edward Catten for the first time. "Should we donate, do you think?"

"Celia's Jaxson and Judith's editor," Alison said to me.

"Celia's incredible," Jaxson said reverently.

"To her male authors," Judith said. "I'm not giving Anna any money. The last time I had a party, she got so tanked, she threw up in my fireplace."

"That was Anna? I thought that was Gemma Carlyle," Jaxson said.

"No," Alison said, "it was Anna. Gemma's the one who got trashed and fucked that sleazy editor from the *Standard* in Judith's bathtub."

"I didn't even invite her," Judith muttered.

"Didn't you fuck that editor in your bathtub last year, Jude?" Alison asked.

Judith bared her teeth in a sharkish grin. "I fucked his publisher."

"Faster than going through a publicist," Alison said.

"Indeed," said Judith.

"I guess if Celia's donating, I had better." Jaxson unearthed his own phone with a sigh. "A hundred? Two hundred?"

"Jesus Christ, fine. Sofia?" Judith asked sweetly. "Want to chip in?"

"Maybe later tonight," I said miserably. Judith smiled at me. *You wanted to fuck an eagle, little girl. Start flying.*

I had a sudden urge to throw my pen at her, overturn a chair, storm out of the café in a shrieking rage; but I quelled it and sat, instead, trying to control my trembling. *Cat fundraiser*, I wrote on my napkin. *Six hundred dollars. A hundred thousand dollars. Celia editor. Anna. Edward Catten. Fireplace.*

"Look at you, working away," Alison said. "I'm wiped out for the day."

"Something new?" Judith asked.

Alison met her gaze, her face absolutely blank. "Same old," she said.

"How's it going?"

"Fine, Judith."

"I thought you were stuck."

"I've been having some trouble."

"The middle's the hardest part," Judith said.

"I keep telling her to show me what she's got," Jaxson said. "She's so secretive."

"Is she," Judith said.

"Leave me alone," Alison said.

Judith smiled like a cat in cream. "Don't be so precious, Als. We're all dying to read whatever you're working on. Why don't you read from it at my series next month? You have to get back on the horse sometime."

"Fuck off, Judith," Alison said, and she wasn't kidding around, either.

"If you ever want to brainstorm—"

"I said *fuck off*."

Judith shrugged.

Outside the café Judith and Jaxson said goodbye quickly, but Alison lingered. "You know, Sofia, if you ever want to send me something, I'd be happy to read it," she said.

"Send you something? Like, in the mail?"

She laughed. "I mean your writing, silly. It can be nice to have someone else take a look. If that's how you like to work, of course."

This is a test, I thought, *and I don't know how to pass it.* "I would love that," I said. "That's, um, really nice."

"Here," she said, digging through her bag for a scrap of paper, writing something, handing it to me. "Email me anytime, okay? And I'll call you next time we meet."

"Great," I said. "I will. See you soon?"

"See you soon, Sofia."

On the walk back to my car, I ducked into an over-priced stationers' and browsed the shelves idly, leafing through letterpress-printed cards, the impression of the type ridged enough to leave shadows on the thick, creamy paper; gewgaws and gimcracks; chipper refrigerator magnets; and fifteen-dollar calligraphy pens until I found what I wanted: a leather-bound journal and a black fountain pen. The salesgirl was checking her phone with her back to me. I tucked them both into my bag.

Back in my car, I pulled out the journal. Its covers were thick board, its blank pages delicate and unlined. Under my fingers, the creamy paper felt like silk.

Big things have small beginnings, I wrote at the top of the first page. I thought of the three of them, resplendent at their table. Jaxson's wry smile, his clear blue eyes. And the tattoo on the inside of his forearm I'd finally seen in full: the stylized rib cage in the shape of a heart and below it *The Bone Girl* etched in a delicate script.

Remember what you came for, I wrote. I put the notebook back in my bag and started for home.

There was a liquor store down the street from the apartment I'd never set foot in but that looked unlikely to ask for ID. It was the work of a moment's deliberation—*bad idea bad idea bad idea* pulsing through me, sweet and reckless and familiar—to cross the threshold and buy a pint of the cheapest vodka on the shelf. The proprietor was grizzled, his sun-leathered skin seamed with deep chasms, but his eyes were kind.

"You twenty-one, yeah?" he grunted.

"Yeah," I said. He winked at me and put the bottle in a paper bag.

Back in the studio, I poured a water glass full of liquor. I was tired of being good.

9.

I dreamed about Earl that night for the first time since I'd gotten to California. The dream was always the same: a confusion of shattered glass and sheeting blood, the anguished howl of metal crumpling, the sick crunch of his body hitting the windshield, his glass-chip eyes, fixed and staring. *Jaxson's eyes*, my dream self thought. I started awake, wide-eyed, heart hammering, willing away the fretful dark. The vodka left me with a hangover that lingered for days, the horizon tilted haywire under a headache-colored sky.

I didn't hear from Alison, and none of them came into the Beane. And yet: hope, that pathetic, feathered stranger to reason. I kept my notebook in my back pocket, jotting down things a writer might notice. The quality of the light at certain times of day, snippets of conversation as they drifted past the register, constellations whose names sounded on my tongue like heroines. I wrote about the ocean.

I did not write about my dreams, which had returned with hellish fury, a whirlwind of splintered bone and smoke, gasoline, blood. I didn't write that I had started drinking again, not lavishly but still in earnest: a thin trickle of spirits, constantly infused, that kept the edges of my vision slightly blurred and the world around me soft as dryer sheets. I didn't write how badly I wanted to crack open my life, send another wrecking ball crashing through the blistering sameness of my days, or how I could feel the old despair settling in my heart like brackish water in a bootprint.

Even Rob, ordinarily stoned into a state of mobile oblivion, commented on my rain-cloud mood. "You're scaring away the customers, man," he grumbled, scratching the hairy slice of protruding belly that, like a bra-burning women's libber, refused all constraints of sartorial oppression. "You gotta stop harshing everybody's mellow."

The temperature dropped into the fifties, and Los Angeles got out its sweaters and holly and tinsel. It was my first snowless winter, and I couldn't help laughing at the afternoon-shift barista at the Beane, Tamara, when she showed up to relieve me in a parka and fur-lined boots. I was still in shirtsleeves, drove from the studio to work with the windows rolled down.

"You're crazy, girl," she said, shaking her head in disbelief. "It's freezing out there."

I'd grown up with annihilating, bone-cracking winters where the snow piled into drifts higher than my head and if you didn't dig yourself out of your house the morning after a blizzard, there was a chance you wouldn't make it at all. Wendy and I tried building an igloo, once, when we were girls, but we didn't have a shovel and only ended up burying ourselves in a heap of new-powder snow, laughing at each other's ice-matted hair and hectic red cheeks. We both adored winter; her mother said we must've been part vampire, impervious to the cold, the way we loved to traipse the frozen roads at night under a sky white with stars, the way we'd get up early enough to watch the sun rise the morning after a fresh snow, rainbow-splintered rays prisming through the ice-limned branches.

I wondered what Wendy would think of it here, where the smoldering sunsets and palm trees and tank-top-balmy afternoons proceeded apace, and the only real signs of winter were the curtains of Christmas lights hung over the streets downtown, the plastic Santas and snowmen in cactus-sprouting front yards, Rob's insistence that we keep the Beane's radio on carols and old standards and put a menorah in the window. True to form, he had neither candles for it nor any idea of which days they should be lit.

I'd never had much use for the holiday itself, but I was lonely as a whistle on Christmas morning, waking early in the pale light on my hard, thin mattress. Rob had given us all the day off, albeit unpaid; we'd gotten a holiday party, too, a few days earlier, free hot chocolates for all and a magnanimous distribution of candy canes. I was used to the café's hours, could never sleep past eight anymore, even with the vodka. I still had most of a bottle left from the night before—the old liquor store proprietor had given me a pint for the price of half, wishing me a happy holiday— and I drank the rest out of a dirty glass and reread *The Bone Girl.* After I turned the last page that afternoon, before I thought too hard about whether or not it was a good idea, I unearthed my phone and called Wendy.

Her "hello" was cautious; she wouldn't have recognized the number.

"Hey."

"Oh my god," she said. "Oh my *god.* You're alive."

"Guilty as charged."

"Where are you?"

"Los Angeles."

"You did it."

"Yeah," I said. "I did."

"Wait," she said. "You did it? Like, you really did the whole thing?"

"Not the whole thing."

"But you—"

"I met him, yeah."

"And?"

"There's a chance," I said. "A pretty small one. But it's still a chance."

"Holy shit," she said. "Holy fucking shit. You are the only person in the entire goddamned world who could've pulled that off."

I heard a wail in the background. *The baby*, I thought. The fucking baby.

"Boy or girl?"

"Boy," she said tonelessly. "Spitting image of his father."

"God help him."

"Fuck you," she said, but I could hear the smile in it.

"Come out here."

"Yeah, sure, lemme just call a limo."

"I mean it."

"With what money?"

"Hitch."

"With a baby?"

"Leave the baby," I said.

She laughed. "Believe me, I've thought about it. I cannot fucking believe you, girl. You did it. You got out of here."

"I'll come back and get you."

"That's not a good idea," she said.

"They're still looking for me?"

"It's only been six months. Not much happens here. Hold on." She took the phone away from her mouth; I heard her muffled voice. "Can't you change him for once?" Stephen in the background, saying something I couldn't make out. Her voice in my ear again. "Sorry, Mom, gotta go. Thanks for calling. I'll see you at the church potluck."

"I love you, slut," I said. "Merry fucking Christmas."

"I love you, too. Call again soon, okay?"

"I'm coming for you, I swear to god."

"Bye, Mom," she said. "Take care of yourself."

A click. She was gone. I threw the phone across the room and buried my face in the pillow and howled out my grief like a child.

And then I took out my notebook and began to write.

Alison came into the Beane by herself on a sunny and unseasonably warm January morning that smelled of jacaranda. I caught her scent before I saw her, a faint trace of that beautiful perfume. I thought I was imagining things. But there she was, leaning against the wall, arms crossed over her chest, her expression unreadable. When the final customer was dispatched to a table, she unfolded her arms and walked up to the counter.

"Hi," she said. "Happy new year."

"Hi!" I said, overeager. "I haven't seen you in a long time. Iced almond latte?"

"You remembered."

"Of course."

"I'm sorry I haven't called you or written you back," she said as I pulled her shot, filled a plastic cup with ice. "The writing you sent me was so great—but then I got sick, and then Jax was sick—we haven't met in weeks—and then it was the holidays, and I'm trying to work on the new book—well, it's not so new, really, I've been working on it for ages, but I guess it's newer than the old one... I keep getting stuck, thought maybe if I holed up for a while I'd get something done, but..." I had never seen her like this before, oddly nervous.

"Is this an okay"—she glanced around—"an okay time to talk?"

"Sure," I said, handing her the latte. "What about?"

"Listen, I had this idea. Why don't you come work for me?"

"*What?*" I asked, astonished.

"Oh, god, I'm sorry," she said suddenly, her voice dropping to a whisper as she leaned toward me, "I'm such an idiot, I didn't think—I shouldn't ask you that here, I'm so thoughtless all the time—"

"My boss never comes in before noon. He probably hasn't even smoked his breakfast bowl yet."

She exhaled in relief. "Okay. In that case—I've been wanting to hire someone for a while? To help out?" Her sentences kept veering upward until they terminated as questions. "I just think if I could focus on the writing and not have to worry about any of the other stuff—and you seem really great, and you're a writer, too, so you get what it's like, which would help a lot..." She trailed off. "It would help a lot," she said again. "To have someone."

There were any number of sensible things I could say to put her off: I barely know you; I've never been anyone's assistant, let alone a writer's; I would have to be insane to quit a job I knew, no matter how tedious, for the chimerical offer of something totally unknown. I had no idea what it was she was asking of me, what she meant by *other stuff*. Her housecleaning? Her laundry? Did she have a child she expected me to rear? I didn't even know how to ask what it was that she wanted me to do.

There are certain moments in our lives when we make decisions understanding that they will alter the course of our future, with no sense of where our new-made maps might lead us. I was no stranger to the reckless gamble, to flinging myself headlong into the abyss, willing into existence the net that might catch me before I crashed into the stony ground below. I liked Alison a great deal. And here it was, handed to me by the universe: the possibility of more of her. Of more of *him*.

"I know this is out of nowhere," she said into the awkward silence. "But I just think—I think it might be good for me to be around someone who's not—who's not, you know." *Like Judith*, I thought but did not say. "I mean, obviously I'll pay you." She named a figure over twice what I was making hourly at the Blissfulle Beane. "I know it's weird. Pretend it isn't. Say yes."

I met her cool, uncanny eyes: grey-green with flecks of gold in them, like a forest pond strewn with autumn-gilded leaves.

"Yes," I said. She put out her slender, fine-boned hand, and I shook it gravely across the counter. I could smell the rank oily odor of old coffee when I moved—I washed my clothes, but there was no point in it, the smell got in the seams, under my skin.

Let her be real, I thought. *Let her be for real.*

The bell-strung door to the coffee shop jangled and a line formed behind her. "I'll call you," she mouthed, as the customer behind her jostled her impatiently; she gave me a shy wave and vanished into the blazing day.

Assistant, I wrote that night in my notebook. *Proximity. Saturnine. Serendipitous.*

"All you have to do is write one true sentence. Write the truest sentence that you know."

Let her be real.

A plea, a prayer, a conjuring.

Please, please let her be real.

She wasn't. Not exactly. But I'm sure you've already guessed that much.

PART TWO

Pompeii

1.

From the outside, Alison's house was unassuming: a one-story grey bungalow with a porch tiled in cool slate. The front yard was planted with spiky grasses and lavender.

I half expected the door to remain snugged closed, or for Alison to be gone, or for her to come out on the porch and tell me she had changed her mind. But she opened the door a moment after my hesitant knock, her hair pulled back into a ponytail that exposed her beautiful cheekbones.

"It's you," she said. "Come in, let me give you the tour. Shoes off, if you don't mind."

That first time I crossed Alison's threshold, I cried. She had her back to me as she led me through one tasteful petal-colored room after another—marble floors in the bathroom and a window in the shower that looked out over a gem-green back garden lively with broad-leaved plants and blooming flowers; silver-grey rafters in the bright, high-ceilinged kitchen, skylights letting in swathes of light; floorboards warm and gold as honey, strewn about with soft, thick rugs that gave deliciously under my bare feet; antique cast-iron bed frame, massive bed piled high with white blankets and pillows, chandelier—chandelier!—sending fragments of rainbow across the rose-pink walls.

"My whimsy," Alison said. My tears threatened to spill over and leave treacherous snail tracks across my cheeks.

Each corner of Alison's house was strewn with treasures: a painting of the seashore, white sails snapping across translucent Mediterranean-blue waves ("Portofino," Alison said, catching my glance, "but you must have been there!" and I nearly opened my mouth to tell her I had never heard of Portofino, so dazed with her glamour was I). Piles of bright pillows sewn with gold sequins and bits of mirrors that caught the light in a dazzle of sparks. A tastefully antiqued coffee table stacked with art books. The open shelves of her kitchen supported thick handmade plates and mugs, an assortment of gleaming appliances in cheery colors, ceramic vases filled with fresh flowers. Things and more things, soft things, tasteful things, things that cost real money—more money than I had ever seen in one place in my life.

Even Alison's books were beautiful: hardcovers with their jackets sheathed in protective cellophane (first editions, I'd learn, some of them worth hundreds of dollars); leather-bound spines stamped in gilt; more art books on the shelves that covered one wall of her living room. My own books, though beloved, were most of them losing their covers, tattered and beaten old things that Wendy and I had passed back and forth like cigarettes until their corners wore down to rounds and their spines split in half. It had never occurred to me that books could be something a person would want to look at and not just read.

But among all the framed prints and original oils, the Art Deco posters and mirrors framed in wrought gold that dotted her walls, there was not a single photograph. No lover, no family, no age-faded snap of toddler Alison rosy-faced and grinning at the beach, watchful parents at her back. Despite the *whimsy*, the carefully chosen furniture, the beautiful dishes and verdant garden, there was some-thing eerily impersonal about her house: like Alison, it was perfectly composed and wholly inscrutable, emerging fully formed from some organic, tasteful void that contained no past, no attachments, no emotion.

"This is my office." She opened a cobalt door with a brass lion holding a ring in its mouth affixed squarely to its center. "Where the magic happens." I followed her into the room. "I really don't show this to anyone," she said, almost to herself.

Walking into Alison's office was like stepping into a jungle; unlike the warm, subdued order of the rest of the house, the office was a riot of so many climbing plants, the walls themselves seemed to be alive. From among the leaves peeped vivid paintings of fantastical creatures; a two-headed dragon winked out from a tangle of spiderwort vines, a minutely detailed pen-and-ink Pegasus took flight from an explosion of pothos, a ruby-red phoenix fluttered behind a blooming orchid. A sun-bleached horse skull gazed sightlessly outward from atop a stack of battered hardbound novels. A drafting table was pushed up under the window, swathed in an avalanche of papers and notebooks, the win-dow itself revealing the same backyard I'd seen from her bathroom. The room smelled faintly of cigarette smoke, and the Amazonian light was warm and green.

The only wall of the room not covered in plants housed floor-to-ceiling bookshelves piled untidily with volumes that spilled over into piles on the floor—these books, all of them, beaten with use. Her copy of *Gatsby* fell open in my hands when I took it off the shelf, and its margins were alive with notations scribbled in different colors of ink, suggesting many rereadings.

"One of my favorites," she said.

"Mine too."

"I think you can tell a lot about a person by their books," she said. "Or you can tell a lot about what they want you to think of them, anyway."

Which one is it with you? I wondered. The pristine hardcovers for show, and the love-worn paperbacks the true story? Her house, I thought, was a façade. It was this room that was her, the frenetic heart beneath the placid veneer.

"It's messy in here," Alison said.

"It's beautiful," I said, reaching out to touch the skull. Alison smiled at me, pleased by my transparent awe. The bone was cool and dry beneath my fingertips. I noticed another, smaller door, almost entirely hidden behind the plants, painted the same deep red as the walls, and firmly closed. A closet maybe, or a bathroom.

That first day, we did very little. Alison took me around her house and made me tea in her bright kitchen. We sat at the counter on her hand-painted wooden stools. She brought out a plate of dense, bready crackers and rich, foul-smelling cheese that clotted in my mouth. We sipped a strong, unexpected tea out of heavy, hand-thrown mugs: licorice and something unidentifiably light with a smoke-dark asphalt flavor underneath. The taste lingered in my mouth for hours.

"You must be hungry for real food," she said unexpectedly, jumping up. "Come, let me take you out to lunch. Your first day deserves a celebration."

"Can I use the bathroom?"

"Of course." She pointed it out.

Like the rest of the house, the bathroom was exquisite: handmade ceramic tiles, chunky hand-cut soaps that smelled of flowers in a china dish, a shower curtain embroidered—embroidered by hand, clearly, in multicolored detail; who even knew how much something like that cost—with a jovial, beret-sporting octopus. More whimsy.

Idly, I opened the medicine cabinet—a habit from the old days I'd never let go—and looked over the glass shelves: face creams labeled in French, tiny jars of oils and potions, a bottle of Black Orchid still unopened in its package, a tarnished heart-sized silver box in the shape of a cat that had a friendly, familiar rattle. I tipped its contents into my cupped palm.

Here was a secret worth keeping somewhere better hidden. A cornucopia of opiates: oxycodone, Percocet, Demerol, codeine, Xanax in a quantity sufficient to fell a dowager.

Oh, god, I thought. *Maybe just one. For old time's sake.*

I pocketed two of the oxys, put the cat back carefully where I'd found it, and ran the taps for a few seconds. I could feel the pills in my pocket, heavy as bullets. It took everything I had not to swallow one then and there.

"Ready?" Alison asked with that blooming smile when I opened the door.

"You bet," I said.

2.

Her car was a beautiful thing, a mint-condition silver Jaguar E-Type Series roadster. "Wow," I breathed, tracing a light fingertip along the voluptuous curves of its hood. "1973?"

"1974, I think," she said, raising an eyebrow. "You know a lot about cars?"

"I used to," I said.

"Goodness," she said with a chuckle. "You seem to know everything." She got in the car and leaned over to unlock the passenger side door. Even now, all this time later, it is difficult for me to ride in a car being driven by someone else. In those days it was nearly impossible. "Are you all right?" she asked.

"Yeah, sorry," I said. "I get—carsick. If I'm not driving."

"Oh, god, so do I," she said, flashing me a smile. "Jaxson says I just have control issues."

Alison drove with a sharp, quick confidence wholly unlike her manner out of the car: decisive and fast and expert, like a girl in a Chandler novel. Though my knuckles were white where I'd clutched the door handle too hard, when she pulled up in front of a restaurant in Koreatown, my breath was even, and my heartbeat was steady.

Over tiny plates of pickles and bowls of bibimbap, I told her about skiing the sharp, white-powdered ridges of the Alps. I told her about diplomats' parties—"Really, writers are nowhere near as boring," I said, which earned a giggle from her—and what I remembered of my mother ("She smelled like amber and chocolate and whiskey and always wore diamonds in her ears") and a lot of other probably very silly things. I had not been much around other people in a long time, and she kept laughing and nodding, as if everything I said was brilliant or charming or both.

"What an amazing life you've had, Sofia," she said warmly. I had forgotten myself in the lambent glow of her attention and embellished rather more detail than was likely prudent. "No wonder you're a writer, with a background like that."

"Oh, well," I said.

"Tell me about what you read at Judith's. Is that part of your novel?"

"It's still—um…"

She laughed. "You're superstitious, aren't you?"

"Yes," I said, seizing on this, although I was not entirely sure what she was getting at.

"I'm the same way."

"What about you?" I remembered Judith's badgering. *Careful*, I thought.

She made a self-deprecating little *who, me?* face. "I don't really talk about what I'm working on, either."

I took a risk. "What was all that with Judith the other day? Why is she so…?" I hadn't thought through the question well enough, but Alison seemed unruffled.

"She thinks she's being helpful, I suppose," she said. "But we're worlds apart as writers. Judith's very commercial. She's a powerhouse. Turns out a book a year, if you can believe that."

"I read the first one," I said.

"Goodness," Alison said. "Whatever did you think?"

"There were a lot of daring battles."

She laughed and propped her chin on her hand and tilted her head at me, considering. "You're awfully talented. And what a backstory. You were wasted on that awful café," she said. "I'm sorry," she added hastily at the sight of my expression. "I didn't mean—"

"No, it's fine," I said. I shrugged one shoulder: elegant, rueful, *the things we do to survive.*

"It can be difficult, making a life," she said, her eyes suddenly far away.

"Here, you mean?" I asked.

"Anywhere, really. I find it so—cumbersome, don't you? All the things that take up a day, all the grubby business of being. Much better to be a monk on a high mountain somewhere, I think; then you know what the purpose of your days are, what you're meant to be doing. Sometimes I wish I had a direction like that."

Alison didn't look like she'd last long in tonsured chastity, but I refrained from pointing that out. "I feel so aimless so much of the time," she went on. "Adrift. I suppose this isn't where I thought I would end up when I came here, and now I don't know what to do with myself. You're from *Europe*, so you must understand. All this sunlight, these healthy people." She said *healthy* the way another person might *leprotic.*

"I don't mind the sunlight," I said.

"I suppose you wouldn't, after all that flitting around the Riviera. I'm from Manhattan. I don't think it's natural not to have seasons. I had to pack all my favorite coats in cedar and mothballs. I'll never see them again, most likely."

"Tell me about New York," I said. "Believe it or not, I've never been there."

"Really? I mean, it's not *Paris*, or wherever your parents used to take you. It's big and dirty and smelly, and the summers are horrific, and the winters are hell, and the train never works, and everyone's in a hurry all the time. It's the greatest place on earth, it really is. If you've never lived there, it's hard to explain. I was broke there for a long time—horribly, horribly broke. I'm sure it's awful being broke anywhere"—*Yes*, I thought—"but being broke in New York is its own special sort of misery. Sometimes I would go to a restaurant I couldn't afford and put a sixty-dollar dinner on my credit card—oh, that's nothing," she said, laughing at my expression, "I know it sounds crazy, but I swear that's not even an expensive *lunch* in New York—just to pretend for an hour that I had a little money.

"But then walking back to the train, you'd catch the sunset in just this way, and the air would be just so, and you'd feel just for a second that you were the coolest girl in New York, and it'd happen like that maybe once a year"— she laughed again—"but that was enough."

"You blend in well here now."

"You know how it is." Her clear eyes met mine. I wondered why she was telling me this, why she'd dropped her guard so quickly and so easily, as if I were the kind of person she could trust. She had no evidence for it, and all I could think of was that she was so lonely in her pretty shell that she'd paid me simply to listen. I didn't know anything about her life, what she did with her days; she thought I was safe.

"Why don't you move back?"

"Closed the book," she said. "Anyway, I don't meet many people out here who are kindred spirits."

I liked the idea of Alison finding something special about me, something that reminded her of herself. I liked it very much.

"I know what you mean," I said.

She nodded, but her eyes had that faraway look again, and I thought she was no longer paying quite so much attention to my own experiences in the world.

"Everyone here is so nice," she said, the word a clear epithet. "No one wants to say anything is bad. Not to your face, anyway. They love to go on for hours about whoever isn't in the room. They've got nothing good to say then. They're all sycophants, is the thing. Someone gets on the *Times* list, and the next thing you know they're all lining up to kiss her ass when the week before they wouldn't have even stood next to her at a party."

"Judith seems a bit like that," I ventured.

"Oh, Jude's an old friend," she said dismissively. "Really, her bark's worse than her bite."

I doubt that, I thought. If Judith were a soccer mom, she'd spike the orange wedges of her offspring's opponents with razor blades.

"We go back a long way."

"And Jaxson?"

Her expression closed like someone pulling the shades. "Everyone always wants to know about Jaxson," she said.

I thought it prudent to change the subject, and I did. "Why did you move out here originally, anyway?"

"Money." She didn't elaborate and leaned forward to brush an invisible speck of dust off my shoulder. I flinched away from the unexpected breach of the boundary between us, the ease with which she crossed it. I had not been touched by another person with care in a long time. I wondered anew at her, the confidence with which she slouched through her world.

Back at her house, she asked me if I wanted coffee, and I said yes, and she said, with a laugh, "I should make you make it." I flinched and followed her into the kitchen.

"What do you want me to do?" I asked. "I mean, for work. For you."

"Well," she said, looking around as though the answer might present itself to her from somewhere behind the coffee maker.

What the hell, I thought again, *am I doing here?*

"I need—I need someone to organize my files. Put my receipts in order for my taxes. That kind of thing." This did not seem like remotely enough work to require the employment of a full-time assistant, but I did not think it wise to point this out.

I cocked my head, put on a listening face. But that was all she was going to give me. "You want me to start, um, filing now?" I asked finally.

"I don't want to make you work today," she said, straightening. "It's your first day. Why don't you just take off early?"

She was paying me by the hour and leaving work early meant more money than I could afford to lose, but she seemed to think she was doing me a favor, and there is nothing so off-putting to the wealthy as poverty.

"Thanks," I said. "I'll see you tomorrow."

"Tomorrow, then," she said, with a cheery wave. The smell of jasmine followed me all the way to my car.

That night I folded the pills I'd taken out of her bathroom in a scrap of paper, mummified them in cellophane, and tucked them under my mattress like a telltale heart. I still have them, actually. I like to think they brought me luck.

Talisman, I wrote in my notebook. *An object that is thought to have magic powers or bring good fortune or to offer the possessor protection from evil or harm.*

3.

So began that spring with Alison, a time that even now comes to me as a memory found in a dream: diffuse, lovely light, one day running into the next in an endless parade of splendors. Those early days were a banquet of wonder, of small, beautiful things I had never known existed; a subtle education in how to choose finely, how to assume the world you moved through was invested in your pleasure, how even humble household objects—the coffee grinder, the duvet cover, the lamps and candles, the silverware, the carpets and the plates in the cupboards, the very cupboards them-selves—could be imbued with the languid weight of luxury.

Each night when I returned to the studio, I wrote down everything Alison let drop in passing, like Cinderella's carriage horse demoted to a crumb-struck mouse; my notebook from that time, long since lost, must have read like a debauchée's to-do list. *Ranunculus* and *Limoges*, *orris* and *ambergris*, *jersey silk* and *napa leather. Escarole, frisée, radicchio, Tulum.*

How can I explain what it felt like, then, the light of her care? I was ravenous for something that felt like friendship. Wendy had been lost to me for nearly a year by then; outside of writing group, I hadn't had a conversation with someone who wasn't a customer or another barista at the Beane since I'd come to LA. Alison made me tea and asked me questions and paid attention to my answers. We ran errands in her silver car, the breeze coming in through its open windows tangling our hair together, my pale strands braiding with her dark.

In the evenings I'd drive my decrepit old car back to the grubby studio I could never bring myself to call my own, as if by refusing to describe it as such I could somehow escape its confines. Standing before the dirty mirror in the dirtier bathroom, the mold of tenants long gone grouting the chipped and broken tiles, I would pull my hair back into a sleek ponytail the way she often wore hers, tilt my head to the side with her quizzical lilt that suggested both gentle displeasure and the certitude that any inconvenience would immediately be remedied. I liked what I saw.

But we were something other than friends, something I did not have the language to name. The discreet white envelope stuffed with cash that she left for me on a side table once a week rendered our relationship in a harsher light, though we never discussed it, or the fact that I was meant to be working for her, or that if she stopped in the middle of some anecdote and asked me to run and fetch her coffee or pick up her dry cleaning or call her personal trainer, I would perform these tasks without protest. She did, after all, pay me more—much more—than I'd made at the Blissfulle Beane; I had enough to keep my gas tank full, to buy more than peanut butter and bread at the grocery store, to be certain for the first time in months that I would have cash enough to pay a month's rent in advance.

It was not enough money to breathe deeply, but it was enough to stave off the worst of the panic that woke me in the wolf hour, my heart pounding and my throat dry, dire visions of lifelong poverty unspooling before me in the pre-dawn darkness as the pinging drip from the leaky kitchen faucet soundtracked my black, ineradicable terror.

I ran errands for her. I ordered books for her—"For re-search," she explained, although they were titles on subjects as disparate as celestial navigation in the ancient world, subversion and ambiguity in fairy tales, the Gilded Age, dogsledding—at the local bookstore downtown that she loved and picked them up when they came in. I sat for long hours with her in the afternoons, drinking her smoky tea and answering her questions about books I'd read and places I'd been (I'd had to do some frantic research at the library) and what I wanted to do with my life, everything from the sort of pets I'd had growing up to the first time I sailed in the Mediterranean. After a few weeks of this, I decided that whatever use she had for me—a friend? a helpmeet? an errand runner?—was at least somewhat permanent, that I was in no danger for the time being of being sent packing. I liked her; I liked her a great deal. I liked the mystery of her and her moodiness, her sudden, radiant smile and her frequent bursts of generosity—paying me extra for a day only a few moments longer than usual, carelessly handing me her credit card at the grocery store and telling me to add what-ever I wanted to her list, buying me three-course lunches at newly opened celebrity-chef restaurants for no reason at all.

And so, as our lives braided ever more tightly together, the question of what she really wanted with me began to fade, until finally I wondered why I had ever bothered to ask it at all.

4.

For several days after I went to work for Alison, I saw no sign of Jaxson or Judith. Judith I could do without, but Jaxson's absence disappointed me, though I knew better than to say so. And then, one morning, as I poked listlessly through a pile of her receipts at her kitchen table—self-help books, matcha smoothies, an alarmingly expensive Ayurvedic shampoo—I heard her phone buzz in the other room and the high-pitched, breathless "hello?" she used when the caller was someone she wanted to please. Her end of the conversation was muffled, but she bounced into the kitchen a few minutes later.

"Writing group is on!" she announced cheerily. "Not the Beane," she added, mistaking my expression. "We don't *ever* have to go there again, don't worry!" She fluttered around the kitchen, fluffing her hair and straightening her clothes, disappeared into her bedroom and reemerged a moment later having swapped out her Birkenstocks for delicate, strappy sandals that showed her toned calves to advantage and smelling more robustly of the complicated perfume she always wore.

"Ready?"

I looked up from her receipts, startled. "You want me to come?"

"I'm not just taking advantage of you." She smiled: this was a joke. "You can think of this" —she waved her hand in one of her habitual all-encompassing gestures— "as sort of like a... mentorship, too."

I guessed the response she wanted was gratitude. "Wow," I said. "That's really—wow. Thank you."

"You have to start taking yourself seriously as an artist," she said sternly. "Consider this your *me* time, okay?" I wondered but could not bear the humiliation of asking if this meant I would not be compensated for the time we spent at writing group together. Most of a weekday was more than I could afford to lose on a regular basis.

"I can't tell you what it means to me that you have this kind of faith in my work," I said.

She smiled. "You have your stuff, right?"

I had my notebook, which I carried with me everywhere now. "Sure," I said. In her bathroom, I ran my fingers through my tangled hair, checked my T-shirt and ragged jeans for visible stains, and rubbed her toothpaste over my teeth with one finger. Jaxson wore dishabille with a wealthy person's easy grace; I just looked poor.

The silver cat pulsed behind the mirror. I'd been so good, so good for so long—the vodka, sure, but that was nothing. I had earned a little treat.

The pill kicked in on the drive. I could feel its benevolent warmth sliding through my veins like molasses. The palm trees took on an effervescent nimbus as they streamed past; the breeze on my face felt like magic. Why on earth had I ever been so foolish as to let this go? Just like that, a few seconds later, desire and care wiped from my brain as neatly as a flipped switch, floating suspended in the generous void.

A throaty-voiced chanteuse crooned from the car stereo's speakers over a sad-synth background: *All I want to do is get high by the beach get high by the beach get high.* Alison circled the block a few times then pulled into a parking spot, her movements sure and efficient.

"Hope you don't mind Dharma House," she said.

I would not have minded if she'd driven me straight into the tar pits. I followed her swinging ponytail into the café.

Jaxson and Judith weren't there yet. Alison left me at a table in the corner while she went up to order food. A moment later Judith stomped in, Princess Snowflake peering apprehensively out of its tote; there was the habitual great kissing of cheeks.

"If it isn't our little ingenue," Judith said, without looking at me.

"Sofia's working for me now," Alison said. "Isn't that great?"

"Working for you?" Judith echoed in disbelief.

"As my assistant," Alison said, wilting slightly under Judith's withering glare.

Judith, however nonplussed, recovered quickly. "That must be such a relief for you," she said. "What with your workload." She sat down in the chair farthest away from me.

"Yes," Alison said, regaining her vim with aplomb. "It's been great. I'm getting so much done. But I wanted her to have a chance to work with us a bit. A pay-it-forward kind of thing. It's important to support other women, too, don't you agree?"

"Absolutely," Judith said, returning her attention to her phone. "Sisterhood is so powerful." I kept my mouth shut and got out my notebook. "Look at you, dear," Judith said. "Maybe next week you'll have a computer."

The door jangled again; this time it was Jaxson, swooping down on us with extended arms. "Als! God, it feels like it's been forever," he boomed, seizing her in an awkward half hug where she sat. "How's the work going, babe?"

"I think I made a breakthrough," she said, looking up at him coquettishly. He beamed.

"That's fantastic. That's so great. Sofia! I haven't seen you in… Wow, how long has it been? Before the holidays, right?"

"She's working for Alison these days," Judith said.

A flash of surprise moved across his face, and then he smiled at me, recovering fast. Separation had done nothing to diminish his intense pull; if anything, he was even more attractive than the last time I'd seen him, so much so that the gelatin opiate wall thinned in his presence until I could feel myself on the verge of tilting toward him.

"That so?" he said. "Great, maybe we'll get to see more of you. I hope she's keeping you busy."

"She's a termagant," I said. He blinked.

"Huh," he said. "I, um—shall we get to work?" In their now-familiar chorus of papers and keyboards and ink bottles, they settled at his command into the task at hand.

As before, they worked for several hours without speaking. I tried not to clock the passage of time in terms of money lost. *Once upon a time, a girl lived next to an enchanted mountain*, I wrote, crossed it out. *Once upon a time. Once there was a girl.*

Once there was an enchanted mountain
termagant
Wendy, I wrote. *Wendy, I miss you. You were right, I guess, that I'd be the one to make it out, but everything we imagined it'd be like out here—it's like that, but like something else, too. Do you remember*
oh, Wen

This time, it was Alison who called a halt. "I'm hitting a wall," she said with a yawn.

Jaxson looked up. "Yeah? Anything I can help with?"

"No," Alison said. "I just need to chew on a few more ideas. I might bounce a few off Sofia later today."

"Really? That's great, Als. Sofia's helping you work?"

"It's good to talk to someone with a fresh perspective," Alison said.

"How nice," Judith said evilly. She got up and headed toward the bathroom, radiating contempt. Princess Snowflake gazed at me forlornly.

"Sofia, can I get you something?" Jaxson asked.

"I'm okay, really."

"I insist," he said gallantly. "Latte? Salad? I Contain Wholeness is really delicious if you can get past the kooky name."

"I'm—just a coffee, then, I guess," I said, rummaging hopefully in my bag for an errant five-dollar bill.

"On me," he said. "Als, come with me? I'm going to get something else, too. I need another pair of hands."

There was a bit of a line; I watched them absently for a minute, Jaxson's solicitous hand on Alison's back, his golden head bent toward her ear. The café was noisy with afternoon custom, and his voice was too low for me to catch much of what he was saying. "…a good idea?" I picked out, and something that was either "what she shows" or "and who knows." Alison nodded vigorously, her ponytail bobbing. Jaxson took his hand away as they reached the counter and placed his order, and I turned back to my notebook. A few moments later, he set a mug of black coffee in front of me before folding himself back into his plastic chair.

"Thanks," I said. They were both empty-handed. I knew better than to ask.

5.

My days with Alison settled into a kind of routine. Mondays for errands: I took her clothes to the dry cleaners— clothes I hardly ever saw her wear, silk dresses and linen jumpsuits, floaty diaphanous clothes that wrinkled easily and demanded great care, organic soaps, and specially selected cleaners screened through a combination of online reviews and alchemy. I got into the habit of occasionally borrowing one of her numberless identical black garments, which made these trips to the cleaner's more engaging than they otherwise would have been. Then the organic grocery store for her pollens and powders and supplements, the bookstore for her orders, the gym for her smoothies.

Tuesdays and Wednesdays she left me in her kitchen, or on her couch, with a pile of detritus to "file" and shut herself up in her office, cigarette smoke creeping out from under the door as she muttered to herself. Sometimes there were whole stretches of a day where she would leave me at her house alone to go on some obscure errand of her own, and I could putter about the sun-gilt rooms, rifle through her bookshelves, try on her lipsticks and skin creams and high heels and dresses like a child pillaging her elegant mother's wardrobe.

Thursdays were usually writers' group—although they did not meet as often, or as regularly, as they had when I'd been working at the Beane. I had the idea that this had something to do with my presence, although none of them said as much. For some weeks Judith ignored me with haughty rigor, deigning to acknowledge me only when I said or did something she deemed outrageous—failed to recognize the name of some peer of theirs or another, for example, or professed ignorance as to the quality of the sushi at Urasawa. The first time she saw my poor old flip phone, I thought her eyes would bug out of her head.

But as one month passed and then another, as Jaxson continued to treat me with a combination of genteel flirtatiousness and occasional deference, as Alison rose to my defense even, Judith relented. Like a battle-scarred old general, she recognized when a sortie was wasted, though I had no doubt she let go her overt hostility only to preserve her energies for a campaign of attrition instead.

It was not long before I spotted the occasional showy, dark crack in Alison's polished veneer. She was always strange about a lot of things: about food (she constantly ordered too much and ate almost nothing), about her computer (which she hid when she was not using it and would not let me touch), about her privacy (once, early on, I made the mistake of knocking softly at the door when she had sequestered herself in her office; she flung it open a moment later, cigarette caught between her knuckles, snapped, "The door is closed for a *reason*, Sofia," and slammed it shut in my face).

She spent a lot of time on the phone, a lot of time writing emails, a lot of time chatting about all the different people she knew—writers, artists, painters, *creative* people, she explained, her sorts of people, New York people mostly but some LA people too—and yet I never knew her to spend time with anyone other than Jaxson, Judith, or me. I wondered more than once if she'd hired me out of sheer loneliness. If that was the case, I did not so much mind; although some afternoons, hot and cross and stuck in traffic, on some purposeless errand, I wanted nothing more than to open the car door and run until I vanished into the heaving sea of smog.

It was another thing that marked the fundamental fault lines of our relationship. When we got tired of each other, only she could leave.

But, for the most part, in those early months, our time together was serene. And despite writers' group—which she did, in the end, pay me for—and Jaxson, Friday afternoons with Alison soon came to be my favorite. On Fridays she went to her yoga class or Pilates in the morning. Afterward she liked to have lunch with me (she paid for that, too, thankfully) in Silver Lake. Over coffee she asked me questions about my week, what I did when I wasn't with her, what beach I preferred (I never went to the beach), my fitness routine (I hadn't one), my favorite restaurants (I couldn't afford any). In order to have something to report, I drove to the Griffith Observatory on Saturday mornings and ran up and down the hill, panting like a hyena. I went to LACMA and the La Brea Tar Pits. I took a photograph of myself standing in front of the backlit yellow wall of dire wolf skulls and texted it to her. I spent a lazy Sunday afternoon in a Venice Beach dive bar watching sun-leathered homeless men push shopping carts back and forth along the boardwalk and scab-kneed, speed-thinned teens pass around joints under the hot pale sun. I made my weekend adventures into a rosary, rationing out each litany, my heavenly reward the spark of life in her eyes when I made her laugh. And her money. If she stopped liking me, I knew what would happen next.

But it was more than that. Her attention was careful; she listened to what I said and remembered it. She tilted her head as I spoke, her grave grey-green eyes fixed upon me, as if I were, in that moment, the only thing in the world that mattered; her pale, lovely gaze was like a drug.

In the end we're all of us longing most of all to be heard, and I've never met anyone who could listen like Alison, not before, and not since—not even Wendy, whose love for me was fierce and reckless and headstrong. Wendy never held still long enough to hear the ends of anybody's sentences. It wasn't that kind of feral, animal-bodied love, humid and tangled, Wendy's burning-hot body asleep in my bed, our stale morning breath in each other's faces, our initials tattooed over each other's hearts with sewing needles and India ink, that I felt for Alison; nothing even close.

But the place Alison made for me was a kind of space I'd had none of in my short life. Alison listened to me as though I belonged in her world, as though I was wise and clever and funny, her attention pouring over me like the green-gleaming light that came in through her garden-facing windows. And I'd never known anyone like Alison, either. Alison, who was wise and clever and funny herself, and a writer besides; Alison, who captivated men like Jaxson. Alison, who'd written a novel and was writing another, who knew the rules of the world she and Jaxson shared like a map she'd memorized offhand, while I bumbled heedlessly through the wilderness, never knowing until now that a civilization like hers even existed.

Wendy and I were the same: fire, fight, desire, will. Alison was older and sophisticated and had beautiful things, and money, and clothes. She could read a menu in French and pick out just the entrée I might like and the right wine to go with it. She had an entire vocabulary for varietals of luxury I did not even know existed. I felt sometimes around her like a puppy called to heel: naive and silly, tripping over my own feet.

But although Alison was closemouthed about her past, I knew she hadn't been born into the life she led any more than I had.

And if she had learned to be herself, that meant I could learn to be her, too.

6.

"You have a real talent," she said one Friday in February. "You're *such* a gifted storyteller, Sofia." She had just come back from Pilates; her hair was piled into a messy bun, and she'd flopped onto the couch with a bottle of water and a bowl of coconut yogurt and bee pollen. Her skin was glowing. The late-afternoon sunlight gave her a radiant backlit halo.

"Oh," I said, embarrassed. I'd just been telling her about my latest fitness adventure, which involved a (highly embellished) collision with a hapless family of tourists on the dirt trails of Griffith Park.

"Do you ever do writing exercises?"

I was uncertain what a "writing exercise" might entail and thought it best to tread cautiously. "Not usually," I said.

"You should try them. I give myself assignments all the time when I'm feeling stuck—works like a charm. You're supposed to write every day no matter what, you know."

I didn't. "Yes," I said.

"But it's so hard sometimes, right? Especially if the work isn't coming. Here, why don't we try a few together?" She leapt off the couch and disappeared into her office, re-emerging a moment later with her computer and a blank legal pad. She handed me the pad, and I followed her into the kitchen, where she pointed me into a chair and sat down across from me at the kitchen table.

"Okay, try this one. How about…" She paused for a second, looking up at the ceiling. "How about—describe a time when you felt afraid."

"Afraid?"

She gestured to the pad. "Just free write. Ten minutes? I'll set a timer."

Was *this* what writers did? I looked down at the blank page in front of me, alarmed. There was no time in my life when I had been genuinely afraid that I had any interest in documenting. What sorts of things frightened normal people? Earwigs, old age, the loss of a loved one. *Unrecognized potential*, I wrote, in a fit of inspiration. Across from me, Alison was typing intently, her eyes fixed on her screen. *I grew up in a world full of promise*, I scribbled. *All around me was boundless wealth and beauty. A universe of possibility.* I quickly concocted a heartbreaking anecdote in which a teacher failed to properly understand my innate sagacity and I was obliged to effect a mighty struggle to prove my worth. This fraudulent recollection took marvelous wing, and I had just gotten to my professor's extensive apology and confessions of inadequacy when Alison's phone chimed ten minutes later and she sat back with a sigh.

"Let me see," she said, seizing the pad from under my nose and scanning my composition assignment.

"This is great," she said.

"Do you think so?"

"Yeah. 'A universe of possibility'—I like that a lot. The way it echoes actual truth? Did you know that almost all the universe is dark energy? Isn't that cool?"

I did not. "Super cool."

She handed the pad back to me. "We should do this more often."

"Sure," I said. "I'd like that."

And so we did. Alison's assignments were sometimes wildly vague, sometimes oddly specific: *Describe the first time you fell in love. Tell me about a thunderstorm you saw. What do you think makes a happy ending?* Once I got into the habit of it, I worked hard at these piecemeal essays, finding within myself a surprising spark of delight. If my own words failed me, I stole lines from whatever books I'd stolen from the library that week or things I'd overheard Jaxson and Judith say—if she noticed this, she never commented.

"This," she said a few days later, tapping the pad I'd handed her. "God, Sofia, this is gorgeous." She'd asked me to write about friendship. I wondered, briefly, if I was meant to write about her.

Instead I wrote about Wendy, changing her name to Mirabella: more suitable for the boarding-school best friend of a quasi-European debutante. Alison skimmed through the pages, flicking each one aside when she was done. "Did you really sneak out of school in the middle of the night and walk a mile to steal *chocolate*? That's amazing."

"We were hungry," I said modestly.

"In December? In Switzerland? You were lucky you didn't freeze to death."

"We had coats."

She looked at me, grinning like an imp. "I think so many women had friends like that when they were young. Someone you'd do anything for."

"Who was yours?"

"Cleome," she said. "I knew her when I first lived in New York. What happened to Mirabella?"

"We lost touch," I said. "Over—a boy."

"That's awful."

"Was Cleome a writer, too?"

"Musician," she said. "She used to play the open mic at the Sidewalk all the time. Bunch of people got their start there, Regina Spektor, Kimya Dawson—anyway, I'd go just to see her, the open mic night went on for *hours* sometimes; they don't stop until everybody has played, so you can imagine—but when she came onstage…" She stopped, her eyes shining, looking at something behind me, something in a different time, a different world. "She was magic," Alison said. "She was like… inhuman. Hold on." She went to her old-fashioned record player, put on a record, flopped back on the couch next to me.

The music was spare and charcoal dark, the singer's words raw and sure: just a guitar and a velvet-textured voice, clear and strong and full of all the heartbreak in the world.

Is it worth singing
All these songs about death?
Only you know me
Only your breath
I can't help wishing
For some kind of road home

So dry your eyes baby
Be glad you're still living
Be glad you're alone

"It's beautiful," I said when the song was over. Alison turned the music down but left it playing. "What happened to her?"

"She killed herself," Alison said. "When we were twenty-one."

"I'm so sorry."

"I never really got over it," she said. "But you learn to live with it after enough time passes."

"It's uncanny, though."

"What is?"

"I was just thinking about that kind of friendship. In *The Bone Girl*," I said. "Jaxson gets it exactly right. I don't know how he did it, but it's perfect."

"I thought you hadn't read it," she said sharply.

Too late, I realized the mistake. "I read it a few weeks ago," I said. "I was curious."

Her hackles went back down. "What did you think?"

"I thought it was really good," I said, truthfully. "I've never read a book that made me feel… seen, I guess. If that makes sense."

"It does," she said. "But it's an act. He never turns it off." She was suddenly upset; I had said something wrong, but I didn't know what. Was she jealous?

"Turns it off?"

"The Jaxson Dace show."

"You don't think he's talented?"

"He's talented, all right."

"Are you—" I stopped, reconsidered. I was on delicate ground. "You don't have to talk about it," I said; this had the effect I'd hoped it would. All that time with her secrets and no one to carry them with her: she was burning up.

"I mean, we are," she said. "Sort of. It started ages ago. When I—he was my teacher, back in New York. That's how we met."

"Jaxson was a teacher?"

"He used to teach writing workshops out of this church on the Lower East Side. I found a flyer right after Cleome died, and I thought, *Why not?* It was something to do. I felt like I had a black hole where my heart was supposed to be. I didn't even think I could *be* a writer; he's the first person who really encouraged me. He told me to write about something far away if I couldn't write what was nearby yet. He was… Well, you know how he is. How he comes across. At first I really believed it was just because he thought I was talented. He told me so all the time. He was older— not that much, but when you're twenty, seven years is a big difference. He seemed so wise. He knew all these writers, he had that face" —we both laughed— "and here he was, telling *me* that he saw something in me that he didn't see in anybody else." She was quiet for a moment. I let the space between us breathe.

"And then when he—when we—for a long time, I wondered if he'd ever seen anything at all, other than somebody he wanted to fuck. It's the same old story for every woman, I'm sure. But the first time it happens to you…" She shook her head. "It made me question everything. Because *I* thought I was good. I thought I had something. And here was this older writer, this *man*, telling me he agreed. But I never knew—I'll never know, really—if anything he said was true. You know the worst part?" But she wasn't waiting for an answer; I might as well not have been there at all, now. Her eyes shone with unshed tears. "The worst part is that I fucking fell in love with him." She dashed angrily at her eyes with the palms of both hands. "And he's nothing, Sofia. He's not worth any of it. He's not worth anything I did for him. He's fucking *empty* inside."

Barry, of all people, had said the same thing.

I should have believed her then, but I didn't. I refused to. She'd been naive; she'd misunderstood. Maybe she'd been obsessed with him, and he'd had to let her down. Wasn't a teacher supposed to care about his students? And he was so wise, so brilliant, so kind. I thought, then, that I was the only one of them who was lying.

Perhaps you've already seen what took me so long to realize; perhaps you saw it coming a mile away. But you have to understand how dazzled I was, for all I considered myself worldly. I was a child; I didn't know a fucking thing about the world. All I'd ever done was read about it in books.

"Anyway." Alison came back to herself. All business. The gesture was familiar by now: Alison the Person putting on Alison the Writer like a coat. "This really is good, Sofia. You should write a little series. 'The Mirabella Stories.'" She laughed. "Do you want me to give you notes? I'd have to keep it for a bit. I have a lot on my plate this week."

Had I put anything in the story that would get me in trouble? Surely not. The memory was clear and sharp as ice:

Wendy and I tramping through snow in the cold dark, the promise of the candy aisle at the gas station carrying us through the night, arriving in with midnight's chill teeth at our backs and slyly palming Skittles and Reese's as we pretended to be arguing over what to buy.

In my story I'd changed our poverty to a charming misunderstanding—"I thought you brought the money!"—the Kum & Go to a *tabac* in Lausanne. Mirabella and Sofia, their slender wrists hung with thin gold bracelets, cashmere cuffs dangling past elegant knuckles—Alison was the one who'd told me about cashmere and how French girls wore their sweaters—their fine scarves pulled close against the lowering snow, giggling and pocketing chocolates, winking at the shopkeeper.

We'd forgotten our gloves, too. That part, at least, was true in both worlds.

You're such a gifted storyteller, Sofia. I thought of Jaxson's golden head bent over hers. I thought of Alison, caught like a rabbit in a wire.

I thought of Earl's fingers around my throat.

"Sure," I said. "Keep it as long as you like."

I was learning patience, after all. I could bide my time.

A few days later, I came to work early. Jaxson's motor-cycle was parked in the street outside. They were sitting at her kitchen table, drinking coffee.

"Hello, you," Jaxson said, turning his smile upon me—dear god, that smile. As if, in that moment, all evidence to the contrary—he wasn't there to see *me*—I were the only girl in the world. "I was just stopping by on my way to the beach to talk to Alison about—um, the new book." His hair was damp from the shower. The condensation-edged outlines of bare feet—much too big to be hers—tracked from the bathroom to her bedroom and back into the kitchen. Alison was unruffled, her serene face impassive as she tilted her yellow mug upward.

"Coffee?" she asked.

"Sure," I said.

"You sit, I'll get it," Jaxson said, jumping up so quickly, he nearly knocked his chair over.

I wondered how we looked to him when he returned, bearing a steaming mug: Alison and I, seated side by side, our twin gazes unblinking. The Furies, united in cool silence?

"I'd better go," he said. "Back to the old notebook."

"See you, Jax," Alison said.

"See you," I echoed in her laconic drawl. He kissed both our cheeks—hers first—and left. A moment later I heard his motorcycle roar to life. The corners of Alison's mouth twitched, and we both collapsed into giggles.

"Okay, you," she said. "Time to get to work."

7.

The summer came brutal and early that year, the drought already ferocious in the first days of June. In the hill towns, well after well went dry. Despite the scorching sun, I kept up with my running. In school, what felt like a thousand years ago but was in truth only one, I'd been on the track team for a handful of seasons. After the first few rather painful weeks, my dormant muscles came alive again. I stopped buying a half-pint of vodka on my way back from Alison's each night. The pills I'd stolen from her that first day lay safely in their paper wrapper under my mattress, insurance against any future calamity. I'd only taken the one, that one time, although I thought all the time about taking more.

I filled my notebook, stole another.

Alison often took me to a coffee shop she liked in Silver Lake: sparse and sterile, postmodern with concrete floors and birch counters and exposed structural ironwork that upon closer examination was holding up nothing at all. I was listing tasks in my notebook while she worked one afternoon—*vegan protein powder, register A spin class Wednesday, new yoga studio (showers/organic products?), email Judith re: drinks w A upcoming*—when an astonishing creature whirled through the door in a cyclone of tendons and black denim and the lingering smell of cigarette smoke. She had the look of those iridescent and gangly black shorebirds one sees loitering about the wharfs. I watched as she placed her coffee order in a staccato bark and surveyed the room, her eyes widening slightly in an otherwise immobile face when they landed on our table. To my surprise, she stomped toward us.

"Alison!" she shrieked in a tremendous, rasp-fletched voice, booming so forcefully across the cement floor that one of the baristas flinched. "God, what a coincidence—I was just talking about you with Judith—how have you BEEN darling—it's been CENTURIES—" She had a strange cadence to her speech, one bellow crescendoing into the next without pause, as though she were shouting from a pulpit.

Upon arriving at our table, she flung her bony arms about Alison's shoulders. Alison looked as stunned as if she'd been shot.

"Celia," she said. "I didn't know you were in town."

Celia, I remembered: Jaxson and Judith's editor. I examined this legendary personage with interest. Her face had been Botoxed into a tundra of pale, immobile flesh. She was wearing complicated black wedge shoes and stiff black jeans so tight, it was a wonder her bony knees could bend. Her hair was dyed an astonishing shade of grape. Her gaunt sternum protruded from an artfully distressed sweater. A cockroach-sized diamond dwarfed her ring finger. She was looking at Alison as though she wanted to wear her like a hat.

"What a coincidence," Alison said, recovering. "How nice to see you. This is my" —the slightest falter—"assistant, Sofia."

"Your assistant," Celia said, the skeptical laser of her gaze razoring over me. "I HEARD about this assistant, HA HA! Judith's told me ALL about you—listen, Als, it's SO PERFECT I found you—Judith's having one of her little THINGS tonight—I'm just in town for a few DAYS for Brendan FAYLOR—so CHARMING— just moved out here from Brooklyn—it's just been an HONOR to work on the new book—and Judith and I had DRINKS the other night, and I said Judith you've GOT that reading series, why don't you have Brendan— it'll be LIKE a party—Jaxson and Minna obviously and probably Rachel Terbinsky and BARRY Koople— Rachel has that new series coming out from Sutton, I was just on a DIVERSITY panel with her, don't you JUST hate those—I keep telling Sal he's gotta stop MAKING me go to those goddamn things, I'm making Forsyth and Montpelier a DUMP TRUCK full of cash—an editor's work is never done, you think writers have it bad, HA HA!—so perfect for you to MEET Brendan and get some inspiration for whatever you're working on NOW—wink wink!" She delivered this entire monologue in a single breath, accenting the *wink wink* by actually winking. "Thank god all the agents are out in New York so we don't have to invite any, HA HA!"

"Oh, I don't—"

"I won't TAKE no for an answer! EIGHT o'clock— don't bother to bring anything—not that you would—HA HA!—I SAID, Judith, you have to get a caterer in for this one just in case—you remember that terrible party after the last festival when Carly Haley GOT absolutely bombed and started screaming at her HUSBAND—what's his name, that banker—"

"Realtor," Alison said.

"Oh, those FINANCE people are all the same," Celia brayed tirelessly, barreling toward an unseen conclusion like a semi whose brakes had gone out, "so AWKWARD, wasn't that?—I don't know why her books SELL so well—I find stories about POOR children so depressing—all THAT meth—"

"Vanilla nonfat latte, extra foam!" bellowed one of the baristas, holding a cup aloft. Celia's head whipped around.

"That's me—must run—so much to do, these IDIOTIC publicists—can't do a thing without me breathing down their necks—so fabulous to run into you—here, I've got an EXTRA advance copy of Brendan's book"—she dug about in her immense leather bag and flung a hardcover on our table—"see YOU tonight!" she bawled as she frittered away with an odd, jerky gait like a greyhound's.

Alison let out her breath.

"Dear god," she said. She rubbed her forehead with the heel of one hand.

"That's Jaxson's editor?"

"Jaxson and Judith's."

"Princesses."

"They're all about princesses in the end," Alison said tiredly.

"She's very energetic."

Alison laughed. "That's the cocaine. Want to come with me?"

"Are you sure that's a good idea?"

"I can't do it alone, honestly."

"I don't think Judith likes me much," I said.

"Everyone thinks Judith doesn't like them," Alison said. I refrained from pointing out that this did not mean that everyone was incorrect. "Come on, Sof. Tell me you don't have plans tonight."

"Jaxson will be there?"

Her mouth twitched. "Not you too."

"No!" I protested, laughing. "I just haven't seen him in a while." Alison had put off the past few weeks of writing group, saying she needed solitary time to focus, although I thought there might be more to it than that. I'd caught her screening her calls.

"Yes, honey, I'm sure Jaxson will be there." She looked down at the book Celia had left her with. "Ugh."

"What's this guy's book about?"

"Teenage boy gets the head of his life from the mysterious goth chick at school, discovers his purpose, something like that," Alison replied. I raised an eyebrow. "I'm serious," she said. "That's a whole genre." She turned the book over, reading from the back cover. "'Touching, whip smart, and pitch-perfect, transcending the constraints of genre to lay bare universal truths.' Jesus Christ."

"You think it'll be fun?"

"It won't be *fun*. It'll be insufferable. But I'm insufferably curious. Celia paid him a million dollars." She winked at me. I felt for a giddy moment that we were coconspirators, working together in secrecy toward some shared goal, infiltrating this bizarre and labyrinthine world in which she operated as a kind of sleeper agent.

I slid the book across the table. "*She, Her, and Me*," I read aloud, turning it over to look at the front cover: a radiantly backlit, highly edited photo of two girls and a boy, all three holding hands: the two girls with each other, and the boy with one of the girls. They were dressed like models in a targeted ad for sweater sets. The girl in the middle had on a lot of black eyeliner and a sultry cast to her features.

"Jaxson says it's dazzling." I pointed to the line of type across the jacket, Jaxson's name cast in a font nearly as large as Brendan Faylor's.

"Celia makes him blurb everything she publishes," Alison said.

"Blurb?"

"It's when an author owes your editor a favor so the editor gets them to say something nice about your book."

"It sounds like an STD."

I read the summary on the inside flap aloud. "'They always say that senior year is the best year of your life. But for Michael Yorick Pemulis, it's the capstone on a career of failure. He's never been to a party. He's never been outside his tiny town of Fairfield, Kansas. He's never even talked to a girl, let alone touched one. Until the day Desdemona Octavia Page walks into his life and turns his world upside down. She's everything Michael isn't: brash, funny, outgoing, adventurous, and sexy. There's just one problem standing between Michael and the most perfect girl he's ever met: her girlfriend, Chelsey.'"

"Stop," Alison said.

"'Can he find the path to true love with a girl who can't possibly love him back?'" I turned to the back flap, where

Brendan Faylor smiled with coy bashfulness, clutching an electric guitar by the neck with one hand and raking the other through his shaggy forelock.

"He looks very sensitive. Look, he's from Kansas. Maybe it's an autobiographical novel."

"Must've been one desperate lesbian," Alison said.

"I bet there's a threesome."

"Oh, god, you're right," she said, laughing. "No, really, stop!" But I was already opening the book, flicking through the rough-edged pages—"They gave him a *deckle*," Alison muttered—until a paragraph caught my eye.

"'If I were the kind of guy who knew how to fall in love, I would have fallen in love with Desdemona Octavia Page the day she took me to the river without Chelsey. The birds were doing the birdiest thing I'd ever heard. The trees—'"

"Birdiest," Alison said in an awful tone.

"'The trees sang tree songs in a winsome summer breeze that ruffled the long layers of Desdemona's rainbow-colored hair and carried her delicious girly smell back to me. Fruit shampoo. Bubble gum. And mystery.'"

Alison put her head in her hands.

"'Desdemona's calves were pale and tawny as she picked her way through the grass—'" I stopped. "They can't be pale *and* tawny."

"Maybe he meant *brawny*."

"Brawny's not sexy to straight teenage boys. I mean, they're not allowed to talk about it if it is, I don't think," I said.

"At least they didn't give him a decent copy editor."

"'...as she picked her way through the grass in front of me. I knew the stories everybody told about the swimming hole. I knew what girls did there. They swam naked. And, not to shock you or anything, I'd never seen a girl naked. Not since my mom. I mean, I didn't see my mom naked recently. I'm not a perv. It was when I was a baby. This is getting weird, right? Everyone's always telling me I take the conversation to a weird place. Not that many people talk to me. And I'm babbling right now because ahead of me, swimming hole in sight, girlfriend nowhere in the vicinity, Desdemona Octavia Page was pulling off her shirt. And she wasn't wearing a bra.'" I paused, skimmed. "I guess Desdemona's bisexual," I said. "There's some graphic erection description, do you want it?"

"*No*," Alison said.

"Poor old Chelsey. Should be some reading."

"Indeed," Alison said. She pushed her chair away from the table. "I feel permanently spoiled. Pestilent congregation of vapors fattening myself for maggots, et cetera. Come on, let's go back. I have something I want to work out before we go to Judith's." She closed her laptop, her mouth set. She drove almost recklessly back to her house, thrust a folder of papers at me and told me to sort them, and slammed into her office. Still holding the folder, I moved silently to the door and put my ear against it.

From within, a faint, rapid clicking as she typed.

I slunk back to her couch, thus dismissed, and rifled through the folder: a disarray of old tax returns and scribbled-on receipts that I investigated briefly and then set on the couch next to me when it yielded nothing of interest. I did not mean to tilt my head back and close my eyes and give myself over to the couch's embrace; I meant to sit with my back straight and order her papers, a model assistant, an upstanding employee, a rising star, but Alison's couch was soft, and I was tired, and the overstuffed pillows in their tasteful subdued stripes were too much. I woke with a start when her office door slammed open, and scrabbled among the receipts as if I'd been ordering them, but she didn't even notice.

"Time to get ready," she said. She got dressed—an oversize, shapeless black shirtdress that somehow looked elegant on her, eyeliner, her heady perfume—while I drank a mug of her strong-smelling tea in my knee-sprung jeans and old T-shirt.

"Well," she said grimly, as though she were leading us to our execution. "I suppose we'd better go."

8.

"Darling!" Judith sailed toward us on a cloud of air kisses, Princess Snowflake mincing at her feet, her gaze skittering past me like someone averting her eyes from an especially grisly car accident. Her voice was high and brash, an unconscious echo of Celia's, as though she'd acquired her bizarre vocal affect by osmosis over drinks. "You *made* it!"

"Wouldn't miss it for the world," Alison said, leading me past Judith into the living room. I recognized many of the guests from Judith's last reading—including, to my dismay, Barry—but the room was markedly more crowded now, and the caterers were busy.

Celia clicked over to us in patent stilettos and a white silk blouse tucked into the waistband of the largest, most unflattering pair of jeans I'd ever seen, vast sails of overdyed denim rigged precariously to her knobby hips. Swathes of fabric had been ripped out to lay bare her ropy thighs.

She had her phone thrust out at us, and her face was twisted into a grimace of aggrieved petulance. "Did you hear?" she boomed. "Another one—all OVER the internet—the hashtag is trending—what a time to be doing BOOK promotion, HA HA!"

"Another what?" Alison asked.

"SCHOOL shooting in"—she consulted her phone—"Ore-gone? Middle school—Salem—isn't Salem the one with the WITCHES—"

"That's Massachusetts," Alison said automatically, looking over Celia's proffered phone.

Celia clucked at her phone. "Brendan won't stop posting his REVIEWS—I don't think it's a good look right now—he's got to learn nuance—I mean life has to go ON these days, HA HA! If we stopped promotion for every terrible thing that happened, we'd never sell another book—but seventeen dead, and with the POLITICAL situation right now—it's so difficult for a writer to navigate, I do understand that—"

Alison lunged for a passing waiter, claimed a champagne flute off a tray. "I think people are pretty scared," Alison said neutrally.

Celia looked around, as if Brendan were lurking directly behind her, taking notes.

"Between the two of us, Als, he does NOT have the feel for social—not at all—it's like he was born on the moon, I swear to god—puts his foot in it with every other thing that comes out of his mouth—I'm trying to help him, but it's an UPHILL slog—"

"It'll be something else tomorrow," Alison said.

"It's TRAGIC—we should sign a PETITION or something—I just feel so helpless—it FEELS like the world is falling apart—the climate—and now all these guns—I was LUNCHING at Barn Joo the other day with MAUNDRA, and she said no one wants to BUY anything except ESCAPISM anymore—I don't know why all the agents at Bond Street INSIST on going to BARN JOO all the time—I'm so sick of their APPETIZERS—"

"I feel helpless, too," Alison said blandly.

"Ceeeeeeelia!" This was Judith now, waving one arm; in the other, she clutched Princess Snowflake, which looked as though it desperately preferred to be elsewhere. I felt a sudden kinship with it. "Darling!" Judith and Celia exchanged air kisses, fresh tragedy forgotten.

"Lovely party—very nice—so glad you gussied up the series a bit for Brendan—you're such a HOSTESS—" Across the room, a woman shrieked. We all looked up. She was standing next to Barry Koople with a look of horror on her face.

"There he GOES again—excuse me—" Celia marched over to Barry, deftly separating him from his hapless victim as Judith observed with interest.

"He's a disaster," she said. "But Celia won't stop him now that he's a *bestseller*."

"I thought they just discounted the e-book," Alison said.

Judith bared her teeth in a sharkish smile. "Everybody hates him except Celia," she said happily.

"Why did you invite him, then?" I asked, genuinely curious. She looked at me as if she had forgotten altogether who I was.

"What?"

"If you don't like him, why keep inviting him to your readings?"

"Look who's here," she said, ignoring me, and there was Jaxson, Minna stone-faced at his side. Judith swooped away from us toward him, already prattling. I wondered if everyone at her reading series went out of their minds. Once a month, like werewolves.

"I'd better make the rounds," Alison said with a sigh. "Sorry. Be right back."

I stood there awkwardly. Jaxson was surrounded by people, and without Alison, I had no one to talk to.

"How thrilling, I've got you alone!" Celia descended on me without warning. "Come, come, come, darling— I SIMPLY must know more about you—" She seized my arm and dragged me to a nearby loveseat, lowering her voice to a hoarse scream that I suppose she imagined a conspiratorial whisper.

"Are you having a good time—certainly you are—what was your name again?—Sally—wonderful—are those jeans McQueen?—surely not out here, HA! HA!—how lucky for you that LA is so casual—I'm so delighted you came, simply delighted—but you must tell me absolutely everything—she's such a mystery half the time—so what's it like, working for her?"

It was the first time I'd heard her ask a real question, and I was instantly wary. "It's great."

"You're so young," she said wistfully. "I could never get away with what you're wearing." She was watching Alison now, who was across the room talking to Jaxson. Minna was nowhere in sight. "Alison's so talented," Celia said, in a way that suggested she did not mean this as a compliment.

"Mmm," I said noncommittally, resisting the urge to pick at the ragged cuff of my jeans.

"It's a difficult business." Celia surveyed the lavish spectacle of Judith's living room with satisfaction. "Incredibly difficult—you have to get so USED to rejection—she never got over the failure of the first book, poor thing—"

"I'm a writer, too," I said.

"ONLY a few writers manage to succeed—all of my AUTHORS do—but so much depends on where you are—if you can capture the right moment—what is she working on these days?"

"She's writing a new book."

"She is—good news! HA! HA!"

"I thought you only published young adult novels," I said.

She stared at me for a moment. "Ah," she said. "YES—that's true—just don't like to see Alison so DESPONDENT—Judith THOUGHT that you might be on hand to EN-COURAGE her—she IS working?"

"Darlings!" Judith shouted from across the room, saving me from responding. "It's time!" Her guests lurched toward the sofas and settees of Judith's vast living room with varying degrees of success. I sat back down, my attempt to escape Celia thwarted. "Tonight we have a very special guest." Her expression strongly suggested this had not been her idea. "Please give a big round of applause for Brendan Faylor, whose book launches next week! Isn't he *adorable*, girls? *And* he's single, can you *imagine*?"

The attendees clapped dutifully as Brendan slunk toward the center of the room. He was even ganglier than he appeared in his book-jacket photograph, his shaggy, dark hair more mop-like, his elbows more prominent, in addition to which he was clutching by the neck an acoustic guitar case covered in band stickers. Alison collapsed next to me on the couch.

"Wow, guys, thanks so much," Brendan said. "Thanks, Judith, wow. I gotta say, LA is a lot more welcoming than Brooklyn!" He beamed at the assembled writers. "Wow, well, okay, so, what you need to know about this book, I guess, is that it's a super unconventional romance." He laughed; dutifully, the audience joined in a second later. "But you guys know I don't do happy endings." He laughed again; this witticism, however, landed in an awkward and confused silence. "So, um, anyway, I'll just, like, read," he said.

There was a peculiarly soporific quality to his voice that became more and more evident as he proceeded. Next to me, Alison's head tilted forward until she pulled it back up with a jerk; moments later, she was tipping toward sleep again. I lost track almost immediately of whatever Brendan was reading—some English class, the hero delivering a scathing takedown of *Wuthering Heights* with the desire to impress one of the lesbians, lots of pauses for laughs that, as a rule, failed to materialize—and let my thoughts drift.

Brendan droned on for an extraordinary length of time. "Just one more short chapter," he said, half a dozen times. The only thing I could make out with any certainty was that Michael Yorick Pemulis had a great deal to say about young ladies' breasts and bottoms for someone who had purportedly never seen a naked girl.

At last, what seemed hours later, Brendan stopped. Alison started awake next to me. "Thank god," she said.

"Thank you *so much*, Brendan—" Judith began, but our ordeal was not yet over.

"I have a special surprise for you tonight!" Brendan interrupted, opening his guitar case.

"Oh dear," Celia murmured next to me.

"That's right, guys," he said, happy as a clam in butter. "I wrote a whole album of songs based on this book, and I want to share a few of them with you." The audience had gone very still, as if hypnotized.

Brendan's singing voice proved a logical extension of his speaking one: a reedy, high-pitched keen that sounded several steps flat to my admittedly untrained ear. His songs were all on the long side. The moment he set his guitar aside, the audience rose as one creature, applauding furiously. *They're trying to drown him out so he can't say anything else*, I thought, and indeed, as Brendan opened his mouth to speak, the applause grew louder, until he was forced to concede the field and retreated to Judith's side, grinning and bobbing.

"Excuse me," Alison said. "I'm going to go shoot myself."

"What was that, darling?" Celia asked, but Alison was already out of earshot as though flung from a cannon.

"She's going to find Jaxson," I said. Celia looked at me shrewdly. I hopped to my feet. "And I'll get us another drink!" I trilled and made my escape.

Everything around me faded. I drank another glass of champagne and one more after that. I had gotten out on Judith's deck somehow, the echo of waves crashing against the sand drifting upward, the smell of the ocean salting the air—I was talking to someone, a blue-haired woman I didn't know—*the book blogger*, I remembered. "You work with *Jaxson*?" she was saying in an awed tone. "Has he told you anything about the new book? We're all just dying to see it."

"He's working on it," I said.

"I heard he was stuck," she whispered in my ear. "I heard he hardly has anything finished at all."

"I'm not supposed to talk about it."

"How do you know him?"

"We're old friends," I said. "I've known him for ages."

Her eyes widened in awe. "From *New York*?"

"Oh yes," I said. "I lived there for years."

"We have to get coffee sometime!"

I nodded agreeably and wandered away.

And then I was talking to someone else—and then I was alone with my hands on the cool, smooth metal railing, two people ten or so feet away from me arguing in low, hushed voices—focusing blearily—Alison and, looming over her slight form, the sculpted bulk of Jaxson.

"Alison," he was saying. "I can't talk about this here. Be reasonable."

"I'm tired of being reasonable," Alison said.

"You know how important you are to me," he said. "Als, you know that. But not here."

"Where, then? When, Jaxson? All these years, and you never—"

"Alison," he said, touching her shoulder. "Baby—" Suddenly enraged, she slapped his hand away.

"Don't you *baby* me, you cheat—"

"Alison—"

"You promised me!" she screamed. "You promised me we would stop lying—"

He put a hand up to stop her. "Someone's out here," he said. "Who is that? Sofia, is that you?"

"Yeah," I said. "I just came out a second ago to get some air."

"Sofia? What are *you* doing here?" Alison snapped. Jaxson's eyes met mine; behind her back, he shrugged, his self-possession descending like a curtain.

"Als, you brought her," he said in the calm, authoritative tone one might use with a large and threatening-looking dog. Her mouth opened and closed again as she stared at me.

"Come on, Sofia, it's time to go. We're done," she snarled. "Jaxson, we're fucking over. I mean it this time."

"Als—" Jaxson said, reaching a hand out to stop her.

But she flung herself toward me, grabbing my arm and hauling me back into the house, through the last traces of Judith's party—Barry Koople, braying drunkenly—Brendan was *singing*—Judith with a fixed smile at his side, her eyes shining with menace—a few more stragglers waving dreg-sloshed wineglasses at one another, their words slurring. Judith saw us, started to say goodbye, and faltered as Alison dragged me across the room and out the front door, slamming it behind her with such force that the frame trembled. She stood panting for a moment on Judith's front walk, her eyes wild, and then gathered herself with visible effort.

"I don't want to talk about him," she said. "So don't ask. I'll drive you home."

She drove without speaking, her eyes fixed on the road. What had I just seen? A lover's quarrel, obviously, but one that seemed final. If she was leaving him, did that leave room for me?

"Why does everyone hate publicists?" I asked in the painful silence.

"They're the easiest person to blame when a book tanks," she said.

I pillowed my head against the passenger window and let myself drift smoothly into sleep.

9.

I woke late the next morning, starting back to consciousness with a jerk. For a long moment, I did not know where I was. The soft, fine blanket, smelling faintly of lavender; the cushions beneath me too thick and giving to be my own hard mattress; even the light gentler and lovelier than the harsh sun that pounded into the studio with relentless force. My mouth tasted like ashes. The night came back to me in bits and pieces. I had drunk champagne. I'd talked to writers. I'd eaten Judith's canapés. A shrimp wrapped in bacon. I'd passed out in Alison's car.

I sat bolt upright. She'd put me to sleep on her couch. I could hear her in the kitchen, moving around. I got up and plumped the couch cushions, folded the blanket as tidily as I could manage, and went sheepishly into the kitchen.

"You're up," Alison said, handing me a steaming mug of coffee.

"I'm so sorry, I never meant to—"

"Don't be silly. Drink your coffee; I've a lot I want to get done today."

"I can leave."

She raised an eyebrow. "I've a lot for you to do as well. Unless you're… discomposed."

"I'm fine," I said quickly, though in truth, the first sip of coffee sent a wave of nausea roiling through me. Her mouth was pressed in a thin line.

"Good. I need to run some errands; I'll be gone for a few hours or so. Can you water the plants in my office, please? And do some laundry? If there's time before I get back, you might tidy up the kitchen a bit as well."

I opened my mouth to protest, saw her look, and closed it again. She'd sent me on silly errands before, but she'd never asked me to do her cleaning for her. I was being punished.

Because I saw her fight with him, I thought. Because I'd seen him get to her.

"Sure," I said. I wasn't entirely able to keep the resentment out of my voice.

"Laundry hamper's in my bathroom," she said. "Cleaning things are in the pantry; the watering can's in there, too. I like to add plant food. I'll be back this afternoon." A moment later I heard the snick of the front door closing lightly behind her.

"Well, then," I said aloud. I went to vomit industriously in her immaculate bathroom.

When I'd put in a load of her clothes, I got the watering can out of the pantry and the jar of plant food (even her fertilizer looked expensive: glass jar with a hand-printed label), filled the can, and carried it, sloshing, into her office. I was surprised she'd let me go into her private lair—she kept it locked when she went out without me—but I saw as soon as I opened the door that she'd either taken her computer with her or hidden it. After setting the can on the floor, I opened the mysterious red door I'd seen on the first day I came to her house.

It was, as I'd thought, a closet, and it was disastrously untidy, even more so than the rest of her office. Papers snowed from the single high shelf; coats—winter coats, leather and wool—bulged from hangers, smelling of mothballs; glittering dresses shed loose sequins across more books, a basket of fabric scraps, a tangled wad of yarn, assorted boxes, a pair of galoshes, and a stack of notebooks.

I took the first one off the pile and paged through it: lined pages covered with her ugly, dense handwriting, nearly illegible. I could make out only bits here and there: *says he's going to help me break out at last and I can't help but think it's* [undecipherable] *I just don't know anymore what I'm doing here in this city* [undecipherable] *alone and forever that way.* I frowned, briefly considered pilfering it for further study, decided against it—what if she missed it, unlikely as that might be?—and replaced the notebook.

The boxes proved unrewarding: more winter clothes, thick-knit sweaters and leather leggings, a pair of knee-high boots so hopelessly crushed that they'd never be wearable again, long-sleeved thermal shirts, and wool tights. Why had she kept all this stuff? I put the last box back where I'd found it, inadvertently releasing a minor avalanche of other articles, and I felt a quick pulse of intrigue when I saw what I'd unearthed: another, smaller cardboard box, the kind you might get from a copy shop to contain your printouts, with *Creepers* written across it in black marker.

The box was full of papers of varying sizes and shapes: printed emails, pages torn from a notebook and covered in handwriting, even a sheet comprising letters cut from a magazine like a ransom note, each annotated with Alison's familiar hand. MERMAID DRAGON MAN, she'd scrawled across the ransom note. I scanned it quickly. GOOD DAY SIR U KNOW MY THOUGHTS ON THIS WORK I HAVE NOT RECEVED A RESPONSE FROM U SIR. IT IS TIME U AKCNOWLED MY CONTRIBUTION TOO THE WORK. The note ended there, but several other pages labeled MERMAID DRAGON MAN continued in the same ominous vein. I set them aside. The emails, from a sender Alison had labeled ROSEBUD WACKO, were so explicitly sexual, even I blushed.

Your messages to me are clear, Rosebud Wacko wrote. *I know this book is for I and I alone, my beloved. I long for you to plunge within my moist petals where I await you in breathless Anticipation. Don't you dare ignore me. Your silence will not protect you from your Destiny. Jaxson, I—*

Jaxson? I thought.

The handwritten letters, from THE SCHOOLGIRL, were most interesting of all. Alison must've thrown away the envelopes; there was no clue as to their actual sender or her location. Unlike the other letter writers, this author seemed to have a solid grasp on the nature and workings of the English language, although she was clearly young. She had written Jaxson a dozen essay-length letters, each on a different theme from *The Bone Girl*: death and desire in the forest, archetypes employed by the novel, the role of mythology. Her letters were not so much threatening as persistent; it was only the last of these, dated several years ago, that approached the tone of the other senders.

I still don't understand why you chose that ending. Why you went the easy route instead of allowing Calliope and Clio a life together. You give Calliope the tools to set herself free from the sorcerer, you give Clio the strength of her journey—by the end, they are more than powerful enough to face him together. And then you tell us it was all in Clio's head. What if it wasn't, Jaxson? What if Calliope killed the sorcerer to save herself?

What on earth was Alison doing with this stuff?

I heard a car door slam outside and jumped to my feet. She'd said she would be gone for hours. Was this some kind of a test? I shoved the papers back in the box, the rest of her things back in the closet in as close an approximation of its original disorder as I could manage, and shut the door tightly just as she came into the house. "Sofia?"

"In here!" I shouted, hefting the watering can and pouring its contents into the nearest potted plant. Her office door swung open, and she peered around the frame.

"Right," she said. "I told you to—you know what, leave that and come into the kitchen, why don't you?"

I set the can down and followed her. I could only imagine what she'd have done if she caught me going through her things—did she know? Had she guessed? Was she readying herself to fire me? I'd be in real trouble if she did; I couldn't afford to lose the work, couldn't afford the time it might take me to find another job, and besides, losing Alison would mean losing all of them, losing Jaxson—

"—wanted to tell you I'm sorry," she was saying, "I shouldn't have been so awful this morning and last night. I feel terrible about it, I just—are you, I mean I don't blame you if you're angry with me, but I—"

"What?"

"I'm sorry," she repeated. "About this morning. I was an absolute bitch. I drank too much, and I—I didn't feel well, and I took it out on you—I wouldn't blame you if you just stomped out the door right now, but I hope you won't. I thought you might not even be here when I got back. I just started to feel so awful about how I behaved…"

"It's fine," I said. "I don't mind."

"Well, that's awfully generous of you," she said. "I take things on in this way and I get so upset, and I've been trying to work on it for ages, but I have this terrible habit of just unloading on whoever's around." She was performing for me, and I didn't know why. "It's not right," she said. "Since we're friends and all."

"Friends," I echoed stupidly.

"Um, listen," she added. "Jaxson and I—I realized last night that he's not good for me. I've decided not to see him for a while."

"Oh, Als," I said, reaching my arms out to her and enfolding her in a hug. "That's so hard. I'm really sorry." I'd never called her Als before; it felt odd in my mouth.

"It's okay," she said, but she was crying, and she didn't let go of the embrace when I did. "I just… I need some space to sort things out. So no writing group for a while. I hope you don't mind."

I did, but I could hardly tell her that. "Not at all."

"And, um, if you—if you run into him," she said. "I don't really want to see him for a while. So you can tell him I need to detoxify my life right now."

"Sure," I said. "You think he'll be around?"

"I told him not to come by," she said. "But sometimes he can be—persuasive. He knows I can't say no to him."

"If you need me to talk to him—"

"I don't think it will come to that. But I appreciate it."

"Right," I said, disappointed. "I didn't finish with the plants, if you want me to—"

"You don't have to do that," she said earnestly,

"I don't mind, Alison. Really."

"Sof, I don't know what I'd do without you. If you *absolutely* don't mind. I suppose you could be a dear and finish the laundry, too. Why don't I make us some more tea?"

"Sounds great," I said.

10.

In the week following her breakup with Jaxson, Alison fell apart. Small things, at first. Her eyes were often bloodshot in the mornings, hinting at long, insomniac nights; she stopped smoking in secret, sometimes even lighting one cigarette off the end of another; I smelled whiskey on her breath more often than not in the afternoons and could tell, by the pinpoints of her pupils and the slight drag of her voice, that she was dipping freely into her stash of pills. None of these things on their own would have been unusual, but taken all together, they suggested a deeper instability, a building crisis of some kind that I would, had I known its contours, have done my best to prevent.

But, in her distress, she was even more secretive than usual, closing me out of her office for sometimes the entire day or running mysterious errands that took hours. I took to keeping track of the tidal ebb and flow of her cat tin, noting the levels of her self-medication and her corresponding moods in my notebook in a shorthand I had developed for this purpose. Her pills were being depleted at an alarming rate and were replaced nearly as quickly, although I had no idea who was supplying them; there were never prescription bottles around her house, which suggested she wasn't getting them from a physician. Not that I'd had much doubt about that. Jaxson called her every day, sometimes several times; each time her phone buzzed, she looked down at it with an expression somewhere between contempt and despair and sent the call straight to voicemail.

I did what I could to soothe her. I went through Alison's cookbooks, taught myself to make the kinds of things she liked—whole grains and steamed vegetables, arranged in her pretty china bowls with garnishes of avocado and miso paste and hand-cracked salt—and brought her meals in the afternoons when I could hear her pacing restlessly behind her office door and the bright-hot light was lengthening slowly toward sundown. I made her an online calendar with her yoga classes and her Pilates and blocks of time marked out as "writing hours." Alison had always been careless about touch; now, I rubbed the knots out of her muscular shoulders, letting her lean into me, her long hair spilling over my hands. I pushed her to meet Judith for drinks.

"You need a friend right now," I told her, although Judith was rather a shark-infested harbor in which to seek shelter from a storm.

"You'll come with me?" she asked after she and Judith had exchanged a flurry of texts. I hadn't intended this result at all, but I said that I would. "Thanks, Sof," she said.

Her relief seemed disproportionate to the occasion, so much so that I wondered why she'd agreed to see Judith at all. That evening, we met Judith at a trendy new place downtown that served bar snacks like bacon-wrapped matzo balls and pork dumplings smothered in cheese, both of which Alison ordered and then left untouched.

"You look great, Als," Judith cooed, her dark eyes glittering. "How are things?"

"You know," Alison said, staring at her drink. She'd poured herself a sizable shot before we left the house, too, though I'd pretended I didn't notice.

"Any progress on the book?"

"Same old," Alison said.

"Mmmm," Judith said, looking over at me and then back at Alison. "If you need any help—"

"I'm fine, Jude," Alison snapped into her whiskey. Judith looked at me over her head and raised one eyebrow. I shrugged.

"If you say so," Judith said. When Alison said she had to go after her second drink, I saw relief flicker across Judith's face. Relief, I thought, and something else, although I couldn't have said what, exactly. Whatever it was, I didn't like the looks of it much.

A week or so after our date with Judith, I was in Alison's living room tidying her bookshelves when a sudden rap at the door startled me half out of my skin. Alison was sequestered in her office. I peered out the window, saw Jaxson's motorcycle parked in the street below. In spite of myself, I smiled.

"Hi," I said, opening the door a crack. "She's not here."

His eyes were bloodshot, the skin around them puffy and discolored. His hair was dirty, and he was wearing an old flannel shirt stained with motor oil; several days' worth of stubble accentuated the sharp lines of his jaw. Dishevelment suited him a lot more than it had suited Earl, but then again, Earl had been poor.

"Can I come in and wait for her?"

"I don't think that's a good idea."

"Sofia, please." His Windex-blue gaze was beseeching. "You have no idea what I'm going through, sweetheart. I'm sure she told you to stay away from me—"

"She didn't," I lied. *Sweetheart*, I thought.

"—but I'm really—I need to see her."

I stepped out onto the porch, closing the door softly behind me. "I think she's just... going through something," I said, looking up at him soulfully the way she used to. "I wish I could help you, I really do."

He put one hand on the doorframe and leaned over me, so close, I could see the fluttering pulse at his throat. "Maybe you can convince her to see me," he said. "Sofia, god, I can't..." He shook his head. "You must think I'm insane," he said. "Look at me. I'm sorry." He pushed himself upright again and shoved his hands in his pockets.

"I can't talk to you about it here," I said.

"Right," he said.

"Give me your phone." He handed it over, and I programmed my number into his contacts. "Get some rest, Jaxson."

"You're an angel, Sofia. I mean it."

"Get out of here before she comes back." On impulse, I stood on tiptoe and kissed his cheek. To my surprise he pulled me close, wrapping his arms around me and burying his face in the curve of my shoulder. "I'll call you," he said into my neck. "Thank you, Sofia. It's really good to see you."

"Don't mention it," I said shakily as he pulled away. "Really."

"Thanks," Alison said an hour or so later. She had come out of her office to make a cup of tea; she added a generous slug of whiskey to the cup without bothering to hide it.

"It's nothing."

"It's not nothing."

I thought about the questions I could ask her and decided against all of them. Her face was closed, an abandoned storefront with its windows dark and empty.

"You want one?" she asked, hefting the mug.

"It's always happy hour somewhere," I said.

Jaxson called me a few days later, on a hot Saturday where the sun came down white and brutal as sheet metal. "Sofia," he said when I answered, and I recognized the smoky rumble of his voice in just that word, felt a little light-headed.

"Hi," I said.

"I know this is kind of last minute, but are you busy this afternoon?" He misread my hesitation. "Of course you are. I'm sorry."

"No, really, it's nothing I can't move to tomorrow," I said. "What did you have in mind?"

"I was thinking about getting drunk."

I laughed. "Suits me just fine. Where?"

"Santa Monica? I know it's a haul for you, but there's this great place down by the pier that's pretty much a straight shot from Echo Park. Or I can come to you if that's easier."

"No, that's great," I said. I'd never told any of them where I lived; there was no reason anyone in her right mind would've driven from Hollywood to Echo Park for a job as generic as the Beane. "I have a couple of things to take care of first—meet you there around five?"

"Can't wait," he said. The charm was instinctual, but that didn't mean I didn't feel it run through me like a drug. "Listen, I feel weird even asking this, but do you mind not telling..."

"Not at all."

"You know how she can be. I don't want her to—"

"Don't worry about it, Jaxson. My lips are sealed. Scout's honor."

"Thanks, sweetheart."

I took the fastest shower of my life, pulled on leggings and a loose, soft, well-cut T-shirt I'd stolen from Alison, spritzed myself with a perfume sample I'd found in one of her drawers, carefully applied a dab of her lipstick, and gave myself a once-over in the grimy mirror. Despite the overhead light's custardy glare, I looked good: all that running had given me a lot of muscle and snacking on the high-end organic contents of Alison's refrigerator had left my skin soft and glowing. I was no Alison, but I'd do. I splurged on a car service. It was more than I could afford, but if I were rendered tipsy and vulnerable *and* carless, I knew, he was too much of a gentleman not to make it his problem. At the very least, he'd pay for my car home.

I would've been far too intimidated to walk into the bar Jaxson had named if I weren't meeting someone with money. The exterior suggested a converted loft building; inside, the ceilings were dizzyingly high, the elegant booths screened by polished black wood, the floor an intricate tile mosaic. The massive bar stretched the length of the room. Behind it, bartenders in vests and suspenders scurried back and forth underneath the looming supervision of shelves that rose nearly to the lofty heights from whence dangled lambent globes, larger than my head, in an even line along the bar. The back bar was of marble and included, in addition to a staggering array of bottles, an old-fashioned library card catalog and rolling ladder; above the ladder's reach, the shelves were stocked not with bottles but with books. It was early in the evening, and the room had not yet filled. Jaxson was seated on a red leather stool at the polished wooden bar, his notebook in front of him, his hair loose and a long-sleeved shirt hiding his tattoos. He had, I noticed, showered.

"Hey," I said, taking the seat next to him and laying one hand briefly on his densely muscled shoulder.

"Sofia!" He turned the full force of his smile on me, and all the air went out of my lungs. "Thanks so much for coming all this way."

"I never get to the beach," I said. "It's a treat."

"I didn't realize you were such a diplomat," he said. "Cocktail?" He pushed a menu toward me. I hoped he was paying. The cocktails had cute, alliterative names and a great many ingredients I neither recognized nor could pronounce. "Whiskey," I said when the bartender appeared in front of me.

"Preference, miss?"

"Neat," I said. "And cheap."

"Nonsense," Jaxson said. "Top shelf for the lady. Do you like rye, Sofia?"

I was already in way over my head. "I have no idea," I said. Jaxson pointed at a bottle, and the bartender nodded at him gravely and winked at me before going to fetch it.

"So," Jaxson said.

"So," I said. "Want to tell me what this is about?"

"Alison won't see me," he said into his drink.

"I'm not sure how you think I can help you."

"You're closer to her than anyone, Sof." I liked the way the nickname sounded when he said it so much that it took a second for me to register what he'd said.

"Me?" I asked, startled.

"Sure. She adores you, you know. Talks about you all the time. How talented you are, how smart, how much you remind her of herself when she was your age."

"She *does*?"

He smiled at my expression. "I know. She's a tough one. Doesn't give you a thing to work with. But trust me, she cares about you a lot. And right now, I think you're the only one of us who can get through to her."

Us. I liked that, too. "That still doesn't answer my question."

"I just need her to listen to me."

"I can't make her listen to anybody."

"You can convince her it'd be a good idea to try."

"That's going to be a tough sell if I don't know what exactly it is you want from her."

"I know," he said. "I'm sorry. It's something that goes way back between us. I don't think she'd like it much if I told you."

I tried a different tack. "I didn't realize you were her writing teacher."

He looked surprised and suddenly wary. "She told you about that?" The bartender set my drink in front of me. I took a sip, grimaced, sighed in pleasure. I was going to let Jaxson pick all my whiskeys from here on out.

"Just that you helped her with the Medea book. That's when you started sleeping with her?" Jaxson, who'd been taking a sip of his own drink, coughed hard.

"Yes," he said after a beat. "We were… extremely close. For a long time. Things got more complicated when we moved out here."

Alison had said she'd moved to Los Angeles for money. "Minna?"

"Minna came after our problems started," he said. "Minna wasn't part of the plan. But I fell in love with her, and she needed a green card, and she's wonderful."

"Not so wonderful that you broke up with Alison."

"Minna's an actress," he said. "She doesn't understand what it's like." I made an involuntary face. "Believe me, I know how it sounds."

"I didn't say that."

"You didn't have to," he said, laughing. "I adore Minna. She has nothing to do with this ridiculous world Alison and I are stuck in. She doesn't give a shit about trying to impress Celia. She doesn't care if Judith hates her guts. She has her own life completely removed from all of it. But at the same time—the thing about writing is that you're so alone for so much of the time. And everything depends on you. An actor has her screenwriter, her director, her costars, the production crew—she can trust that if the final work crashes and burns, it's not all on her shoulders. It takes a village to fuck up a movie. Fucking up a book is a one-man show. Alison gets that. Alison gets me. In a way that Minna never can. I'm not proud of it," he said. "Or making excuses. That's just how it is."

"Does Minna know?"

He raised an eyebrow at me.

"None of my business. Fair enough." I was acutely conscious of the warmth of him next to me, the incremental distance between our thighs on the leather stools, the salt-breeze scent of his hair, the way we were talking: world-weary, wise, like equals. What else did I have to offer him? "You know Alison has a drug problem, right?"

That, I saw, he had not expected. "What?"

"You didn't know?"

"I mean, she drinks too much sometimes, but so do all of us."

"I'm not talking about drinking."

"You think that has something to do with the way she's been acting?"

"I doubt it's helping. Who would she be getting drugs from? Prescription stuff."

He shook his head, alarmed. "I heard a rumor Brendan's been dabbling in the trade, but I can't imagine Alison buying from him. She can't stand him."

"Brendan the writer? Can anyone stand him?"

He grinned. "He's something else, isn't he?"

"You said he was dazzling."

"Perils of the post. Another round?" I shrugged, and he signaled to the bartender. "What kind of drugs do you think Alison's doing?"

"She's my friend," I said, looking up at him and running a finger along my collarbone.

"Come on, Sofia. If she's doing something that's putting her in danger, you have to tell me. Tell Judith, at least."

"Tell Judith?" I asked, startled. "Are you serious?"

"I know Judith can be—well. But she cares about Alison. Ah, okay, so your poker face is not entirely impermeable. She and Alison go way back."

"The three of you."

"Yes," he said. "If Alison's in trouble, please, Sofia. You have to tell us. Even if she makes you promise—I don't know, whatever she's probably made you promise."

The second drink went down even more easily than the first. "She hasn't made me promise anything. Why does she have your fan mail in her closet?"

"She showed you those?"

"Not exactly."

He cocked his head at me. "You do contain multitudes. My agent has me save the weirdest ones in case anybody gets stalker-y. But I don't like to have them in the house. Once they pile up, I give them to her, and she keeps them for me. Did you read them?"

"Some of them. Why *did* you end *The Bone Girl* that way?"

"I thought you hadn't read it."

"I read it the week I started working for Alison. It's beautiful."

"Wow," he said. "Thanks."

"You must hear that all the time."

"Not from people whose opinions interest me."

"Are you flirting with me, Jaxson Dace?"

He moved his knee an inch closer to mine and leaned in close. "I wouldn't dream of it, Sofia Bencivenga," he said.

"Poor Minna."

"Minna's fine."

"Poor Alison, then."

"Alison isn't speaking to me right now, if you'd forgotten why I called you."

"I hadn't. You didn't answer my question."

"Which one?"

"Why did you end the book that way? I read that girl's letters. A little obsessed, but I don't disagree with her critical opinion. You've got the two sisters willing to die for each other—to kill for each other—and then suddenly it's all a weird hat trick and one of them isn't even real?"

He moved back in his chair but left his knee where it was. "Yeah," he said. "That's a long story. One more?"

The whiskey was singing its merry little ballad of trouble in my belly, but I had stopped caring halfway through the first drink. "Why not," I said. When the bartender brought the third round, I lifted my glass to Jaxson's. "To bad decisions."

His eyes really were heart-stopping, but his smile was the thing that could gut you like a trout. "To bad decisions," he echoed, clinking his glass against mine. "And to the Schoolgirl, wherever she may be. Vassar, most likely."

"Maybe she'll be your publicist one day," I said.

He laughed. "She still writes me sometimes. Well, she did."

"Creepy stuff?"

"No," he said. "Pretty smart. Anyway, Celia wanted that ending."

"Celia?"

"Yeah. What did she say about the ending again? It's been a long time."

I tried to remember the lines of cursive. "Something about you giving Calliope the tools to set herself free and taking them away again."

"That sounds about right. The original ending was much different. Calliope and Clio put the sorcerer in a box and set him on fire, and they run away together. Into the wilderness. They build another world together, just the two of them, and live out the rest of their days in peace and quiet."

And then, casual: "That was Alison's idea, actually. I talked to her a lot about the book while I was working on it."

That was Alison's idea.

Clio and Calliope.

Cleome.

No way, I thought. *No fucking way.*

After all this time with them, how could I possibly have missed this? I felt the truth blow through me like a hot wind off the dead hills, sere and harsh, the smell before a wildfire. I was a little fool for not having slotted the pieces together months ago. Judith's constant offers to help Alison write. Alison and Jaxson's fight. Suddenly I wanted to get away from him, just long enough to un-ravel all the knotted threads I held and weave them into a pattern that made sense. I thought of Celia, cornering me at Judith's party. The years since *The Bone Girl* had been published. Did Celia know? Was Alison supposed to be writing the second book, too?

Was it possible that Jaxson couldn't write a book at all?

I loved *The Bone Girl*, loved it through and through, the taxonomy it offered for the only other true love I'd known in my life: the way Wendy and I had lived and breathed and fought and wept for each other, the willingness we'd both had to chuck aside our lives for each other, to sacrifice whatever the world asked of us to keep each other safe. I'd marveled at Jaxson's uncanny insight into a bond I'd thought only girls knew. I'd been trying all these months to pick apart his implacable façade to find the bloody heart beating within, the source of that life-altering story.

I'd been looking in the wrong place all along.

The boldness of it nearly winded me. I'd fallen for him in no small part because of *The Bone Girl*. It didn't hurt that he was beautiful, that he was kind and funny and wise, that he treated me like someone who mattered, but I'd loved him before I'd ever met him, loved him from the first time I'd turned the last page.

Only, the book was a lie. Everything I'd believed about him was a lie.

And the book Alison was working on, the book everyone kept asking her about, the book Jaxson was supposed to be writing: They had to be one and the same.

Jaxson took another sip, oblivious to the galaxy of revelations unfolding inside me. My hands were shaking as I lifted my drink. "Anyway," he said, "Celia said it wouldn't sell."

"And you listened?" He was wrong about my poker face. He couldn't guess what I was thinking, because he didn't notice a thing. The heat coming off me should have burned him like a ray gun out of an old space story.

"I was broke," he said. "The ending you want is a luxury. The ending the world wants pays the bills."

"Kids are ghoulish little fuckers."

You fucking monster, I thought, everything I felt for him blowing wide with rage. *You let those girls die. You let Celia ruin their lives for money.*

He laughed. "Something like that, yeah. Who told you that?"

"Barry."

"He would know."

"Barry has *children*?"

"Four daughters and three ex-wives. I know, it defies imagination. At least the wives can get away from him."

"Did you know about Cleome?"

Jaxson went still. "She told you about that, too?"

"Yeah," I said, casual, hoping my voice was steady. "We were talking about the kinds of friends you have when you're young. Girl stuff. Like in *The Bone Girl*."

"Right," Jaxson said. "We talked about that a lot, yeah." He drained the rest of his drink in one long swallow.

"So, what's the second book about?"

"Trade secret."

"Come on."

"Really, Sofia."

"I thought we were friends," I said.

"We're the best of friends, sweetheart. But Celia would have me drawn and quartered if I told you. I had to sign a million nondisclosure agreements. Even Judith doesn't know."

"Does Alison?"

He didn't blink. "Nope," he said.

"Celia must be really on your case."

"Indeed," he said. "Now, either I'm going to keep drinking here with you and end up doing something I will very much enjoy and almost certainly regret, or I'll settle the check and put you in a car. Your decision."

This time I was the one to lean in close. I put one hand on his chest—skin and muscle, bone and blood—and my mouth against his ear. I heard his breath catch.

"It's not cheating on your wife and your girlfriend if I make the first move, is that it? No thanks," I said, low and soft, and then I pulled away. I'd meant it. But he laughed through his nose and signaled for the check.

"You drive a hard bargain," he said.

"You have no idea," I said.

We stood outside the bar in silence while I waited for the car he'd called to arrive. He was careful to keep a good few feet of sidewalk between us. I pulled a pack of Alison's cigarettes out of my bag, offered it to him, and lit one for myself when he shook his head.

"Promise me you'll talk to her," he said. "Promise me, Sofia."

"I'll do my best," I said.

"Thank you." He looked away. "I really do care about her."

"I'm sure you do."

The car pulled up. I climbed in and shut the door on his goodbye.

11.

As if she could sense the newfound knowledge burning white-hot in my heart, Alison's behavior became even more erratic. On Monday, she shouted at me for overwatering her ficus, and fifteen minutes later, apologized in tears; on Tuesday, I overheard her screaming into her phone at the poor assistant at her yoga studio; on Wednesday, she told me I'd never done anything worthwhile for her, and an hour later, seemingly oblivious, she pulled me close to her, crying and telling me she could not possibly continue to survive without me. I brought her a cup of tea and rubbed her shoulders and told her she was beautiful.

We stopped going to coffee shops or yoga or funny vegan cafés; we did not sit for long, leisurely hours at her kitchen table, drinking tea or whiskey and talking about books; she no longer pretended to give me tasks. She spent most of her time shut in her office chain-smoking and talking to herself. I heard her clicking on her laptop from time to time, but mostly she made no sound at all, and I imagined her staring out the window, cigarette caught carelessly between her fingers, turning slowly to a long column of ash.

At a loss for activities, I dusted her bric-a-brac, alphabetized the hardcovers shelved in her living room, scoured her kitchen, mopped her floors. I unearthed a stepladder from her broom closet and spend an afternoon painstakingly cleaning the individual crystals of her chandelier until it sparkled like a tiny, private constellation. I watered her plants—after that first morning, when she'd demanded it of me so imperiously, she had increasingly entrusted me with their care; I found the task oddly soothing—and spent hours looking through her books to determine the best method of nourishment for each species and variety.

But mostly I was a wreck: exhausted, on edge, racking my brain for the right words to soothe her. I had no idea if she'd guessed what I now knew, if her flare-ups of fury with me were displaced rage at Jaxson; I had no idea what she was up to, if she'd abandoned the second book altogether or if she was planning on finishing it and presenting it to him triumphantly after all. How could she live with such a lie? And how, now that I knew the truth, could I?

In that week Alison was my entire life. I dreamed about her. I replayed our conversations, obsessively picking through her words as though they would offer me some clue as to how to unravel the knotted warp that had snagged us. Jaxson texted me so constantly that I had to hide my phone for fear she would see his messages, which were all about her. *Als ok today?* or *did you talk to her yet?* or *does she seem better?* That sort of thing. Most of these messages, I ignored; if I responded at all, it was with a terse *she's fine* or *haven't talked about you.*

I wanted to call him up and scream at him: *I know what you did.* But, naive as I might have then been, I hadn't gotten as far as I had by being stupid.

On Thursday, she came out of her office, sobbing. "It's not working!" she howled. I was in the kitchen, making tea. I went into the other room, this project temporarily abandoned.

"What's not working?"

"You wouldn't understand, Sofia," she said. She covered her eyes with her hands and sank down into the couch. I sat next to her and patted her awkwardly on the back. She leaned into me, weeping. "I—can't—do—this—" she sobbed into my shoulder. "I can't."

"Can't do what?"

She scrubbed hard at her eyes with the heels of her hands. Her eyes were bloodshot, her cheeks hollow. "This book," she said. "I can't finish this book. I've never been stuck like this in my life."

"You don't have to finish it today, Alison."

She looked at me as though I had uttered some piece of Vedic wisdom.

"You're right," she said. "I just need to take a break. Come back to it with fresh eyes." As if on cue, her phone pinged. Mine buzzed in my pocket. We both checked our screens.

got Jude to set up drinks thing pls make sure she comes
and then,
make sure u come too, Sofia

"It's Judith," she said. "Just in the nick of time. Want to get a drink with her?"

"Won't Jaxson be there?"

"Probably," she said. "But I'm not going to live my life in a convent."

"If you're sure," I said.

"No, I'm not sure," she said. "But I think I stopped caring. Who keeps texting you?"

"Phone company," I said. "I haven't paid my bill in a while."

"Ugh. Ghouls," she said. I put the phone away. She went into the kitchen and plucked the whiskey bottle off the shelf, raised an eyebrow.

"Make it a double," I said.

Judith's drinks thing was at the same bar where I'd met Jaxson. Alison delayed our departure until the last possible minute—changing her clothes, muttering over her shoes, refilling her jam jar with more whiskey, disappearing into her bathroom and reemerging with her pupils shrinking. By the time we got in the car, Jaxson had already texted me three times.

The bar, this time, was packed. Alison put one hand on my shoulder and stood on tiptoes, scanning the room. "This was a mistake," she said. "Let's just go."

"We drove all the way down here," I cajoled. "One drink. Then we can go."

"Fine," she muttered. "There they are." I spotted the blue-haired book blogger and then the gold of Jaxson's ponytail. Edward Catten's stewardess was waving an empty martini glass around, hanging prettily off Brendan's shoulder. Alison slid through the crowd like a shark on a blood trail.

"Ladies." She gave the book blogger a dainty hug, pointedly ignored Jaxson. He gave me a look over her head. I made my face into an absolute blank, and he moved back into the chum of writers. To my dismay, I recognized Barry Koople.

"Where's Jude?" Alison asked.

"Not here yet," said the book blogger, who turned now to me with bright eyes and bushy tail and caught at my hand. "You promised me gossip." She giggled.

"I did?"

"At Judith's!" A hazy memory coalesced. I'd talked to her on the balcony. "I want to know all about working with Jaxson!" Her exaggerated whisper seemed loud as a bellow, but thankfully Alison was deep in conversation with Edward Catten's Anna and did not notice. "Is he a good" — she paused significantly— "*editor?*"

"Mmm-hmmmm," I said, extricating my hand from her clammy grip. I wondered if she went through a lot of pillowcases. Maybe blue-haired persons invested in a special kind. She had a tattoo, I saw, on her forearm, near the crook of her elbow. Jaxson's tattoo: the heart drawn in bones. A *Bone Girl* tattoo. I considered, briefly, whether the catharsis of stabbing her in the eye would be diluted by the subsequent jail sentence. That book was not written for the likes of her to see themselves within.

"I have lots of tattoos, but that's the most important one. I love him," she said. "Don't you just love him?" She bumped her hip coyly against mine and leaned in for the kill. Unclouded by champagne, her features were alarmingly murine. "I want to know everything about him," she murmured. "And the new book—"

"Judith's here," I said. "I'd better go say hello."

But Edward Catten's stewardess was already clacking past me, wobbling dangerously on her heels. "Judith! Just the Cruella de Vil I was waiting for. That's for Edward, you bitch!" she screamed as she drew her hand back and slapped Judith hard across the face.

The high buzz of conversation died immediately, and a hush fell across the entire bar. Judith's eyes widened; her own hand flew to her cheek, where a sizable red mark bloomed.

"I will fucking end your career," Judith said, in a calm, low voice that carried far.

Anna was clearly several sheets and an additional schooner to the wind. "You contributed to Edward's fund-raiser and then asked for a *refund*!" she shrieked. "Who steals from a dying cat?"

"Do you want to know why, Anna?" Judith took a languid, menacing step forward. Anna drew herself up indignantly.

"Hoo, boy," someone said behind me.

"Do the words *purple-prosed, anti-feminist trash* ring a bell?" Judith asked in a tone that, had I not known her better, I would have mistaken for friendly.

Edward Catten's Anna blanched and tottered backward. "I don't know what you're talking about."

"You knew what you were talking about when you told Gemma Carlyle you wrote it anonymously for Alexandra's blog," Judith said calmly.

"I didn't—I would never—I swear, Judith, it wasn't— Edward *needs* us—" Anna looked around wildly in search of an exit.

Judith smiled, baring all her teeth, and leaned forward, tapping Anna's breastbone with her forefinger. Anna flinched.

"Don't let the door hit your giant ass on the way out," Judith hissed.

Anna backed away and burst into tears. The blogger rushed to her side and escorted her, sobbing, out of the bar. Judith looked wonderfully pleased with herself.

Chatter resumed at a higher pitch. The blogger reentered the bar sans her weeping charge a few minutes later, took out her phone, and typed furiously.

"Wow," I said to Alison.

"Judith really shouldn't google herself."

"There's nothing wrong with Anna's ass."

"You have to understand that a Bloody Mary is the closest thing Jude's had to a solid meal in the past twenty years," Alison said. She eyed Alexandra and downed her whiskey. "God, that's about to be all over the internet. Poor Anna."

"Why isn't Judith mad at Alexandra instead?"

"Anna's a big deal. Alexandra's the kind of person who hangs out in bookstores waiting to be recognized by her fans."

"I thought Alexandra wasn't famous," I said.

"She waits a long time. Want to say hi to Judith and Jaxson? I'm going to go get another drink."

"Sure," I said. Alison beelined for the bar.

The other writers were giving Judith a wide berth.

"Hi," I said.

She made a face as though she had eaten something sour. "Look at you," she said. "So laid-back."

I looked down at my jeans. "I left the McQueen at home."

Her mouth twitched. "It's just not the *same* without you at writing group."

"Got your quota of blood for the night, Jude?" Jaxson rumbled from behind me. He bent to kiss my cheek. Judith's eyelid flickered.

"I'm just getting started," Judith said, looking about. "I hope that wretched animal dies horribly."

"Anna?" I asked.

"I meant the cat," Judith said, "but god knows no one would miss Anna, either."

"Sound the klaxons," Jaxson said, amused. "The kraken has been released. Think you and Als will be back at writing group next week, Sof?" he asked me. Judith's other eyelid flickered.

"I hope so," I said. "Alison hasn't been feeling well."

"Is that right," Judith said. Her basilisk stare had landed upon me again. "She sounded fine on the phone."

"You've been talking to Alison?" Jaxson asked, surprised.

"We've been chatting about her new book."

"Have you, now," Jaxson said.

"I think there will be developments on the front we discussed shortly," she said stagily. Jaxson glanced at me, and Judith smiled. "Oh, Jax, don't worry. *Sofia* doesn't know anything about Alison's book. Do you, Sofia?"

Go fuck yourself, you old bat, I thought. "Nope," I said. "Not a clue."

I drank a lot that night—everyone there did—but Alison drank easily twice as much. I should have kept an eye on her, but I was tired of being her custodian. I lost her after my third or fourth whiskey; I said a lot of things to a lot of people at the bar; I flirted with Jaxson and then lost him, too; I watched as Barry approached woman after woman, their faces fixed in wary grins, and thought about what Judith had said about him selling well. How naive I'd been to think that the lubricant of this storied world was talent. Here, as everywhere, it was only money.

"Fucking forget about it!" Alison's voice cut across the bar noise. I left off midsentence and looked around. She was talking to Jaxson; Brendan, who'd been dogging Jaxson's heels for the entire evening, was with them, too.

"My, my," Judith murmured next to me; as was her wont, she had materialized out of nowhere. Alison screamed something else incoherent and slammed away from Jaxson and Brendan, heading for the bar. "I think she's had bit much to drink, don't you?"

"Not my job," I said curtly.

"Isn't it?" Judith asked. "She's embarrassing herself, Sofia. I'd think, as her protégé, you might want to intervene."

Jaxson's eyes met mine across the bar. He gave me an intense, beseeching look.

"Poor baby," Judith said next to me with a private little smile. "He doesn't know *what* to do. Come on, Sofia." Judith seized my elbow and marched me toward Alison.

She was already in the middle of a monologue, the bartender nodding at her with a pleasant, vacant smile. "...because ultimately, it's a myth about the punishment of female confidence," Alison said, punctuating her points with the highball glass. "Arachne isn't wrong, not at all; she tells the truth, shows the gods as the corrupt and foolish creatures that they are; she bests Athena at her own craft—what she's punished for is not her arrogance but the fact that she's right and no one can stand it—hi, Sofia, Judith, I was just telling—what was your name again, sorry?"

"Justin," the bartender said.

"I was just telling Justin about the fucking patriarchy," Alison said. "And you know who upholds the fucking patriarchy, Justin?" The bartender dried a glass on a white dish towel and put it carefully on a shelf. "Fucking women, Justin. That's who upholds the patriarchy. All those bitches back there making excuses for all those men. Celia doesn't even care that Barry's a fucking serial harasser as long as he's making her money. Celia doesn't even care that Jaxson—"

I held my breath; he'd come up behind Alison without her noticing.

"Alison," Jaxson said. "Not here." Judith watched.

"No? Then where, Jaxson? Where do you want to have this conversation?"

"Alison, please," Jaxson said. No one else was close enough to hear us, but I could almost see the fear coming off him. "Please, let's talk about this later, okay?"

"Alison, darling," Judith interrupted. "If you're not going to think about anyone else, you might at least think about your future."

Alison stared at her, glassy-eyed. "Fuck you, Judith," she snarled. "And" —this to Jaxson— "fuck *you*. Fuck you *both*." She waved grandly around the bar. "Fuck all of you fuckers!" she yelled.

"Alison, let's go home," I said, touching the hand with the now-empty glass.

"Wan' another one," she said.

I cut my eyes at the hapless Justin.

"I think you've had enough," he said affably. Alison's habitual response to being told what to do was violent opposition, but she only looked at him and giggled.

"Justin's looking out for me," she said. "What a sweetheart." She blew him an air kiss; I seized this opportunity to grasp her arm gently but firmly.

"Want me to drive?" I asked.

"Fuck you too, Sofia," she said tonelessly. "*She's* paying my tab," she added.

"Funny," I said.

"I'm serious, I don't have my wallet."

"How can you not have your wallet?"

Expressionless, Justin busied himself with the register, returning with Alison's check before drifting a significant distance from us down the bar.

"I didn't bring my wallet. Just use a card or something, I'll pay you back."

"I don't have a card."

"Come on."

"I'm serious, Alison." I realized I was holding her shoulder more tightly than the situation warranted; I let go, and she slouched back against the bar and stared at me with a belligerent light in her eyes. "I don't have a card," I said again.

"Who doesn't have a card?"

I didn't have a bank account, either, but that wasn't any of her business. She pouted. "Can't you just use cash, then?"

I looked at the bill. Her tab was more than she paid me in a week.

"I don't have this much cash, Alison."

"You're my assistant," she said. "You figure it out."

I almost walked out on her, then and there; I'd never been so angry with her. She'd been cruel to me before, in passing, but never, ever like this. Jaxson reached past me and examined Alison's bill in silence. He pulled out his wallet and slapped a card down. Justin rematerialized and swept the card away. I looked away from them, toward the door and freedom, willing the hammer of my heart to slow its beat.

She was only drunk. She didn't mean it.

I had nowhere else to go.

"Take it out of my check," Alison said, listing slightly.

"I think we're all settled up," Jaxson said, his voice cold.

"You and Judith think you have it all figured out, don't you? Just you wait until I tell everyone what a fucking liar you are and see how that works out for you—"

"Don't you dare threaten me," he said. "After everything I've done for you—"

"After everything *you've* done?" Alison screamed.

Justin returned and set Jaxson's card and receipt on the bar, clearing his throat politely.

"Come on, Alison," I said. I felt suddenly ancient and exhausted and more than a little sad. "Let's go."

"This isn't finished," she said to Jaxson and Judith. "Not by a long shot."

"*Alison.*" I pulled her arm. "Come on."

She jerked her arm away. Without another word, she marched toward the door. I gave Jaxson and Judith an apologetic shrug and followed her. I could feel their eyes on my back the whole way to the door.

Outside, Alison had lit a cigarette and was rummaging for her keys with her free hand. "Why don't you let me drive?" I said.

"I'm fine," she said. "I'm not that drunk."

"You're pretty drunk."

"No, I'm not."

"I really don't think—"

"Shut up, Sofia."

She pulled out of her parking spot with a screech of rubber that made me wince.

"What was all that about?" I asked, although I had a pretty good idea.

"You're taking his side now?"

"I'm not taking anybody's side, Alison."

She jerked the steering wheel to the right, narrowly missing a row of mailboxes, and pulled the car to a stop on a broad patch of shoulder overlooking the ocean.

"Really?" Her entire body was alive with rage; I thought she was going to lunge across the gear stick and strangle me. "Do you think I don't see you? Looking around my house? Writing everything down in your notebook? You think you found out all my secrets, huh? So, tell me, am I good enough for you, Sofia? You think you can take him away from me? You think my work is shameful? Do you think my life is that funny?"

"No," I said. I met her eyes. "I don't. I think it's beautiful."

Her mouth opened, and she stared at me for a long time, her eyes shining with unshed tears that gathered and finally spilled over. She dashed them away angrily and slumped back against her door.

"I know what you're like, all of you! Wanting to know about me and Jaxson, you and Judith and Celia, all you vultures—you think I'm fucking crazy, don't you, Sofia? You're writing everything down for *him* because they all want to get rid of me! You think Judith could do what I do? You think Jaxson could?"

"Alison, I'm not taking notes. I don't know what you're talking about."

"Eighteen years," she said dully. "Eighteen years I've known him, and all this time, he's been sucking everything out of me until I have nothing anymore, do you understand? I have nothing left, Sofia, nothing. No stories, no soul. I'm forty years old, and I've never done anything that anyone will remember me by. I don't even have children, I don't have a family, I have hardly any money left. When I'm gone, there'll be nothing—nothing that isn't his—all I want is to do something of my own—"

She began to cry with huge, ugly noises that tore out of her chest, out of some ragged animal place beyond pain or rage or sadness. I leaned over the gearshift and put my arms around her and held her while she shook so hard, I thought her bones would fly apart. She was saying things that did not cohere as words or even anything recognizable as language, and I did not try to calm her or stop the torrent but let her cry herself out as the dashboard clock ticked through the gelid blast of air-conditioned minutes, until she could manage a breath that did not break open on a sob and leaned away from me.

"I'm sorry," she said.

"You don't need to be."

"Sofia—" A breath. I waited. "I'm running out of stories."

"You can't run out of stories. What about the Arachne story? You were just talking about a new story."

"Jaxson hates that story," she said.

"Why does that matter?"

"Because," she said. "You know, don't you."

I didn't say anything. She wiped her eyes, pulled a cigarette out of her pack with trembling fingers, lit it, exhaled hard, offered me the pack.

"Cleo would've hated him," she said. "She hated men like that. She used to say the reason men make so much terrible art is because they've never had to learn how to see anything other than themselves. She would've seen through him in the first five minutes. I'm such a fucking fool."

She looked away from me, out toward where the ocean heaved itself listlessly at the white sand. "I'm sorry I yelled at you back there. You didn't deserve it. You don't deserve any of this bullshit."

"It's okay," I said.

"I don't know what I'd do without you."

"Well," I said, embarrassed.

"I mean it. Having you around, it's—it's been a lifesaver." She sighed. "I didn't mean to get so fucked up."

"Do you want me to drive?"

"Can you? It's a manual."

"Of course."

"Right. Europe. They teach you all that stuff there."

We traded places—she, moving unsteadily; me, practiced and sure-footed, despite the whiskey. There was a quality to driving in California that I loved more than anything else about that state: the way that speed flattened the horizon, the immense expanse of sky, hurtling into fifth gear as if flinging yourself into some great void of possibility devoid of past or future.

Driving Alison's glorious car was like flying—this late at night, swallowing miles along the freeway, the palaces of Malibu speeding past in a hazy blur of new money and starlight. That chlorinated fever dream of the West, cocaine jitters and white-sand beaches, all the things I had thought I'd find in California, real again with the wind in my face and the engine roaring beneath me, one big gorgeous gasoline dream.

Was this what it felt like to be Alison, to be rich, to know only the wants of the heart and none of the needs of the body? Her head lolled against the window as I drove, the tears drying to traces of salt dust on her cheeks, her eyelids fluttering closed, and I thought that I might drive forever into the bottomless future, drive until the car combusted into sparks, drive until I forgot everything I had ever been and everyone I had once dreamed of becoming.

I used to drive like that back home, but back home, the light had been different and the sky heavy, the grasslands monotonous, the car smelling indelibly of old cigarette smoke and fast food, Earl's aftershave and the pomade he used on his hair. I had known then that I was not happy, but that was before I dared to imagine myself as a person who might have, if not happiness, at least a life that was mine. That was before Earl died, before I came west, before Alison shook me loose from my moorings and into a brave new world.

But even back then, even before Alison, I'd been hungry for something bigger. Something like this: the silver car, the silvered night, the whiskey in my blood, the girl sleeping next to me, as lovely as hope.

I put my hand on her shoulder when I pulled into the tiny garage in the alley behind her house, and she came awake with a start. "Jaxson?"

"It's just me," I said gently.

She blinked for a few seconds and then shivered awake. "Sorry. I was out. I said—"

"It's fine. It's forgotten."

She smiled. "Bless you. It's late, yeah? Why don't you crash here?"

Her walk was lolloping. I'd never felt more clearheaded. Inside her house I pushed her long hair out of her eyes, and she leaned into me, the smell of her clean as salt. Her kiss tasted of bourbon.

Her skin was as smooth as I'd imagined it to be, but there was nothing soft about her, just lean muscle and long bones, her breasts small enough to fit in my palms. She fell asleep almost immediately afterward, as if she'd been knocked unconscious. I lay beside her, alive with fear and elation, until dawn paled the sky outside her windows. I slid out of her bed as easily as I'd fallen into it. She did not stir. It was entirely possible that I would never see the inside of her house again. I gathered her soft black dress from the floor where it had fallen, pulled it over my head, and closed her bedroom door behind me.

I stood for a long time in her living room, and then I went into her bathroom and opened the medicine cabinet.

I considered pocketing the cat tin; what I didn't use, I could sell until I found some other job, but that would certainly bar her door to me if the night before had not. Instead I skimmed a judicious take off the contents, enough to keep me over bliss's threshold for a while if she fired me. I could still smell her perfume, mixed now with her sweat, on my skin.

In her office I fingered the broad-leaved green plants, drawing deep breaths of the jungled air, memorizing the riot of color and disarray coming to life as fingers of new sunlight shafted through the windows. And then I saw it: the computer, on her desk. She hadn't put it away when we went to the bar.

There was no noise, no movement, from the bedroom. I opened her laptop; no password. *O Alison*, I thought. So like her: to hide the laptop but not protect it, to build a life of secrets in the hope that someone might come along to untangle them. Had she meant for me to find it like this all along?

Her desktop held only documents, no photos, no music, no apps or games. I opened her email. She had dozens of unread messages: business offers from Nigerian royalty, inspiring missives from an entity billing herself as a "life coach," product recommendations from Sephora, a notice from her bank that her credit card bill was overdue. I made an instinctive mental note to remind her to pay it.

I was careful to leave the unopened emails alone and scrolled through her history: online bill notifications, car service receipts, bank statements, shipping notifications from athleisure companies. The bland minutiae of her catered and cushioned life. Nothing from Jaxson. But one very interesting message from Judith a week earlier, one line only, no subject:

If you don't finish it, I will. He doesn't need you as much as you think.

I'd read Judith's books. I knew as well as Alison did that Judith never could've written anything like *The Bone Girl*. Not with a million monkeys and a million typewriters and a million years.

But did Jaxson know enough to realize the same thing? Did Celia?

And did it even matter?

I thought of all Jaxson's fans, the breathless legions spilled out at his feet. I thought of Alexandra's tattoo. I thought of the movie, which had stripped all the beauty out of Alison's masterpiece and flattened it into a cheap story of pretty dresses and CGI monsters. I thought of Judith and Brendan and Barry and Anna.

How many people even knew a real book when they found one?

I closed Alison's email and looked through her file directory. She had written a lot of notes to herself, ideas for essays and outlines for short stories. In a folder labeled ATH-ENA, she'd saved different versions of the Arachne myth and pages of her own commentary, a hastily sketched out chapter or two—nothing all that compelling, and nothing that compared to the beauty of *The Bone Girl*.

I clicked on a folder titled FUCK THIS FOREVER.

"Bingo," I said to the plants. Five years' worth of files, beginning with FuckThis_November Draft. I opened the most recent file, from July.

*Our footsteps crunched across the new-fallen snow.
Overhead, a spill of stars bright as moonlight, the constellations Mirabella herself had taught me: Orion and
his gleaming belt, the twins of Gemini, Hydra the water monster.*

*"My mother used to tell me the sky is full of ani-
mals," she'd told me once, long ago. The night was sharp
and cold and clear, though at its edges, we could see the
black silhouettes of piling clouds. We'd forgotten our
gloves; we pulled our frayed cashmere cuffs over our bare
knuckles. A gold chain looped gracefully across Mir's elegant, bony wrist. "Do you ever think about running*

Oh, Alison, I thought. *Oh, no.*

The long conversations, the writing exercises, the confessions she'd doled out to me like meal rations. I'd thought
she'd seen herself in me, thought she'd picked me out as a
rare gem, solitary and self-sufficient, a mirror to her own
aloof and wild nature. I'd thought any number of things.
All of which she'd let me.

All of which had been wrong.

The full draft was two hundred or so single-spaced
pages. I didn't dare read the whole thing, but a quick skim
was all it took to recognize it. It wasn't finished; the text
was peppered throughout with comments she'd written in
all caps—FILL IN HERE or THIS SCENE MOVES EARLIER, FIX
THIS PART.

But I knew the story by heart, because it was mine.

An orphaned girl with a glamorous, slightly shady past;
boarding schools; ski slopes; a cruel, wealthy boyfriend; a

flight to the West Coast and attempt to reinvent herself. Mirabella and Sofia at the *tabac*. She'd added her own chapters between the work I'd done for her, but she hadn't changed a word of what I'd written.

She hadn't even changed the names.

I was so angry, my hands were shaking. They'd lied to me, all of them, but Alison had lied to me most of all. *Assistant.* She'd wanted someone whose life she could pillage, a lost little girl like me whose story she could steal, whose words she could seed among her own.

And if I complained, who would care? Who would even believe me?

Alison muttered aloud in the bedroom. I held my breath, waited. She was silent again. I closed the file, shut the laptop, checked that I'd left it as I found it.

And then I let myself out of her house and walked to my car, not allowing myself to look back.

12.

I suppose Alison and I had more in common than she knew. We'd both loved girls who were sisters to us in darkness; we'd both left them behind to fall under a certain kind of spell, though she'd come out of the nightmare with a different set of scars.

We'd both chosen wrong.

I have always understood the effect people like Jaxson had on other people, especially women; have in the past been susceptible to the pull of charisma myself, before I learned better. Earl was no Jaxson, but he'd had the same magnetism, the same animal grace. Jaxson was no Earl, either: Earl would've eaten Jaxson alive.

The first time I'd gone out with him, girlish and aflutter, he hadn't bothered with the niceties of high school boys: dinner or a movie, egg creams at the Main Street drugstore, letterman jackets draped around my shoulders. Earl was older, and meaner, and had lived for a long time in a world I knew nothing about, a world of hard, cruel men and the hard, cruel things they did for money, a world with no place for the girlish and the cordial. He'd marked me differently out of all the other girls that surrounded me, knowing something then that I did not know yet about myself: my own capacity for appetite, and the reckless streak that burned through me like a welt of lava.

He'd driven me in his joke of a muscle car out to a bluff at the edge of town, cigarette knuckled between the long-fingered hand that dangled out his car window, his dark hair combed back with pomade like a fifties greaser's. The cicadas poured out of the cracked earth like water that summer; all around me the sound of their wings rose in a world without wind.

Earl finished his cigarette without speaking, turned to me, wrapped a hand, once, around a fistful of my hair, pulled my head back, and said low into my ear, "Your body is made to get fucked," and instead of laughing or hitting him or running from the car, running away from what even then I had a strong inkling would be the worst decision of my short life, I felt warmth flood the crotch of my school-girl's cotton underwear and my breath catch in my throat. His smile was not kind; he knew he had me, knew I'd let him push me into the back seat and slide his hand up my sweat-slick thighs, under my dress; and I knew what was coming next, met it with the wide-open wonder of a girl going outside for the first time.

I had bruises for weeks afterward, from his hands, from where the gear stick had slammed over and over into my hip. For days I dreamed only of his face, his eyes empty of anything other than desire; of the way he looked at me; of what it felt like to be the object of such devastating want. Whatever ran between Earl and I was not, was never, love; it was something more base and more enduring, as though we had been wired for it by some grand engineer who liked to lean down from time to time and dabble in the lives of animals.

After all these years, after everything, despite what came after, it still brings a flush to my cheeks to think about what sex with Earl had been like at first, the ecstatic knife-edge where cruelty met desire. I had never been paid attention to in that way, was too young to know how different being wanted is from being known.

Wendy had known what was good for me back then, warned me off him—Wendy, who'd known my appetite for trouble since we were just kids, wholesome and stalwart Wendy, who played varsity girls' basketball and turned in her homework on time and whom everyone loved but who, for reasons known only to her, loved me best of all.

She'd almost made it out, too; there were rumors of a scholarship her senior year—to the state school, sure, but even that humble leap would've pulled her light-years away from the suffocating gravity of the black hole that held us. Thanksgivings at Wendy's house, fleeing Mamie and Pops and the trailer full of old cigarette smoke and overflowing ashtrays, Wendy's brothers and sister clean scrubbed in their holiday best, the hush that fell when her father came into the room in a dirty undershirt and sweatpants. He was a sticker at the slaughterhouse—three hundred throats an hour, he used to boast—and the blood never came out from under his fingernails. We were all terrified of him. Wendy wore long sleeves even in summer. I didn't need to ask why.

The nights we'd slept under the slide in the elementary school playground, curled into each other like cats, neither one of us willing to bear any longer the hellscapes we were meant to call home. How could I ever forget the boredom, the flat sky, the flat land, the flat days running one into the other without anything to distinguish them or to suggest that any day to come might bring some relief from the shattering dullness? How could I forget that all-consuming longing for somewhere, anywhere, anything but there? How could I forget the abyss that had swallowed all attempts to bridge it: drugs, sex, cheap alcohol, bad decisions, blood.

Wendy, my first and only and oldest friend. Wendy, who'd seen me through everything, who'd helped me get free. Wendy, her dark hair, her dark eyes. We'd sworn oaths to each other, the way young girls do. Digging into our wrists with a pocketknife, matching the ragged wounds in a bloody kiss. I still have the scar.

She was smart, smarter than me. Fierce. Strong. She could have been anything she wanted once she got out of that place. But then she'd gotten pregnant, and Stephen had done what was expected of him and married her, and the fragile blossom of her alternate future withered where it bloomed.

And now Earl was dead, and Wendy was fifteen hundred miles away. My own Clio, stomping through the long grass, her hair wild and her heart mine. So beautiful, Wendy—not the kind of beauty you found out here, money-eyed and waxed and radiant with creams, but something fiercer, raw, unshaped by outside forces. I thought of everything Wendy had done for me, the promise I'd made her when I left, the copy of *The Bone Girl* she'd given me.

To see ourselves in a book like that—it had changed everything.

How ironic, then, that the book we'd fallen in love with, the book that had altered the shape of our lives, that had named what we felt for each other, was built on a lie.

And the woman who'd written it had stolen the story of us.

13.

On Monday morning I let myself into Alison's house with the key she'd had made for me after it was clear—to her, anyway—that I wasn't going anywhere.

I was expecting—well, after all this time, it's hard to say what I was expecting. She hadn't changed the locks, at any rate.

She was in the kitchen, eyes bright and hair freshly washed, looking better than she had in weeks. "Hey, you. Want coffee?" she asked.

"Sure," I said. "Thanks." She poured me a mug and handed it to me, her face guileless. There was nothing in her manner that suggested the preceding Friday night had even happened, let alone that she remembered it.

I know what you did, I thought. *I know. I know.*

"Drink up," she chirped, "*lots* to do today! I was hoping—"

A sudden pounding on her front door interrupted her, and her face transformed in front of me, its supple mask of cheer splitting to reveal the grain of worry beneath.

"Can you get that?"

"I don't think—"

"Just tell him to go away," she said. "Make something up. I don't know. Don't tell him I'm here."

"Okay," I said and went to answer the door.

How had I been tricked by the new-minted flash of a penny before the tarnish coats? It was so easy, now, to whiff out the sillage of his fraudulence, sharp and cheap as the afterburn of drugstore cologne.

"She's not going to talk to you," I said.

"Let me in."

"No."

"Come on, Sofia."

"She isn't here."

"Bullshit."

"Yoga class or something. Come back later." I shut the door, but he stopped it from closing with his boot.

"What's gotten into you?"

"What's that supposed to mean?"

"You're different. You're acting different."

"I'm tired."

"I really need to talk to her," he said. "After the other night—" He trailed off.

I waited. "After the other night?"

"Just let me in, Sofia. ALISON!" he shouted. "GOD-DAMMIT, ALISON!"

"Jesus Christ," Alison said from behind me. "Quit yelling at me, and go home. I can't help you anymore, Jaxson."

"I'll find someone else," he said. "I really will this time, Alison."

"No, you won't," Alison said calmly, and then she slammed the door in his face.

She marched past me into the kitchen. When her phone rang, she refused the call. After it rang again for the fifth time, she switched it off and put it in a drawer.

"What are you going to do?" I asked.

"Everything's fine," she said. "I did a ton of work this weekend."

I bet you did, I thought. Was that why she'd fucked me? For reference material? Sofia and Mirabella scissoring gamely as the scene coyly fades to black?

"He'll get off my case as soon as he sees the draft."

"That's good," I said.

"Really, it's the best work I've done in years," she said blandly. "You're such an inspiration, Sofia. You're so healthy and stable. It's been good for me."

"Your credit card bill's due," I said. "You should probably pay it today."

The rest of that week was surreally calm. My phone remained ominously silent; Jaxson had given up texting me. I thought that likely did not bode well for Alison. She busied herself in her office, typing furiously. She wrote out longhand lists of things to do, clothes she wanted, trips she would like to take—

"Have you ever been to the Bahamas?" she asked me, scratching away with her fountain pen.

"Not since I was a girl," I said.

"We've *got* to go, then," she said, returning to her paper.

On Friday morning she greeted me with an uncharacteristically manic smile. Her cheeks were flushed, and her eyes had a hectic glint that I did not like the look of.

"You're not doing anything on Saturday, are you?"

I never was. "I can cancel," I said. "Why?"

"It's Jaxson's birthday. He's having a party. Want to come?"

I stared at her.

She clapped her hands. "Great, it's decided! Wait until you see his house. You think Judith's place is a mansion, holy wow!"

"But I mean—I'm not invited," I said.

"I'm sure he'll be happy to see you. You can borrow a dress from me if you don't have anything to wear. I'm going to make everything right between us, you'll see. We can all go back to normal. Have you seen that black dress I was wearing last Friday?"

"No. You finished the book?"

She tsk-tsked me. "You're not supposed to know about that, Sofia! You'll get me in trouble."

"Okay," I said. "Sorry. Sounds fun."

"Good," she said. "It's a date." She winked at me.

If I'd known what would happen that night, would I have gone with her?

It's hard to say. Who's to say I wouldn't be living just as well if her death hadn't set me on the strange and marvelous path that unfurled in its wake? Would she still have died, if I hadn't been there? Or would the events of that night have transpired differently in my absence, so that even now she would be puttering around her golden kitchen in the sleepy hours after dawn, smoking her first cigarette of the day in her little office, opening her computer to begin her work, while I lived some other unimaginable life in a dream-soaked city too distant at this remove to name?

Alison told me once about the many-worlds theory, that every possible outcome of decision spins outward into its own complete universe, that all possible histories and futures are, somewhere, true.

Yeah, I thought. *I've read that book, too.*

The night before Jaxson's party, I dreamed of Earl. When I woke in the dawn-paled dark of the studio, I thought I could see his blood on my hands, but it was only a trick of the shadows.

But Alison, I might have said, *the many-worlds interpretation applies to particles, not people.* Whatever divinity shapes our rough-hewn human ends does not, I imagine, truck much with waveforms. Alison was a romantic, but she didn't like to be wrong. Maybe I should have told her.

The world we have is the world we get, Alison. There is no other life.

But those are only daydreams. In this and every other universe, Alison is dead.

I drove to her house around seven that Saturday as instructed. I knocked instead of using my key. When she answered the door, she had a glass of whiskey in one hand already, and her hair was wet from the shower. I was wearing cutoffs and a T-shirt but at least I, too, was clean.

"God, you can wear anything and look good," Alison said. Her mood was still infected with that eerie and suspicious buoyancy. She breezed me into her bedroom, threw open closet doors. "I have a million things that will fit you," she said. "We're nearly the same size."

It was true; I was a few inches taller, but otherwise we were. Alison's body was beautifully maintained, well-moisturized and regimented, toned by years of spendy classes, but sheer poverty along with my reacquired running habit had thinned my own frame down to the bone. She pulled dress after dress off her hangers, tossing them on the bed in a careless, haphazard pile without any overlying organizing principle. I did not know the rules. Should I pick a good dress or one that looked so much like the others that she was sure not to miss it? Should I find something I could not possibly ruin, or should I pick something luxe, hoping not to embarrass her? But she left me no room for indecision once she pulled her bounty from its carefully arrayed racks and turned to me, hands on her hips.

"Take off your clothes," she said, ignoring my flinch as she pulled dresses from her pile and held them up against me.

I'd done a lot of things in my short life, but I'd never stripped in full daylight in front of a beautiful rich woman in her house of lovely things. It was too much, it was more than I'd signed up for, letting her Pygmalion my bitter, lonely life into a terrible facsimile of her own wealth and brightness.

Something moved through me so completely, I thought I would catch fire. To this day, I couldn't tell you whether it was hatred or love.

"This one," she said decisively, pressing her selection against my shoulders. This close, her skin smelled musky sweet: spicy perfume, a whiff of the whiskey she'd poured into our tea, and underneath it, some other smell that was irreducibly, ineluctably her, a smell that was as familiar to me as my own and as exotic as the far plains of Mars.

"It's great," I said, meeting her depthless gaze, the upward flick of her mouth as she registered the challenge and returned it. I wanted to hit her in the face, throw her to the ground and tear her hair out, I don't know. Eat her alive.

The dress she gave me was beautiful. Alison wasn't the kind of woman who'd put you in something frumpy out of fear of being outshined. It was made from supple, suede-y silk, somewhere between grey and purple, cut on the bias and with a complicated draped neck. "No bra," she said authoritatively, and I heard the soft *whuff* of laughter before she swallowed it as I turned my back on her to modestly undo the clasp. *I'll show you*, I thought and slid my underpants off my hips as well, and then I lifted my arms, knowing what she saw, the long muscles of my back and legs, the high curve of my ass—less toned than hers, maybe, but still nearly two decades younger—the way my hair fell, loose, nearly to my waist. I made her put the dress on me, her hands smoothing the loose silk over the curve of my hips, her breath at the nape of my neck, as if she were the servant and I her mistress, and for a moment, the luxury of it, of being waited on, of her yielding, made me forget my place.

"It suits you," she said quietly. "Look what we've made you into." She stepped out of the way so I could look at myself in her mirror. I looked like myself through a filter: softer, more graceful, leaner.

I looked like her.

"Just don't bend over," she said. "Unless you're ready for someone to take it off you."

Alison shrugged into a dress of her own, upscale, slinky black cousin to mine.

"Lipstick," she said, pulling open her drawers and coming up with a selection of tubes that she fanned out and held out to me like a magician offering a shuffled deck of cards. I picked a discreet, neutral red; she shook her head and handed me a blood-bright one.

"Too much," I said.

"It'll look good on you." I put it on while she watched. She was right; it did. "You can put it in here," she said, handing me a little black leather clutch. "Keep them both."

For herself, only gloss and then a spritz of the perfume she always wore.

"Want some?" she asked.

I offered her my throat.

14.

Jaxson's house lay at the end of a long drive overhung with blooming jacaranda. The way was barred by high wrought-iron gates covered in metal bears gamboling through a field of metal roses as metal birds swooped overhead, their feathers cast down to the finest line of each barbule. Alison leaned out the window, deftly flipped open a metal toadstool to reveal a keypad, and tapped a series of numbers. The gates swung open before us silently, and Alison breathed out.

"He didn't change the code," she said, which should have been my first clue that something was wrong.

If Judith's house was a monstrosity, Jaxson's was a leviathan erupting from the bowels of the earth in a concatenation of balustrades and gargoyles and turreted towers akimbo, a vertiginous assemblage of stone and wood and stained glass extruding structural anomalies as though it were being possessed by some eldritch and ancient force. White oleander surged up its sides like sea-foam. Immediately behind it, the ocean tumbled and roared with a vigor that suggested it, too, had been summoned to this particular place through ill-omened augury.

"Holy *fuck*," I breathed.

"It's poisonous."

"The house?"

She was looking at the oleander. "Chronic poisoning causes depression and hallucinations, but it doesn't take much to kill someone; a hundred grams is enough to poison a horse, and a person wouldn't need nearly as much. Tremors, seizures, paralysis, and then eventual collapse." Her voice was dreamy. "A woman killed herself in this house in the thirties—made a tea out of the blossoms. The flowers are the most poetic way to go, but any part of the plant is equally toxic." Her eyes focused again. "The house is sort of awful, isn't it? But I think it's rather grand, in its own way. It was built initially as the set for a black-and-white silent horror movie in the twenties, and then it just kept..."

"Metastasizing?"

"Something like that. The movie never ended up getting made—starlet died under mysterious circumstances, director had an affair with the leading man, that kind of thing. Quite an era."

"Quite a house."

"He loves it," she said. "He loves being a writer so much. The awards, the interviews. He's so good at it. He does all the things that writers do except write."

"Alison," I said. "What are we doing here?"

"I'm almost done with the new book," she said. "But this time, it's mine. I'm not giving it to him. And I'm going to go inside that house and tell him."

We looked at the house, both of us holding our separate thoughts.

It's mine. For a fleeting moment, I wished I'd never met Alison, met any of them; I would have traded everything Alison had given me in that moment if I could have *The Bone Girl* back as it was the first time I'd read it, marvelous and untainted and pure.

And then I remembered the flat, bare prairie and Wendy's eyes huge in the dark and Earl's hands around my throat, and I let the book go, let it go for good.

I'd come here to be someone else. I didn't need a book to become that girl anymore.

"Why did you write *The Bone Girl* for him?" I asked.

I thought she hadn't heard me, she was so far away. Wherever she'd gone, it was a world I couldn't see into.

"I just wanted her to have a happy ending," she said finally. "Celia wouldn't even give me that much."

I thought of Cleome's lean, bare voice in the dark. A perfect thing preserved forever, like a bee's wing in amber. And, for once in my life, I was tired of lying.

"I think it's time for me to do something else," I said.

"What?" Her gaze snapped back to me.

"To move on. Find another job."

"Are you serious? After everything I've done for you? You can't just quit, Sofia. You can't just quit like this. Where will you go?" What she meant: *What will you take from me?* "Do you seriously think you can find something better?"

"I don't know," I said. "I just want... I want something else."

"You're not going to tell anyone about *The Bone Girl,*" she said. "You wouldn't dare."

"I don't care about that," I said.

"What will I do without you?"

"Finish the next book yourself," I said.

A beat. Forget my poker face; Alison's reigned supreme. "What's that supposed to mean?"

"You didn't even change my name, Alison."

"What?"

"'We'd forgotten our gloves; we pulled our frayed cashmere cuffs over our bare knuckles. A gold chain looped gracefully across Mir's elegant, bony wrist,'" I said. "You didn't change a single word."

"I have no idea what you're talking about," she said coolly.

I couldn't help it; I laughed.

"Sofia," she said, her voice raw now, and after all the months I'd spent with her, I still couldn't tell if the emotion was real. "Please. You're my only friend."

"I'd hate to see how you treat your enemies," I said.

She looked at me for a long time in silence, her eyes sheened with a film of rising tears, and then she got out of the car and slammed the door behind her.

I watched her walk into Jaxson's house. She'd taken the car keys with her. I didn't have my wallet or enough money for a car, and it was a very long walk back to Hollywood.

"Fuck," I said under my breath. The urge to call Wendy ran through me like an electric shock. I thought of the little liquor store down the street from the studio, my own bed, as sorry as it was, my own horizons.

After tonight, I told myself, *you'll never have to see any of them again*. I got out of the car and followed the path to Jaxson's threshold.

15.

The immense front door, which was carved in a pattern of leaves and vines, was like something from Tolkien. I tried the wrought-iron lever without knocking; the door opened smoothly and silently. The noise of the festivities echoed through Jaxson's cavernous foyer, which was as baroquely ridiculous as the exterior of the house: walls plastered to look like the uneven surface of a grotto; chandeliers bristling with actual candles; more statuary in varying degrees of deshabille. I walked toward the noise of Jaxson's party.

The room—*hall* was a better word for it, maybe; it was immense and stretched the full length of the house and was packed with people—had been decorated to look like a safari lodge. The walls were covered with detailed canvas murals of acacia-sprouting horizons and blue skies and yellow grasslands; faux-fur rugs were strewn across the stone floor, some of them complete with fake animal heads and paws, their felt teeth bared; bolts of canvas swooped from the ceiling like the billowing folds of a tent; the caterers, I saw with some horror, were dressed in loincloths and beaded halter tops. The whole effect was that of an airport bar done up in spectacularly poor taste. I could not imagine how much this decor had cost. I did not want to know.

The guests were costumed as animals, their faces covered by masks. I recognized Jaxson from his frame and the tattoos creeping out from his black shirtsleeves; he was wearing a panther mask and pert black cat ears. Minna was impossible to disguise; she was dressed as a cockatoo, magnificent crown of white feathers pinned to her hair, white dress a sharp contrast to her flawless skin. I wondered if her costume, an animal distinctly absent from the savannah, was a dig at Jaxson's choice of theme. Tonight she did not look serene so much as utterly contemptuous.

An elephant—complete with a horribly phallic rubber trunk—was chatting up a sexy antelope in one corner; a sexy bird of some kind was flirting with something that might have been a turtle; a legion of sexy lionesses capered about; I saw a hippopotamus and a tower of giraffes. Everyone was yelling and already drunk.

"Thofia." Judith's voice was unmistakable and so were her heels. She was got up as a tiger. Her mouth bristled with plastic fangs, which gave her an exaggerated lisp, and her eyes gleamed dangerously behind an orange-and-black striped mask. "Doesth Jaxthson know you're here, darling?" The *darling* was set with barbed wire. She pushed the mask up, where it sat atop her head like a startled hat.

"Alison wanted to surprise him."

"Alithon'th here?"

"Why do you care?"

Judith spat her fangs out into her palm, tucking them away in her handbag. "Where is she?"

I shrugged.

"What do you mean, you don't know where she is?"

"She went in ahead of me."

Judith narrowed her eyes at me. "Why?"

"She was really upset."

"About what?"

"Something about Jaxson's book," I said innocently. Judith's face underwent an abrupt transformation.

"You stay here," she said. "I'm going to find her. And when I do, *both* of you are leaving this house. Understood?"

I shrugged again. She stalked off. Someone had left a mask on the marble mantel of a massive fireplace big enough to hold a witch's cauldron and the witch herself. I tucked it under my arm and went to find a bathroom in which to wipe out the present.

When I came out a while later, mask in place and opiates fizzling dreamily through my sinuses, Brendan was lounging against the wall in what I believe he considered an alluring manner, giving me a freighted and knowing look. He had the dismembered upper half of a stuffed bear affixed to his head at a strange angle, and he was wearing brown sweatpants.

"Hi," he said. "You're Alison's friend."

"No," I said.

"Whatcha doing in there, Alison's friend?"

"Nothing."

"Want some more?" He rubbed his nose suggestively.

"What?"

He looked around and lowered his voice, although no one was within earshot. "I said, do you want more?"

"I don't know what you're talking about."

"I'm holding," he said importantly. "It's for research. For my new book. I'm, like, going inside the culture of drugs. You know?"

"I don't know a thing about drugs, Brendan."

"I could show you, if you wanted. I like your dress," he said.

"Do me a favor, Brendan. Stay the fuck away from me," I said and pushed past him.

"Hey!" he yelled at my back. "You know where to find me if you change your mind! You'd be helping *great litera-ture*!"

I wandered away from the main hall, down convoluted corridors and past oddly shaped rooms of different sizes, stained-glass windows set into the thick walls, and hall-ways that looped back on themselves, until I found myself in a room that looked familiar. The ceiling was made of the same rough, fake stone as the rest of the house, but the walls were straight and even and painted a clean, soothing white. One wall was covered in floor-to-ceiling bookshelves. Be-hind a massive oak desk and an imposing leather chair, a set of French doors opened onto a balcony.

It was the room he'd been photographed in for the *Times* interview. There, in the corner, his pile of legal pads. I wondered what he'd really been writing all those years. I sat in the desk chair, the leather worn in the shape of his body and smelling of him, and thought of how thrilling the girls Wendy and I had once been would have found this trespass. The lair of the master himself. I wanted to call her from his chair, to tell her what I now knew—but no, I thought.

I could never tell her. The lie of it would ruin her.

The top drawer of his desk was full of fountain pens. The second was full of letters, mostly unopened. I recognized Alison's handwriting, the creepy cut-and-paste of Mermaid Dragon Man, the beautiful cursive of the Schoolgirl; otherwise, the envelopes were from unfamiliar senders.

I heard Jaxson's unmistakable voice in the corridor, followed by Alison's. There was no escape down the hall. I would have to try my luck out the French doors. The balcony was dark, the room brightly lit; with any luck he wouldn't notice me. The railing was low, barely knee height. Some distance below, the ocean heaved and moaned against an outcropping of rock. The tide was out, the moon a swollen gold whitewashing the stars.

"—that's great, Als, really great," he was saying. His back was to her; I could see her face over his shoulder as they walked into the room. Her look, if he'd caught it, would have turned him to stone.

"Yes, it's good news," she said stagily, slouching up against a bookcase. "I'm thinking of sending it out. Under my own name."

He turned around, stunned. "What did you say?"

"I thought I'd see how it did in the world."

"It's under contract, Alison."

"You're under contract," she corrected.

"Why would you do this? Are you unhappy? Do you want more money? I know things have been tight lately, I should've advanced you something for the—"

"You owe me way more than money," Alison said. "You owe me my entire career."

"Your career is over, Alison," Judith said from the doorway. Minna stood next to her; their arms were folded in unconsciously identical poses of disdain. "You wrote one book over a decade ago. It tanked. No one's going to bet the prize money on *you*."

"Judith—" Jaxson began, but Judith cut him off.

"No," she said. "I'm done watching this bullshit opera. You want to go out there with your little masterpiece, Alison? What do you think will fucking happen? Someone will *care*? The only reason anyone in this house even knows your name is standing right next to you. Finish the book, and take your fucking check. Or I'll do it. And no, maybe I'm not the *great writer* you are, but I know how to make a *fucking* deadline, which is a lot more than anyone can say for *you*. Just go home."

"I'm not going anywhere," Alison said. "I'm going to tell everyone in this goddamn house—"

"And you think they'll believe you?" Judith's voice cut over hers like a whip. "You're so drunk, you don't even know how pathetic you are."

"You *bitch*," Alison whispered.

"I don't think—" Jaxson tried again.

"No one cares what you think, Jaxson," Judith said. "Go back to your party."

"But—"

Minna looked directly at him, her eyes flat and deadly, and he wilted.

"*Go*," Judith said. He stumbled past her, his shoulders slumped. She sighed and raked a red-taloned hand through her hair, dislodging her mask, and threw it to the ground in irritation. "I mean it, Alison. Go home. Consider yourself lucky if Jaxson still wants your fucking book in the morning."

"Why do you always take his side?"

"Als, right now I'm siding with your dignity," Judith said.

"I can't live like this anymore." Alison wept. "I can't. Jude, it's all over, I want to *die*, I can't do this, I can't—"

"Get yourself together, Alison. You'll feel better when you sober up," Judith said. "Now go."

"Vitun huora," Minna said under her breath. I didn't know what it meant, but I could guess.

Judith shook her head. "Come on, Mins, I'll get you a drink," she said. "You can throw it in his face if you want. Goodbye, Alison."

Alison crumpled to the floor, sobbing. They left her there like a dirty rag, all alone.

I could have done a thousand things in that moment other than what I did. I could have gone to her, put one hand on her shoulder, said her name until she came back to me. I could have confronted Judith and Jaxson at her side. I could have held Alison tight and helped her to her car and driven her home and put her to bed and, in the morning, forgiven her. Maybe she'd just been lying for so long, she didn't know what the truth looked like anymore.

Goodbye, Alison, I thought instead. I felt tired and old and sad and alone. Curled around her own misery, moaning into her hands, she didn't even see me as I walked past her on my way to the door.

I'm no Orpheus. I didn't look back.

16.

The party was even more chaotic than it had been moments ago, although I could pick out Celia's piercing squawk easily over the general melee. Jaxson had a lot of friends. I looked over the room, searching for someone lost, lonely, or bored enough to take me home this early, when the libations still flowed freely and the snacks tables groaned under the weight of their burdens. Jaxson and Judith were nowhere to be seen.

"Nuts, isn't it?" The voice by my side was bemused.

"Yeah," I said, casting a glance sideways. He was fresh-faced in that sweet California way, exuding charm and good health, sporting high-tops that even I could pick out immediately as expensive, and looking at me with frank interest. Perhaps the night was not lost after all. He had on a headband with a pair of lion ears but was otherwise undisguised.

"You a writer?"

"Yes," I said. "You?"

"Nah, I'm the help," he said, turning his gaze back to the party. "Jaxson's gardener. He likes to open his home to the little people."

"Ah," I said.

"Young adult?"

"Too many princesses."

He laughed. "Princesses paid for this palace."

"I thought they were paupers," I said.

"As long as my paychecks clear, what's the difference? I'm Oliver," he added, offering me his hand, which I held longer than necessary. He kissed my knuckles like a little prince.

"Sofia," I said.

"Who are you here with?"

"Myself."

"Good news for me."

"Is it?"

"It is."

I touched my collarbone with one fingertip, then my mouth. He was tall enough that I could look up at him coquettishly. "Do you want to—"

A piercing scream cut across the room, throwing the entire party into a sudden confused silence. Another scream rang out again before devolving into a high, keening sob; there was a clatter of running footsteps—more voices now, piling on top of that unearthly howl—"Jesus, call nine-one-one!"—"Is that?"—"Oh my god!"

Oliver unfroze himself from our startled tableau and took off in the direction of the hubbub. I ran after him. The commotion was coming from Jaxson's library, where a great confusion of persons was milling about, weeping and shouting and climbing over one another and collapsing into faint piles on handy bits of furniture. The glass doors at the far end of the room had been flung open, and more people were clustered there, peering over the edge of the balcony.

Minna, who must have been the source of the initial scream, was in Jaxson's arms on a sofa, looking stunned. More than one person was shouting into their cell phone, their overlapping voices rising progressively in competition and lending the room the feel of a stock exchange trading floor.

"*What* is going on in here?" Judith bellowed, flinging open the door to the library with a resounding crash that had the sudden damping effect of a blanket thrown over the room, exactly as she'd done just fifteen or twenty minutes earlier.

"Malibu!" I heard Barry bray into the abrupt stillness, and then he looked up at the now-quiet room and dropped his phone on the floor.

"Does someone want to *explain* this to me?" Her authority in the situation was unaffected by the fact the house over which she presided was Jaxson's, not her own. Only Minna's high, soft keening continued over the silence.

"It's Alison," Jaxson said heavily, raising his shaggy head from where he had been whispering into Minna's ear.

"What has she done *now*?" Judith snapped.

Slowly, regally, Jaxson set aside his wife and got to his feet.

"Judith," he said. "She left a note on the… Jesus Christ, she jumped off the…" He covered his face with his broad hands, and his shoulders crumpled.

"She's dead," he said into his palms. And then he began to cry.

I did go home with Oliver in the end. After the police had arrived in a wail of sirens and flashing lights, after the ambulance—the EMTs carefully picking their way down to the rocks where Alison's body lay, haste obviously unnecessary—had come and gone away again, bearing its sad burden, after the cops questioned all the partygoers—no, hardly anyone had even seen her; no, she hadn't been invited; no, she hadn't seemed well lately; suicide... well—one doesn't want to think about it, but she'd been so unhappy, and her *career*—

I bore my own questioning with stoic patience. When the police officer asked me my relationship to Alison, I said, "Friend," and then clarified. "Best friend." It was, after all, not entirely untrue. The sergeant interviewing me, a white woman with permed black hair scraped back in a bun tight enough to pull her eyebrows into a permanent expression of faint surprise—nodded sagely.

"You have any idea she was this upset?"

"She'd been drinking—I didn't realize—I didn't think it would come to this," I said.

"These things are always a terrible shock, kiddo," she said gently. "I'm sure there was nothing you could have done."

The night was a blur, and not just because of the alcohol; the proceedings had about them the feeling of an elaborately staged melodrama without intermission or climax that dragged on until morning showed along the horizon and the stars snuffed out. Everyone was crying, including people who couldn't possibly have known her at all; the floor was littered with animal masks and bits of fake fur, and a broken glass lay in a puddle of blood-colored liquid that I belatedly realized was only wine. I was conscious of very little that was happening around me.

"Hey," someone said behind me, a warm palm finding the small of my back. I knew without looking that it was Oliver, could smell his lovely grassy whiff of gasoline and sea air. "You okay? I mean—sorry, that was—"

I wiped my eyes and came away with a damp smear of Alison's mascara on the back of my hand, which made me start to cry again.

"Want to get out of here?" Oliver said gently in my ear, and I melted into him, the warmth of his body pressing against mine, the pulse of his throat next to my lips. His breath caught in his throat, and his hands came up to find my shoulders; I felt the current running between us.

"I'll take that as a yes," he said. I raised my head and looked about me one last time; at Jaxson's house, which I would likely never see again; at Minna still huddled on the sofa next to the open balcony door, surrounded now by police officers; at Jaxson weeping freely and somehow manfully; at Judith, screaming something about a lawyer; at Brendan and Barry in a corner looking as shell-shocked as old veterans catching an echo of "Taps." I hated all of them with every corner of my heart.

"Come on," Oliver said, gentling me away from there. He led me by the hand like a child through a warren of corridors and rooms all the way to a beautifully restored old pickup truck parked outside a side entrance. I thought someone would stop us, but it was as though we were invisible, enchanted trespassers in Jaxson's fairy-tale palace. Oliver opened the passenger door for me, but I pushed him against the side of the truck and kissed him; his hands tightened in my hair, and his mouth met mine hungrily; we would have torn each other apart, I think, had we the teeth and claws of predators, but instead he pushed up Alison's pretty dress and groaned when his fingers found my dripping sex. In one ferocious movement, I tore open his belt buckle and shoved his jeans to his knees, and then he was inside me, his breath hot and fierce in my ear as I wrapped my legs around him, and when I called him *Earl*, he only grunted hard and fucked me harder and said nothing, absolutely nothing at all.

On the long winding ribbon of the coast freeway, he took my hand and brought it to his mouth, and I put my fingers between his teeth and he pulled over and I climbed on top of him before he even turned off the engine. The sun was well over the horizon when he brought me to his apartment, a studio—no roommates, thank god—as anonymous and shabby as the one where I lived, its sole distinguishing feature the abundance of surfing paraphernalia strewn across its balding carpet, and laid me on his bed.

"I didn't know you were a fan," he said, touching the tattoo at the curve of my hip. Wendy had its twin, in the same place. We'd gone to a shop in Des Moines on my sixteenth birthday and let a dirty-haired old biker set the mark into our flesh.

"I used to be," I said. "Come here."

It was a long time again after that before he fell into a restless, dream-twitched sleep and I disengaged myself from the sweaty tangle of his sheets and long brown limbs. Awake, he was handsome, but asleep he was beautiful, his eyelids fluttering and face slack and vulnerable, the rapid pulse at his throat, his prodigious cock softened and dried semen streaked across his muscular thighs; as limp and exhausted and lovely as the *Pieta*'s spent Christ.

I stood watching him sleep for a while.

I could stay here, I thought. I could wait for Oliver to wake up, and scramble eggs for him, and make him fall in love with me, and start over again as a different person. Marry him, have sunny little California babies, eat avocados, learn to surf. The bubble of this imagined life hung, shimmering and complete, before me in the cool apartment.

And then it burst into iridescent fragments, and I put on Alison's dress and went out into the hot, bright afternoon.

The first afternoon I would know without her: the first afternoon of all of them, stretching ahead of me for the rest of my life—the life that had, for better or for worse, been irrevocably altered by her entrance and was now stripped bare and bone-dry once more under the cruel yellow-white sun. The country that had revealed itself to me, however briefly, that enchanted garden on the other side of the hedge, shuttered away from me for good: Who was I to become, now, without her?

I had seen, in her company, a kind of life I had not known existed, a life I had dared to imagine as my own. To let go of it now was a pain as great as the knowledge that she was dead, that I'd never again knuckle the tightness out of the muscles at the base of her neck, sling my arm around her waist like a sister, catch out her low, sweet laugh, or the cool-green flash in her absinthe-colored eyes when I said something clever.

I knew I couldn't just leave Jaxson's party and return to an ordinary life. Not after what I'd seen, what I'd done, what I'd written, who I'd been. But, for the moment, the way forward seemed barred to me. I had been cast unceremoniously from paradise, with the path of return yet unclear. I wanted, as I always did, to call Wendy, but for the first time in my life, I had come to a place where she could not follow me. Now, I was truly on my own.

I thought of that first morning in Alison's house, the gold light on the floorboards, Alison, greyhound-slim and smiling, opening the door to Faerie, to a world so lovely, it seemed impossible that it could be real. The fact it hadn't been lessened not at all its loss.

Dry your eyes, I thought, *and be glad you're still living.*
My old life was over now, again, for good.

PART THREE

After Me,
the Flood

1.

It's easier than you might think to disappear. Certain avenues will be denied to you: stock options, picket fences, credit cards. But consequences, as one of Jaxson's—Alison's—heroines might have said, only matter to the faint of heart.

There is a degree of entrepreneurship involved in becoming a one-woman, cash-only economy. If asked for identification, it is best to demur. You cannot sign a lease or open a bank account or put a bill in your name, you'll need burner phones and fake resumes and a lot of ingenuity, but all these things are a small price to pay for a past as blank as clean paper and a future you can make into a palimpsest with as many layers of text as you like. A new life for the cost of a used Toyota.

I would know.

The first time I tried to get away from Earl, the bruises still livid stripes across my throat, was the second time he almost killed me. I hadn't gotten very far, just to the county line. I was trying to hitch. I saw his truck coming from a mile away and knew I wasn't going anywhere else anytime soon.

"Get in," he said when he pulled up next to me.

"I just wanted to get out of town for a few days," I said. Wendy had family a couple of counties over, family that was kinder than her dad. My backpack was full of Earl's money and Earl's pills, a reverse dowry. Earl didn't say anything until we were back at his father's. He stopped the truck and came around to the passenger side and opened the door like he was a gentleman, pulled me out of the truck by my hair. I won't waste your time telling you what happened next.

"Next time, you're dead," he said when he was done. He left me in the dirt and went into the house. He took the backpack with him.

"Oh, baby," Wendy said that night when I went to her. "Baby, you gotta get out of there." Earl's father was content to let lie my endless falls down the stairs, all the doors I walked into, my many slips on icy streets, but Wendy knew what Earl was long before I did. She washed my hair for me that night in her dirty bathtub and held me when I cried. I only ever cried in front of her.

"He's gonna kill you," she said.

"I know," I said. I didn't recognize myself in her mirror, dull-eyed, frozen with fear, a heifer headed toward a slaughter she knew was coming and could not summon the will to avoid.

"What if—"

"What if what?"

"The sisters," she said. "What if they'd just killed him? They'd still be together. They'd be together in the forest forever."

"Earl's not a sorcerer. He's the fucking devil."

"Nobody's too scary to die," Wendy said.

She was supposed to come west with me. We'd talked about it for years. About what it would be like out there in Jaxson Dace's sunny world. Once Earl got hold of me, we talked about what it would be like to be free. The night of the car accident, I showed up at her house at three in the morning, covered in his blood, and she didn't even blink. Put me in the shower, stuffed a duffel bag full of clean clothes, nicked the keys to her brother's truck, and drove me a hundred miles. When she finally pulled over next to a used-car lot, the sun was coming up over the prairie. She handed me a paper bag full of twenty-dollar bills.

"What is this?" I asked. "Where did you get this?"

She wouldn't look at me. "For the baby," she said.

"The baby?" And then I understood. "Oh, Wendy. No."

"I called the clinic in Des Moines," she said, her voice dead. "They can't—I can't do anything without my parents' permission. My dad would kill me. I'd have to drive to, like, Colorado. I don't even have a car. Stephen wants to get married."

"Wendy," I said. I took her hand and squeezed it, tight. "Wendy. Come with me anyway. We'll figure something out."

"With *this*?" she asked, gesturing to her stomach.

"I don't care."

"We don't have any money."

"We don't need any money. We'll find money."

"I can't, Shar. I can't do this. Oh my god, I'm so scared."

"It'll be okay," I said, although I didn't believe my own words. "Whatever happens, it'll be okay."

"Just promise me you'll make it work out there," she said. "Live for both of us."

"Wendy—"

She leaned over the gearshift and put her arms around me, and I have never in my life loved anyone as much as I loved her then, and I never will again. The smell of her, sunlight and Herbal Essences shampoo. The softness of her hair. Our twin scars. People used to mistake us for sisters even though we looked nothing alike. Our names were always linked in other people's mouths. Shariandwendy. Wendyandshari.

"I can't leave you," I said into her hair. "I can't."

"Yes, you can," she said.

And I did. But I never meant to do a single moment of this alone. All of it, always, was for us. The endgame was never Jaxson. It was always her.

I tell a lot of lies. But I never forget my promises.

2.

After her death Alison gained a level of prestige she had never earned as a living, breathing woman. Her fall made the front page of the *L.A. Times*, the *New York Times*—"Woman Falls to Her Death at the Home of Millionaire Children's Book Author," her first profile in that esteemed publication—the *Chicago Tribune*, even a number of international outlets. It was Jaxson's fame, and money, that pulled the eyes of the world to her diver's arc, but it was her beauty, her mystery, her inscrutable gaze and siren's hair that kept them there.

She was described in a number of places as Jaxson's *close friend*—which, I am sure, Minna loved—and in others as his protégé, an insult at best considering she was a forty-year-old woman who'd published her first book years before she'd written his.

Her novel was dug out of obscurity and gone over meticulously in the papers; it was described repeatedly as a "lost gem," a "precocious and astounding glimpse of what should have developed into a tremendous talent." (That was the *New York Times* again.)

I still think about how unfair it is that dying was the only thing she ever did that anyone noticed.

She haunts me now in the language of what I've learned. How to pour a good wine and let its body fill the broad-blown belly of the glass. How to pinch fabrics between my fingers, test for weft and weave. Leather on cool nights, linen in the sun. How to move like a woman who is always leaving.

Sandalwood, bergamot, vetiver, ghosts.

3.

I did nothing the day after Alison died but watch shadows move across the ceiling in the heat-soaked studio, elongating and contracting and elongating again as the sun sank, burning into the skyline. I knew I'd have to go back to the Beane and beg for mercy. Alison had owed me a couple hundred dollars when she died, a subject that seemed in poor taste to take up with the police, and I was as close to dust broke as I'd been in a while.

Rob the hippie pretended indifference at first. What was it to him if I'd fallen on hard times after leaving him in the lurch, didn't I know how hard it was to train replacements when people just up and quit, wasn't I sorry now that I had thrown over a hell of a decent job, I deserved to have to think about what I'd done, et cetera; throughout this philippic, I nodded so violently, I thought my head might fly off, which would at least have the likely effect of stopping him talking. After he had wallowed lavishly in moral superiority, he gave me my job back, as we'd both known from the first that he would. I even talked him into a raise.

I fell back into my old life with an ease that made the time I'd spent with Alison seem like the lingering impression of a dream. Had I been that girl, however briefly, who sweated next to Alison in her Bikram studio, who drank fine tea in her garden as the sun came over the palm trees, who circulated in her clothes at Judith's parties on the silvery coast? That Sofia vanished in a matter of days, a radio signal from a distant galaxy too faint to be collected by the unsubtle instrument of memory. I had to think of something else before I faded away completely. I'd had no real plan in mind when I'd told Alison the night of Jaxson's party that I'd wanted to do something different; I wasn't even sure now that I'd meant it.

I thought of calling Jaxson, or even Judith, but I needed time to think before I took another leap without looking.

There was no guarantee I'd land so lucky this time.

A dark-haired man I didn't recognize came into the Beane on my first day back. He had on a fedora and a pale-grey trench coat, although there had been no rain for months. He put one elbow on the counter and looked at me in a way I did not like.

"Sofia Bencivenga," he said.

"Who the fuck are you?"

"A friend."

"No, you're not."

He smiled. "All right. Guilty as charged." He pulled a wallet out of his jacket pocket, flashed a badge at me. "Ray Soames. Detective." My heart dropped into the pit of my stomach.

They found me, I thought, an icy sheen of terror sweat gathering swift under my arms. *Oh my god, Wendy, they found me.*

"What do you want?" My voice was level, my expression mildly surprised; all this time, all these lies, I was an artist.

"I have a few questions about Alison Keene."

I blinked. "Alison?"

"You were at the party where she died?"

"Yes," I said, cautiously.

"Did you witness her death?"

"No. I came into the room after she jumped." Waiting, just waiting, for him to say *Earl*. Or *Iowa*. Or any of it.

He looked around the Beane. "Step down for you, isn't it? Your friend Judith tells me you used to work for Alison."

I handed him his coffee in a paper cup. "Lids are over there, and milk and sugar." He took out his wallet, but I shrugged. "Don't worry about it."

He threw a dollar on the counter anyway. "Can't have any accusations of taking bribes," he said. I put the dollar in my tip jar and refrained from telling him a twelve-ounce coffee was three-fifty. He sauntered over to the lid station and liberally doctored his coffee with milk and a steady stream of sugar.

He'd timed his visit well; it was late afternoon, business was slow. I snatched a towel out of the bleach bucket and whipped it savagely at the already spotless counters. If this wasn't about Earl, why was he here?

"I didn't work for Alison when she died," I said.

"Care to elaborate?"

I looked down at the counter, up at him. "I quit," I said quietly.

"Why was that?"

"It could be complicated, working for her. Just the two of us?" I put a Valley tilt into my sentences. "Like, we were like sisters? But I totally needed my own life." I widened my eyes. "Do you think—is that why she—oh my *god*?"

He gave me a bemused look. "I wouldn't worry too much about that, Sofia. I'm sure she was dealing okay with the loss. Anything you want to tell me about her state of mind?"

"I'm pretty busy, Officer."

"Detective. Indulge me," he said, casting a sardonic eye over the nearly empty room. One patron still lingered at the corner, watching us over his laptop with wide eyes, but as soon as the detective looked his way, he shifted his gaze to the window.

"What do you mean, her state of mind?"

"Before she died."

"That night?"

"That night, the days leading up to it, the months you worked for her—come on, Sofia, don't you find it suspicious that she fell to her death when no one was around to see it?"

"Why is that suspicious? She was sad," I said. He waited. "Do you think someone *killed* her?"

"Do you?"

"She left a note," I said. "Jaxson said so."

"Did you see it?"

"No."

"You really think she got sad, got high, threw herself over a balcony in a room that suddenly happened to be deserted in the middle of a 'massive'—that's your friend Judith's word, by the way—party, right at the moment she was seized by the urge to die?"

"I mean—she was upset," I said. "I don't think she was, like, thinking clearly?"

"Was she making any long-term plans before she died?"

"She said something about spending a week in Turks and Caicos."

"Turks and Caicos? Expensive, isn't that?"

"I wouldn't know."

"She give anything away in the weeks leading up to her death? Possessions, money, favorite pieces of art?"

"She loaned me a dress the night of Jaxson's party. She let me borrow her stuff all the time." I looked down. "She was, like, really generous."

"Did you know she didn't have a will?"

"Is that important?"

"Lot of money, lot of nice things…" He shook his head. "Girls like that don't like to leave things messy. She have a history of drug use?"

She wasn't a girl, I thought. "Like, no? Why would someone kill her? Who could do that?"

"You tell me. So, our host for the evening. That would be…" He pulled out a notepad. "Jaxson Dace?" The notepad was for show; there was no way he didn't know Jaxson's name, especially considering the way he pronounced it. "Anything you want to tell me about Alison and Jaxson's friendship?"

"No."

"They were unusually close, weren't they?"

"No."

"Was his wife jealous?"

"I never talked to her. I didn't know she spoke that much English."

"Because she's *Black*?"

"Because she's Swedish."

"Finnish." The notebook again. "'I think they all think I don't speak English. But that's fine, I don't particularly want to talk to any of Jaxson's dreadful little friends anyway,'" he read. "Her English is very good, in fact. Why doesn't she like Jaxson's friends, Sofia?"

I smiled in genuine delight. Score one for Minna.

"Alison and Jaxson were lovers," he said. It wasn't a question.

"It wasn't, like, any of my business?"

"She's dead, Sofia. She can't fire you."

"I quit."

"Right."

"She was a private person. So were her friends."

"Ah, yes," he said, turning pages, letting me see they were all covered in his tiny handwriting. "Her friends. They have a lot to say about you," he said. "The thing is, Sofia, that Sofia Bencivenga doesn't exist."

"You could've fooled me," I said.

"Come now, sweetheart, you're smarter than that. Cops *do* know how to use the internet. So tell me: What's your real name?"

I thought fast and hard. "Wendy," I said. "Wendy Reyes."

"From Italy, huh?"

"From Iowa."

He laughed. "Why'd you change your name, Wendy Reyes?"

"It's Los Angeles. Nobody cares about Wendy Reyes from Iowa."

"Fair enough." He wrote down the name. "Am I going to find anything interesting when I look into Wendy Reyes?"

"No."

"You a writer, too?"

"What?" I asked, startled.

"All these people are writers. I'm asking if you are, too."

"Sure," I said.

"Got an agent? Celia your editor?"

"I'm between agents at the moment."

"Jaxson. Judith." He turned a few pages. "Barry. Brendan. Pretty important, aren't they? These people all make a lot of money. They're prestigious. They win awards. People look up to them."

I tried to imagine using the word *important* to describe either Barry or Brendan and failed. "I guess."

He stared at me for a long moment and then wrote something down.

"Alison wasn't invited to that party, was she?"

"I didn't know until Judith told us to leave."

"Why didn't she leave?"

"I don't know."

"She argue with anyone that night?"

"Like, no?" If he didn't know about the book, I certainly wasn't going to be the one to tell him.

Did he really think someone had killed Alison? Judith, Jaxson, Minna—all of them had been in the room just before she died; all of them had a reason to want her dead, though I couldn't imagine Minna caring enough to kill someone over Jaxson. She seemed more like the type to clean him out in a divorce. Judith would hire a hit man, some Mafia don she scrounged up out of central casting.

Jaxson? I thought. If he'd thought she was never going to give him the book, if he'd thought she was going to go public? Jaxson was a lot of things, but he'd never struck me as dangerous. Then again, I'd never seen him up against a wall.

"Don't go anywhere," Ray said. "I'd like to talk to you again."

I leaned forward slightly, giving him a glimpse down the low-cut neck of Alison's T-shirt. "I'm not a girl with anyplace to go, Ray," I said.

He raised an eyebrow.

"I don't believe that for a second, *Wendy*," he said. "I'll see you soon." And then he was gone.

4.

That night I got a curt mass text from Judith: *Als memorial 2pm saturday she wld have wanted u there*, followed by the address of a church downtown. Alison, as far as I knew, had never set foot in a church. I wondered if Judith even realized she'd invited me. The list of other numbers was unfamiliar and long. Jaxson called me a few minutes after Judith sent the message.

"Hi," he said. "I'm sorry I haven't called. It's been messy around here for a few days."

"It's okay," I said, although it wasn't, not really.

"How are you doing?"

"I keep dreaming about her."

"That sounds about right." He was silent for a while. "Can I see you?"

"I'm busy tonight," I said, which was a lie. "Friday?"

"That sounds great. Sofia—" I waited. "I'm sorry," he said. "I know how much you cared about her. This is really hard."

"Yeah," I said.

"If you need anything—"

You can't even begin to imagine what I want from you, I thought.

"Thanks, Jaxson."

"See you tomorrow," he said.

We met at the same bar. He was a creature of habit, for all his worldly, well-traveled air. Same cafés, same parties, same friends. I wondered if he ever got bored of being Jaxson Dace, if he ever wished he'd stayed whatever good-looking, ordinary nobody he'd been before Alison's book made him into himself.

He came through the door a little after I got there, sat next to me at the bar and held me for a while. I held him back. He hadn't shaved, and there were dark circles under his eyes. The bartender brought him his drink without asking what he wanted.

"It's good to see you, Sofia," he said, when he let go.

It was good to see him, too, although I didn't want to admit it. I finished my whiskey fast and ordered another. So did he.

All right, I thought. *It's going to be like that.*

We got so drunk, we could barely walk. The bartender was the same one who'd listened to Alison yell about the patriarchy. Justin, I remembered. "I'm sorry we're drinking so much," I said to him at some point, "our friend just killed herself," and after that he refilled our glasses each time they emptied, unasked, until the room whirled around us, a vortex with the two of us at its still, unbeating heart.

When there was no one else in the bar, we realized the bar was closed and had possibly been closed for some time. Justin had been a good sport about it. Jaxson left him a tip that was bigger than our considerable tab.

"She was a terrible tipper," I said, and he laughed.

"I know," he said. "I was always on her case about it. Walk down to the beach with me?"

I found that I could walk after all.

At night the pier was lit up like a circus, the spokes of the Ferris wheel a radiant neon, the smooth water mirroring red and gold and green. We walked away from it in silence along the beach. The waning moon was a pale sliver, the city too bright for many stars. The air was clean as salt. I took my shoes off and slung them over my shoulder by the laces, padding over the cool, damp sand, and after a while, so did he.

"How long have you been surfing?" I asked.

"All my life," he said.

"You can surf in New York?"

"Sure. You can surf Long Island, you can surf anywhere."

"What's it like?"

He stopped walking and looked out at the water with his hands in his pockets. The edge of a wave rolled over his toes, but he didn't move, didn't even look down. "It's not like anything other than itself. On the water I think with my body, not with my head. It's the only time I feel like myself."

"That sounds beautiful," I said, and meant it.

"Did Alison give you anything before she died?"

"Like what?"

"I don't know," he said. "Anything. Something you could remember her by."

"That cop asked me the same thing."

"Which cop?" he asked, startled.

"That detective. Ray. He said he talked to you and Judith. He came and talked to me at work," I said.

"What else did he ask you?"

"If Alison seemed suicidal."

"What did you tell him?"

"He asked if Minna was jealous."

"Does he think *Minna*—"

"I don't know," I said.

"That's crazy. Minna would never—"

"I know."

"I don't know why he keeps asking questions. I don't know what he wants."

"I think he thinks someone killed her," I said.

"That's crazy," he said again. "That's *crazy*."

"I know," I said, watching him. "I know."

"I feel so terrible," he said. "I could have stopped her. If I'd just told her—"

"There was nothing you could've done," I said.

"There were a million things I could've done," he said. "She was hard up for money; I could've helped her out, I could have asked Celia to—I had no idea she was so—" His voice broke. "Jesus," he said. "What a fucking mess. I can't believe she's dead. I keep thinking I'll turn around and she'll just be there. Laughing at me."

I stepped toward him, took his hand, put my head on his shoulder. He rested his chin on the top of my head. "I know," I said.

"You even smell like her. Sofia," he said. "I don't want to go home. Tell me I don't have to go home."

I thought of the apartment, the awful walls. The cheap slats of the blinds. The roaches in the kitchen. At least it was clean. As clean as I could get it, anyway.

"Where I live isn't very nice," I said.

"I just want to be somewhere I've never been," he said.

"You don't have to go home."

He pulled me to him, not for a kiss. I put my face in his chest and let him cry into my hair.

"I loved her," he whispered. "I loved her so fucking much."

"I know," I said. "I loved her, too."

As drunk as we were, we did right by each other. He was a courteous lover and a generous one, and I was in the mood to return the favor. It was a long while before we left off, our sweat smelling of whiskey and each other. I'd lit a candle I kept around in case the power ever went out—you never lose the habit, growing up in tornado country—and in its golden light, with his golden body, the apartment was almost bearable.

"So many books," he said, looking around for the first time.

"Mostly from the library." Wendy's copy of *The Bone Girl* was hidden behind a milk crate. I'd had a hard time looking at it the past few days.

"No pictures," he said. "She never kept pictures around, either."

"I keep them in my head."

"Alison told me your parents died when you were little," he said.

"Yeah," I said.

His eyes were soft and sad. He bent over me and kissed my forehead. "Thank you," he said. "I'm sorry."

"It's okay." I was still drunk, on the edge of saying something I couldn't take back. *You don't have to leave. I love you.* Although neither of those things was at all true.

"What happened?" he asked, touching my hip, where I'd put an adhesive bandage over the tattoo.

"Walked into a door."

"Poor kid," he said. He smoothed a piece of hair behind my ear.

"You better get back," I said. "It's almost morning."

"Doesn't matter," he said. "We can sleep in, get breakfast somewhere if you want."

"It's Saturday, Jaxson," I said. He stared at me.

"God," he said. "Oh, god. For a minute I forgot she was dead."

The sky was clouded over, but slats of blue gleamed through the veil by the time I parked down the street from the church. I had done my best with what I had: sober makeup, hair pulled back, black pants, and a black button-down shirt. I was exhausted, catastrophically hungover.

I looked terrible; but Alison's dresses were too sexy for the dead.

The interior of the church was like something out of a bad sitcom. Although the room's bones were lovely, all Art Deco columns and lofty ceilings and patterned tile floors, every effort had been made by the church's leadership to counteract this inherent grace with mint-green paint and cheap plastic folding chairs in irregular rows. A series of posters was taped crookedly to the walls, featuring aggressively multicultural groups of persons engaged in various activities delineated in type emblazoned across the top edge: CHARITY (extending hands to a teary, fly-spotted child of indeterminate African descent), BAPTISM (gazing raptly at a wailing white newborn as it was dunked into a tub of water), ALMS (grinning like maniacs, dropping coins into a basket).

The folding chairs were packed with people: some I recognized from author events or panels Alison had taken me to, but others gawped about them, starstruck, presumably looking for Jaxson or there for the clichéd but unmistakable appeal of a sad pretty rich girl's suicide.

The casket—closed, thank god—presided at the front of the room, heaped with a hideously tacky, gargantuan wreath of white roses. Beside it, an easel displayed a picture of Alison I'd never seen, a picture that had to be years old— her smile was sunny and untroubled, her face airbrushed to an uncanny smoothness, the camera's focus as soft as a shopping-mall glamour shot.

I spotted Judith, hovering at one edge of the room like a malevolent specter, and next to her a woman who, although I did not know her, had something familiar about her eyes and mouth. Her skin was as tanned and wrinkled as old leather, her lips puffed with fillers and glistening pinkly, her lashes mascaraed into such dramatic spikes that I could see them from across the room, and her hair, bleached a nuclear yellow, was teased up into a cloud that moved as a single unit as her head swiveled back and forth on a stalklike neck that was, improbably enough, several shades darker than her face. I waved at Judith; she didn't see me, but the creature at her side did and gave her sleeve a tug.

Judith looked my way, and an expression of displeasure flashed across her face before she replaced it with an unconvincing smile.

"*So* glad you could make it," she said, mincing toward me.

"Thanks for inviting me."

"Mmmm."

She hadn't meant to, then. "Quite a turnout."

Her lip curled, and for a second, I almost liked her. "Rubberneckers," she said in a voice that could have curdled milk.

"This church is something else."

"Only place she could get on such short notice that would do a Mormon funeral," Judith said.

"Mormon?" I asked in astonishment. And then, absorbing the entire impact of her sentence: "*She?*"

Judith jerked a thumb at the woman she'd been standing next to, who had now got hold of Jaxson and was crying on him with much gusto. "Sister. Flew out from Salt Lake last night."

"I didn't know Alison had a sister."

"Half sister, technically. She's been a *wonderful* surprise for all of us," Judith said lethally. "She's not handling the death well, as you can see."

I could. Jaxson, his face a mask of abject terror, was holding the sister at bay by the elbows while she sagged forward, sobbing hysterically and attempting to fling herself into his arms. He gave Judith a beseeching look.

"I suppose I'd better go and rescue him," she said. "Want to come? Up close she's even worse."

Up close the sister looked to be from hell. Her mourning ensemble consisted of a constrictive, hot-pink tailored number that resembled a nine-year-old's idea of a Chanel suit. Cantilevered breasts emerged at a perilous angle from its upper realms, while its bottom half exposed a startling amount of tanned leg and veiny feet crammed uncomfortably into pink patent pumps. The sister's eyes were red and bloodshot; I wondered if she was stoned. Judith had said Mormon, though; I didn't think they were allowed at the medicine cabinet.

I remembered something Alison had said long ago, and the sister suddenly fell into place: the Mormon missionary father—possible murderer, or at least manslaughterer, of her mother—who'd spirited the family off to Salt Lake. He must have remarried after her mother died, though Alison had never mentioned a sister—and no wonder, given the personage before me, who now turned her tear-sodden face to me and said in a reedy warble, "All her friends have been so kind. Are you a famous writer, too?"

"Yes," I said. Behind the sister, Jaxson barked out a harsh, surprised laugh that he tried to pass off as a sudden coughing fit. Without looking at Jaxson, the sister reached behind her and hit him on the back, several times and hard. I caught a strong whiff of cheap gin. I was almost certain they weren't allowed to drink, but perhaps that was only in their native lands. Weren't they not allowed birthdays? Everything I knew about Mormons I got from *A Study in Scarlet.*

"That's the Jehovah's Witnesses who can't have birth-days," Judith said next to me. "Mormons are the ones with the magic underwear."

"We refer to it as the temple garment," the sister said. Her smile had become rather rigid.

"Magic undergarments," Judith said sweetly.

"I think we should take our seats now," the sister said. She turned and marched stiffly away from us.

"Are you *high*?" Judith asked me, leaning forward suddenly.

"No," I lied.

"Give me one."

I rummaged in my bag and found the Altoids tin in which I kept the remnants of my pilfered stash. Judith flipped it open expertly and gulped down one of Alison's pills.

Having paid the price of admission, I followed her to one of the plastic folding chairs. Jaxson was already seated. His hair shone like spun gold; his sober dark suit was tai-lored to emphasize the manly bulk of his shoulders and slim lines of his waist. The shadows under his eyes brought out their entrancing blue. He looked a lot better than I did. He looked magnificent, actually: Byronically devastated hero mourning his comrade, fallen on the battlefield of art. No wonder so many women lingered in his wake, eager to offer consolation.

Minna was prominently absent.

The other mourners filed into their seats, and a hush descended on the hall. A small white man, dressed nat-tily in a black suit and red tie that contrasted unfortunately with his pinched and reptilian features, stood and rested one hand on Alison's casket.

"Welcome, everyone," the man began. In the front row, the sister emitted a single choked sob, dabbing at her spikèd lashes with a white handkerchief. He nodded gravely. "We are gathered here today to remember Alice's life and comfort those she has left behind on this stage of her journey. Alice's sister, Tiffany—"

"*Tiffany*," Judith muttered next to me.

"—has asked me to be here today to discuss the spiritual aspects of our lives and how death relates to the overall plan God has for us. Let me take a few moments now to reflect on the purpose of life and how Alice's" —he took a stack of white note cards out of his suit pocket, glancing down at the top one, and cleared his throat— "er, Alison's actions prepared her for the next step on her path toward God."

Judith snorted, and he looked up from his cards. "Alison was among us as a—er—as a" —the cards again— "a virtuous woman who chose the path of righteousness. And though today is a sad day of parting, it is not a tragic day, for Alice is rejoicing at this very moment in the spiritual world, the celestial kingdom, at the side of our Lord and Savior Jesus Christ—"

"I thought they got their own planet," Judith said.

"That's the Scientologists," I said, happy to be helpful. "They go to the afterlife facility on Venus to be recycled."

"A very sad day," the priest repeated loudly. "But Jesus Christ overcame the obstacle of physical death for all of us and, through his suffering and death on the cross and resurrection, cleared a path for us all to find the way to our

Heavenly Father. We may always turn to Jesus Christ in times of trouble, for he is able to help us endure any trial or sickness in the physical world. And together we must rejoice now, for although Alice did not share our faith, in her death she has shown us the path to the right hand of the Savior and the way to our final rest in the spirit world, where those of faith who have passed before us await us with open arms—"

I looked around. Jaxson had buried his head in his hands; Judith's face was bright red with suppressed laughter; a number of people were weeping in a stagy, impersonal sort of way. Ray was in the back row with a notebook open on his knee like a college student at a lecture. What the hell was *he* doing here?

I saw Celia, too, looking particularly ratlike, done up in a little black skirt suit, her weathered skin adorned with two bright stripes of red blush. I wondered if she'd flown back out just for the funeral.

For a moment, before I turned back to the front of the room, I almost thought Alison was sitting next to me, covering her mouth with one hand to hide her smile; for a moment, I forgot completely that this whole bizarre farce had come about because she was dead, that I would never be able to laugh with her again, or drink tea with her in her kitchen, or page through her sleek dresses; she was gone, gone for good, and nothing of her was left behind for me to hold on to. Alison at the wheel of her silver car, the wind in our hair, the honeyed rasp of her laugh.

You're such a storyteller, Sofia. I felt tears start in my eyes and lowered my head to keep them from Judith.

"...for death is not an ending but the threshold we must cross to enter our immortal lives," the priest droned on. The mourners were silent. A fly buzzed loudly in the still air. It hovered, osprey-like, over the sister's head before diving with sudden precision into the teased yellow cloud of her hair. She shrieked and slapped ineffectively at her head with one pink-taloned hand. A murmur rippled through the assembled mourners. Judith, unable to hold it in any longer, screamed with laughter.

"Immortality," the priest said again, working valiantly to raise his voice above the fracas. "Sister Tiffany—"

He opened his hands in a plaintive, hopeless gesture, and the white note cards fell in a wave to the floor.

Jaxson at the podium was another thing altogether. It was easy to see him as the world saw him, as I myself had seen him less than a year ago, as I had seen him for a few hours the night before: charismatic, brilliant, gorgeous, wise. The illusion was so reassuring that I found myself comforted, though no one knew better than I did the falsehood at its core.

"Alison meant so much to so many of us," he said in a grave voice that carried beautifully. He had the actor's trick of looking out at a point just over the audience's heads so that it seemed he was making eye contact with each of us individually. "She was funny and kind and talented and unlike anyone I've ever known. She was—" But then the composure wavered, and his voice broke. He paused. "I—" He stopped again.

The audience rustled nervously. He pulled a piece of paper out of his jacket pocket, unfolded it, and read in a flattened, toneless version of his rich baritone, not looking up from the paper.

> *Let those who are in favour with their stars*
> *Of public honour and proud titles boast,*
> *Whilst I, whom fortune of such triumph bars,*
> *Unlook'd for joy in that I honour most.*
> *Great princes' favourites their fair leaves spread*
> *But as the marigold at the sun's eye,*
> *And in themselves their pride lies buried,*
> *For at a frown they in their glory die.*
> *The painful warrior famoused for fight,*
> *After a thousand victories once foil'd,*
> *Is from the book of honour razed quite,*
> *And all the rest forgot for which he toil'd:*
> *Then happy I, that love and am beloved*
> *Where I may not remove nor be removed.*

When he was done, he stumbled away from the podium and out of the room without another word.

5.

"That was certainly an UNUSUAL service," Celia said afterward over the funeral meats. "Publishing is FULL of Mormons," she added to me conspiratorially.

"Really?"

"Stephenie," Judith said. Her pupils were miniscule black points.

"Well, yes," Celia said, as if this remark had been in poor taste. "But Annemarie Vincent is one too—and Alyssa Carpentier—she's got to be worth millions by now—"

"Alyssa is?" Judith asked, looking slightly more alert at the mention of money. "Maybe I should convert."

The sister had organized a wake in the church hall's basement, catered with tragic plastic platters of salami and squares of fluorescent cheese and Ritz crackers.

There was no alcohol. The sister was huddled in a corner with her sage; the writers, milling about with cocktail napkins piled high with cold cuts, ignored her entirely. Jaxson was nowhere to be found.

"Should we go to the liquor store?" I overheard someone say behind me.

"I heard the sister got the house," Judith said. "No will and no other next of kin." Without the pill she probably would have thrown a fit when she realized the room was dry.

"I heard that, too," Celia said, craning her head around until I wondered if it would spin a full circle like a possessed person in the movies. "I can't really imagine that PERSON being related to Alison, can you—I mean—do you think it's some KIND of scam—Judith, you didn't invite BRENDAN, did you—I'd better go say hello—"

She stared at the far end of the cavernous basement, where fluorescent lighting flickered ghoulishly off Brendan's pasty face. I hadn't noticed him during the service. I wondered if he'd shown up for the food. He seemed the type.

"I don't think he's seen you yet. You're safe for now," Judith said, examining her own sleeve with rapt interest.

"I'm so sick of him—thank god he's making money—but you know he's just intolerable—"

"I know," Judith said.

"Ladies." Ray's notebook, at least, had been put away. He had even donned a dark suit for the occasion. "I'm sorry for your loss."

Celia pulled out her phone and began texting without even looking at him.

Judith stared at him. "What are you doing here?" she asked.

"Paying my respects, ma'am," he said. A muscle in Judith's cheek tightened. "Miss," he corrected smoothly.

"Do you really think that's *appropriate*?" Judith asked.

"I have some follow-up questions for you both," he said.

Judith gaped. "You *what*?"

"Just wrapping up the investigation."

"Are you seriously conducting police business at my friend's funeral? Her *body* isn't even in the ground yet." Judith was as irate as I had ever seen her.

I had to give Ray credit; not everyone had what it took to face her. "Just doing my job, ma'am. Miss."

"Not here, you aren't," Judith said. "I'd like you to leave now before I call the—" She faltered. "If you'll excuse me, I need to see to the flowers." Judith clopped away on her spindly heels, her back rigid with fury.

"Nice to see you again, Sofia," he said.

"Likewise," I said. "Ray."

"What exactly did Alison do for a living, Sofia? No one seems to be able to tell me."

"She was a writer."

"Drugs have anything to do with it?"

You have no idea, I thought. "I should go help Judith, Ray."

"All right," he said affably. "You see Jaxson, tell him to give me a call."

I waited until midnight to put on black leggings and a black hoodie and drive to Alison's. I parked a few blocks away from her house and circled back on foot, casting an eye about me, but the block was deserted and the blinds in the neighboring houses were drawn. Still, I pulled my sweatshirt hood up and kept my head down as I slipped up the porch steps and tried my key; it turned easily. I closed the door behind me and stood for a few seconds, listening, before I went any farther.

The bungalow had an eerie, absent quality that was more than the sum of the darkness, the stale air, the gathered heat, the faint skin of dust gathering on the coffee table and the shelves. The kitchen tap dripped a solemn, erratic rhythm in the dark. I could smell something decaying underneath the familiar amber layers of the incense she loved, her scented candles, her perfume. Gradually the darkness softened as my eyes grew accustomed to it, and when I could make out the print of the spines on her books by the lingering glow from the streetlamp, I moved softly through the living room and toward the office door.

It was closed but not locked, as it had been when we left her house together for the last time, the night that already felt as though it had happened lifetimes ago. The disorder within was not Alison's characteristic tidal debris of paper scraps and notebooks and unread books and receipts. The closet was open, manuscript boxes pulled out and their contents scattered, her journals tossed across the room; her books were splayed on the hardwood floor; her desk drawers were open, pens and notepads flung against the walls as if in a fit of rage.

Someone had been here looking for something, and there was only one thing that Alison kept in her office that anyone who overlooked the bounty of the rest of the house would want to steal. I had a pretty good idea of who that someone might be.

Well, well, well, I thought. Perhaps Ray was on to something after all.

I searched the room quickly and methodically, putting things away as I looked through them. She hadn't taken the laptop with her to the party, which meant it was here, unless whoever had come to the house first had beat me to it. But I didn't think they had; the mess had a spiteful quality to it.

I stood in the center of the room and let my eyes unfocus, turning in a slow circle with my fingers outstretched, as if they were antennae tuned to the particular frequency of a small laptop laden with secrets, until my empty gaze landed on the coral-colored rug underneath her desk chair. It was rumpled against its rubber matting and littered with trash from her desk, but it had not been moved. It was the only spot of order in the room.

I toed the rug aside, and there it was: a square of wooden flooring that did not match the wood around it, with a tarnished old brass finger pull that laid flush against the boards. I hooked a forefinger through the ring and pulled. The hinged wood swung open, revealing a milk crate-sized compartment packed tight with fat stacks of bank-fresh hundred-dollar bills and Alison's sleek laptop in its black leather case.

"Shit," I whispered, fanning through the cash. So much for money troubles. Then again, I knew how much Alison spent in a month. This stash wouldn't have lasted her all that long. And now that she was dead, Jaxson would never have to pay her again.

He'd probably only fucked me to see if I had the computer myself.

Did she give you anything before she died? Anything to remember her by?

I lit one of Alison's cigarettes. *I'm going to bring him down*, I thought, exhaling out my nostrils in a long, steady plume the way Alison always did when she smoked. *I'm going to ruin his life, Als.*

It'll be my very first good deed.

I found a capacious leather bag in the closet, shoved in amidst the fur bombers and high boots, stuffed in the money and the computer and the hollow silver cat, rattling with pills, from her bathroom, and headed for the door. But, with my hand on the knob, I reconsidered. The house and everything in it, everything Alison cherished and adored, everything she had chosen with care and intent and a keen sense of greater purpose, had been her sanctuary. I could hardly bear the thought of the crab-clawed sister, veiny and screeching, like some ghastly funhouse-mirror facsimile of the Alison I knew and loved, pawing through Alison's beautiful things, her clothes and tchotchkes, her balms and oils, her jewelry and silk and sequins and lace.

I couldn't carry her dishes, her fine copper pots or her selection of imported whole-bean coffees or her luxurious furniture, her percale sheets or her Belgian linen duvet cover; I couldn't take with me her life, preserved whole like a butterfly in amber. But I shoved handfuls of her silky clothes into the leather bag, the strappy sandals she'd let me wear once and that fit me as though made custom for my feet, the full bottle of Le Labo perfume she'd just replaced and a random selection of her face creams and potions and film-noir red lipsticks; a box full of the heavy silver and turquoise jewelry she'd collected but never worn; the books I knew she loved best, their margins full of notes and their spines broken from rereading. The overstuffed bag smelled richly and completely of her.

I paused again at the front door; the street was empty, the night black and moonless and still. I tapped the bottom of the bag—superstition, really—to make sure I could feel the hard contours of the laptop, and then I skimmed quickly down her stairs and back to my car.

I stopped at a gas station on the way home and bought a pack of Lucky Strikes with one of her hundred-dollar bills; the attendant went over it huffily with a counterfeit detection pen, but in the end, he took it.

"Lighter too," I said, and he looked at me as if I had asked some outlandish favor. I was about to say something sharp when I thought of Alison's way with service workers, her benevolent and oddly comforting superiority, and I smiled generously at him with her characteristic, inquisitive head tilt—*I'm so sorry, but I* did *say dressing on the* side—and he softened.

"Thank you," I breathed gently when he handed me my change.

"You have a nice night, miss," he said.

"You too, honey," I said.

I threw Alison's key in a storm drain in the parking lot on the way back to my car. Startled, a grey coyote scuttled out from behind a patch of jasmine and froze in the road, staring at me with its yellow eyes, before darting into the bushes again.

6.

I slept restlessly that night. I chased Alison through the deserted streets of a broken city, her white dress flashing in the shadows as she ran from doorway to yawning doorway. I followed her into an empty, whitewashed warehouse where light streamed through broken windows in pale sheets and Alison was always just around the next corner. Even as I ran, the walls fell away to reveal a sordid old carnival, merry-go-round decaying into the earth and the scaffolding of the Ferris wheel rotten and collapsing, the flutter of her gauzy skirt like a flag taunting me as it disappeared into a maze of rusting metal and dirty clown costumes and splintering signboards heaped against each other in the bare dirt.

I woke up early, though I'd only been asleep for a few hours, wondering if the visit to her house itself had been a dream; but no, there was the leather bag, pregnant with treasures, resting plumply in the corner of the studio where I'd left it. I pulled out her gorgeous antique silk kimono, embroidered with a blaze of roses, and wrapped it around my bare skin; touched her perfume to my wrists and collarbone and behind my knees, the way I'd seen her do so many times; and counted the money I'd taken from her office.

Thirty-six thousand eight hundred dollars.

I sat back on my heels, staring at the neat piles. It was more money than I'd ever dreamed of seeing in one place.

I stuffed the money back in the bag and shoved it into one of the empty cabinets that leaned precariously away from the kitchenette's wall. I'd have to find a better place for it—safe deposit box? But that required paperwork I wasn't about to fill out, likely a bank account I didn't dare open. Hiding the money could wait. I was starving, and now I was rich. I dug through my drawers and found an ancient Chinese take-out menu that some enterprising delivery person had left tucked under my door ages ago and I hadn't ever thrown out. I picked out dishes Alison never would have touched—sesame noodles swimming in oil, spring rolls, pork dumplings, fried rice, more food than I could possibly eat in a day. I called in my order with unrestrained glee and opened her laptop while I waited for my smorgasbord to arrive.

A brisk rap sounded against my door. "That was fast," I said, surprised, as I opened it.

"I was just in the neighborhood. Mind if I come in?" He was wearing the trench coat again and smelled of cologne, something classier than Jaxson's that made me think instantly of old Westerns.

"I'm in the middle of something, Ray." He looked down at the kimono, and I remembered to be tractable. "Can we schedule something for later? At the... station?"

He smiled at me winningly. "Just a few more questions, and I'll be out of your hair, Sofia."

I kept my own smile fixed in place while I went through my options, and then I opened the door to let him in. He took in the entire apartment with a single glance that betrayed nothing, his gaze landing on the open laptop.

"Working on something, Sofia?"

"I'm busy." I slammed the laptop shut and pushed it into a corner.

"Mind if I take a look?"

"I really don't understand what it is you think I can help you with."

He walked to the grimy window, observing the dismal view of the street below. "That's an expensive computer."

I waited.

"Alison get that for you?"

"Sure."

"She in the habit of buying you expensive things?"

"It was for work."

"So technically it was hers?"

"Technically it was mine."

"Should probably give that over to the sister, shouldn't you?"

I waited again. He turned to face me, leaning against the sill. "You don't think Alison killed herself, either, do you, Sofia?"

"It doesn't matter what I think."

"Who broke into her house last night?"

"Someone broke into her house?"

"Neighbor saw somebody coming out of the house at three in the morning and called the police."

"Did they steal anything?"

"Hard to say. The sister's never been inside. You'd probably be the only person who could tell."

"I didn't know the sister even existed until the funeral."

"Was Alison Mormon?"

"God, no," I said.

"How much do you know about Jaxson?"

"What's that supposed to mean?"

"Let me rephrase that, Sofia. What do you know about Jaxson that you aren't telling me?"

"I…" I trailed off, looking torn. "It's none of my business."

"If Alison didn't kill herself, it's certainly my business."

I walked toward him until we were close enough that I could have reached out and touched him. "Why do you think Jaxson killed her?"

"Why do you think I think Jaxson killed her?"

"Because you keep asking me questions about him."

"There's something all of her friends aren't telling me," he said. "I think you know what it is, Sofia."

"'They say the rich can always protect themselves and that in their world it is always summer. I've lived with them and they are bored and lonely people,'" I said.

He was delighted. "I didn't peg you for a Chandler fan."

"There's a lot you don't know about me, Ray." The kimono slid off my shoulder. His eyes moved involuntarily toward my bare skin and away as quickly; but it was too late, I'd seen the change that came over his face in that instant, felt the sudden charge in the air between us. I needed time to think about what to do next. I rested my fingertips lightly on his chest.

"Why did you really come to see me, *Detective*?" I said, in Alison's throaty purr.

He cleared his throat and moved as if to pull away, but there was no conviction in it. His hands came up to my face, first one and then the other, and he cupped my chin in his palms and drew me toward him. As the kimono fell all the way to the floor, I registered faintly behind me another thunder of knocking, but my takeaway feast had moved down my to-do list somewhat in priority, and after a while, the deliveryman gave up and went away. I could hear him grumbling all the way down the hall.

Ray fucked like a man who'd be easy to fool. Afterward he propped himself up on one elbow and pushed my hair out of my eyes.

"I shouldn't have done that," he said.

No shit, Ray, I thought.

He traced one finger around the tattoo on my hip. "What is that, a rib cage?"

"A bad decision."

"It looks familiar."

I took his hand in mine and brought it to my mouth, bit him lightly. "I'm starving."

He forgot the tattoo. "Let me take you somewhere else. Get you something to eat."

"Sounds good to me."

He ran his thumb along the line of my collarbone, tangled his fingers in my hair. "God, you're trouble," he said under his breath. "Trouble, trouble, trouble."

"If one of her friends killed her, I want to find out who it is."

He leaned back and laughed. "On the other hand, it didn't take all that much to make you cooperate."

"Who says I'm cooperating?"

"What do you call this?"

"Collaborative investigation," I said. "Put your clothes on and take me out to breakfast."

His car was perfectly ordinary. I scanned the dashboard, twisted around in my seat looking for—I don't know what, a hidden panel that slid out of the headrests to confine prisoners in the back of the car, signs of a secret arms cache, evidence of drugs stolen from an evidence locker.

"I'm off duty," he said, amused, as I played with the automatic locks and rolled my window up and down for good measure. "Civilian car."

"Huh," I said. "Where's your gun?"

He gave me a look but opened the glove box to reveal a handsome little snub-nosed Ruger revolver. "Leave it!" he protested when I reached for it. It was as warm and heavy in my hand as a human heart.

"It's loaded," I said. "Isn't that illegal?"

"Jesus, put it back," he said.

I returned the handgun to its nest. "How did you find out where I live?"

"I'm a detective, Sofia. Finding things out is my job. Don't you want to know where we're going?"

"Surprise me," I said, watching palm trees flash by out the window. We were headed toward Venice.

Like Alison's, the car was a manual. Each time he shifted, he brushed his hand across the inside of my thigh; at first his touch was light, plausibly accidental, but when traffic slowed our passage, he let his palm rest at the place where the hem of my cutoffs met my skin. I shifted downward in my seat, still looking out the window, let him work his way inward from there, listened to his breath change and hoarsen, shifted my own breath to match it, as if being finger-banged in Los Angeles traffic by a cop with bad habits was the hottest thing that had ever happened to me. I let loose with an operatic yell, and he returned his hand to my thigh, content in his mastery of my person.

The diner he'd picked was an honest one, none of the faux-rustic affectation Alison had favored. The aproned waitress wore a name tag that read DOROTHY in yellowing letters; she greeted Ray by name and addressed me as *hon*; my fried eggs tasted of cooking grease, and their farm of origin—likely some sorrow-ridden horror show of a factory—was not listed on the stained and dog-eared menu. Ray dug into his own breakfast, a stack of pancakes encased in a resinous coating of syrup, with evident relish.

"You didn't answer my question," I said, starting on my hash browns.

"Which one?"

"Any of them. Why don't you think Alison killed herself?"

He took a clear plastic bag with a scrap of paper inside it from his jacket pocket and handed it across the table to me. "Don't take it out."

I studied the paper for a minute: *I DON'T WANT TO LIVE LIKE THIS ANYMORE.* Under this line was scrawled a huge, jagged *A*.

"That her handwriting?"

"I don't know." I examined it again. "Actually, it sort of looks like Jaxson's."

"Yes," he said. "It does, doesn't it?"

"Where did you find this? Do you think it's, like, fake?"

He pushed his plate away and leaned back against the vinyl booth. "Let's say she wrote it. What didn't she want to live like anymore?"

"I don't know," I said.

"Why go to the party in the first place? Why not kill herself at home?"

"Maybe something happened at the party that upset her. Maybe she fell by accident."

"You don't believe that any more than I do." He pushed one last piece of pancake through his syrup. "And that doesn't explain the note. Either she jumped or somebody pushed her. What aren't you telling me, Sofia? Did something set her off that night?"

"I told you everything. I went with her. Lost her. Judith told me to find her and take her home. I was looking for her when I heard Minna scream. You know the rest."

"That's not *all* the rest."

I shrugged. "I went home with, um—" Oscar? Omar? I couldn't remember.

"Oliver."

"I went home with Oliver, and after that I cried for a week, all right?"

"That's not the rest of the story I was talking about."

"That's the only rest I got, Ray."

"You always deal with your friend's suicide by having sex with strangers?"

"I don't have a lot of friends."

My phone buzzed with an incoming text message. I looked down.

I NEED TO TALK TO YOU.

"Something wrong?"

"Nope," I said.

He threw some bills on the table without waiting for the check, stood, stretched. "I'll be right back." I watched him walk to the men's room, shot a quick look at DOROTHY, who was idly refilling sugar shakers, and then leaned forward casually, tugged Ray's jacket onto my lap under the table, and went through his pockets until I found his notebook.

I flipped through the notebook quickly. I was unsurprised but still mildly disconcerted to find several pages of scribbled notes about me—how long I'd worked for Alison, my background as filtered through a variety of lenses with differing degrees of accuracy. He'd talked to Judith and Jaxson and Oliver and a handful of other people whose names I recognized and who'd been at Jaxson's party.

On a page by itself, he'd written *Patricia Smith— JACKSON????* and an address in Venice Beach. I tore the page out and stuffed it in my pocket.

But there were other notes, too, that made a lot less sense. He'd scribbled a pyramid with a foot extending out from either side; at the apex, he'd written MURDER in all caps, with question marks over the pyramid's sides and JACKSON at its right foot. Under that, ARISTOTLE, underlined twice, and SEE KING—ON WRITING. I heard the bathroom door open and put the notebook back where I'd found it just as Ray came out of the bathroom, whistling.

I need to talk to you too, I texted Jaxson.

The response came immediately: *WHEN?*

"I'm not done asking you questions," Ray said, slinging the jacket over his shoulders.

"I'm all out of answers, Ray."

"Someone was selling her drugs," he said.

"Is that your motive?"

"Could be."

I thought suddenly, incredulously of Brendan, lurking around outside the bathroom at Jaxson's house. *I'm holding.*

"Brendan," I said.

He laughed. "*That* guy? You've got to be kidding me."

"He tried to sell to me at Jaxson's party."

"Wow," Ray said. "Just when you thought you'd seen it all." He sat for a moment, thinking. "Come on, my little Nancy Drew," he said finally. "Let me take you home."

"I'll get a car."

"I'm not done talking to you."

"Then you'll just have to see me again," I said.

I left him standing there, hands in his pockets, grinning like a dupe.

7.

The liquor store proprietor reached automatically for my usual plastic half-pint of paint-thinner-grade vodka, but I shook my head.

"My ship came in," I told him, pointing at a random bottle of whiskey on the top shelf. The seams of his ancient, wizened face rearranged themselves in a terrifying metamorphosis that I belatedly realized was a smile.

"You have a good day, miss," the proprietor said. I gave him ten dollars over what the bottle cost. He'd been good to me over the past months.

Back in my apartment, I called the downtown police station, Ray's card in my hand. When the operator came on, I asked for Detective Ray Soames. There was a pause while the operator clicked away, and then: "I'm sorry, honey, can you repeat that?"

"Ray Soames," I said. "A detective. He's investigating a murder."

More clicking. "Well, he doesn't work for us," the operator said. "Sure you got the name right?"

"I'm sure," I said, feeling a delicious glow of triumph blossom in my gut.

"You want to leave a message for any of the other detectives? Is this about an open case?"

"No, thank you," I said. "I must have gotten mixed up."

"You have a good day, dear."

"You too."

I looked him up on Alison's computer with my neighbor's Wi-Fi; it was that easy. Ray Soehms—different spelling, same face—was a low-level employee of American Pride Investigations, whose logo comprised a startlingly executed collage of bald eagles and American flags; his profile, next to a small, blurry, but unmistakable photograph of a several-years-younger Ray, indicated that he offered protective escort, personal injury investigation, mystery shopper services, and business surveillance. In his spare time, he enjoyed reading and writing crime novels.

"Got you, idiot," I said aloud, sipping my whiskey. Someone could've hired him, but I doubted it. None of Alison's friends had any reason to want her death investigated, and the sister certainly didn't. The aspiring-novelist line in his bio was motive enough for his interest. No wonder he was after Jaxson. I thought of that hokey old television show about FBI agents who chased aliens and the evil cigarette-smoking man whose career enforcing the law was but a smoke screen for his failed career as a novelist. Ray'd caught wind of Alison's fall, seen the names attendant, and seized his chance to pony up to the big leagues. Impersonating a cop had to be some kind of felony, at least.

He was a fraud, but he liked to take risks, and the fact he wasn't a cop didn't mean he wasn't dangerous. If someone *had* killed Alison, his poking around could dislodge all sorts of subterranean creatures that were better left out of the light. Despite the care I'd taken, he'd found my apartment in a matter of days. I didn't like to think what he might find with a little persistence and a dash of luck.

I stared at Alison's computer screen, chewing thoughtfully on one of the Montblanc pens I'd palmed off Jaxson's desk at his birthday party. I had a good hand, but the dealer wasn't done laying out the game yet.

My phone rang: Jaxson. I let it go to voicemail. He called again. And again. The fourth time, I picked up.

"Sofia," he said. "You've been on my mind."

"Okay," I said.

"Can we meet?"

"Okay," I said again.

"Same place?"

"Tonight?"

"Yes. In an hour?"

"Okay." I hung up and went to put one of Alison's dresses.

To my surprise, Judith was at the bar with Jaxson. Their heads were bent together as if in study. I stood behind them for a moment, watching, and then I cleared my throat.

"Hello, Sofia," Judith said. "Have a seat." Jaxson moved over and gave me the barstool between them. Princess Snowflake was in its bag at Judith's feet. It looked up at me and licked its nose in a disconsolate manner.

"Hi, Sofia," Jaxson said. "Thanks for coming." He put a hand on my shoulder. "I know this is—I know this has been—"

"A very difficult time," Judith supplied. Jaxson took his hand away.

"Yes," I said and ordered a whiskey off the highest shelf I could point to. Judith stabbed savagely at an ice cube with the plastic straw in her drink, which was pink and looked to have bits of shrubbery floating about in it.

"How have you been?" Jaxson asked.

"I miss her," I said.

"I miss her, too," he said.

"We all miss her," Judith said. "Isn't that her dress?"

"She gave it to me before she died."

"They say people do that," Judith said flatly. "Has that awful detective been to see you, Sofia?"

So that was what this was about. "The cop?"

"Yes, the cop." Judith frowned. "Is there *another* cop?"

They hadn't made him, then. "No, just the detective."

"What did he ask you?"

"He wanted to know if I thought her suicide note was real."

"Did you?" Judith was on the alert now, like a rat terrier.

"I said I couldn't tell."

"Of course it's real," Jaxson said.

"Yes," Judith agreed. "Of course." She was silent for a second. "I wish we'd gone through that room before we called the police," she said.

"You don't think she killed herself?" I asked.

"Obviously she killed herself," Judith said coolly. "But I don't think the police think she killed herself."

"They found some of her letters in my desk," Jaxson said.

"I don't know why on earth you kept them," Judith said. "She was *unhinged*."

I thought of Jaxson's file of obsessives. Ironic that she'd become one of them herself.

"Did she give you anything else before she died?" Jaxson asked. "Besides the dress? Like her computer?"

He was as guileless as a child. "No," I said. "I don't know what she did with it."

"It's not in her house."

"Someone broke into her house," I said.

"How do you know that?" Jaxson asked.

"The detective told me."

"Did they take anything?"

"He said it was too hard to tell."

"The sister doesn't have her computer, either," Judith supplied.

They know I have it, I thought. *They just can't prove I have it.*

"Mmm," I said. "Do the police know about it?"

"No," Jaxson said. "I'd like to keep it that way."

"What's on Alison's computer?"

Jaxson shifted uncomfortably in his stool. "Er... photos," he said finally. "Some pictures I'd... rather Minna didn't see."

"I see," I said. I looked at them. "You think the police think Jaxson killed her."

Judith threw back the rest of her drink with a grimace. "I'm afraid so," she said.

"Did you?"

"Jesus Christ, Sofia," Jaxson said, staring at me in shock. "How can you even say something like that?"

But Judith was looking at me in a newly appraising way.

"Did you?" I asked her.

"What's gotten into you?" Jaxson asked, angry now. "How dare you, Sofia?"

"No, Sofia, I did not kill Alison," Judith said, all business, "and neither did Jaxson. This confusion with the police is very unfortunate, but it's all a misunderstanding. I'm sure we can clear it up. But I would *appreciate* it if you could tell me if that detective comes around asking any more questions."

"There's still Minna," I said. "And Brendan."

"Leave Minna out of this," Jaxson said.

"You didn't," Judith said.

"My wife did not kill Alison!"

"Jaxson," Judith said sharply. "No one is saying she *did* kill him. Only that, in the eyes of this horrid *detective*, she *could* have, and so could *you*, and so could *I*. We must think like the *police* if we all want to get *through* this." She looked at me again. "What do you know about Brendan?"

"Was Alison buying her drugs from him?"

"What drugs? What kind of drugs?" That was Jaxson.

"I wouldn't know," Judith said primly. "Did the detective ask you about that?"

"Yes," I said.

"What did you say?"

"That he'd offered me drugs at the party."

"He did?" Jaxson, still bewildered.

"Oh, Jaxson," Judith sighed. We sipped our drinks in silence. "He seems rather more likely to inspire murder than to commit one," Judith mused.

"We could frame him," I said. "I mean, just enough to give that detective something to do."

"*Sofia!*" Jaxson with the outrage again. "What are you *talking* about?"

"You know," Judith said, "that's not a bad idea."

"I can't believe I'm hearing this," said Jaxson, looking back and forth at us. "I can't believe…"

"Unless *you'd* like to confess and save everyone a lot of trouble," Judith said.

Jaxson shut up.

I pulled out my phone. "Give me Brendan's number."

"Aren't you the intrepid girl detective," Judith said.

"Nancy Drew in La-La Land," I said cheerfully.

"Is that safe?" Jaxson looked worried now, his moral outrage of moments earlier abandoned.

"Sofia strikes me as a cat who lands on her feet," Judith said. She scrolled through her contacts, read me Brendan's number. I dialed. He picked up on the second ring.

"Hello?"

"Hi, Brendan. It's Sofia."

"Who?"

"Alison's friend."

"The hot one?"

"If you say so. Hey, remember when we talked at Jaxson's party?"

He breathed noisily for a moment on the other end. "No?"

"You said you could help me out."

"I did?"

Jesus Christ, I thought. "You said you were holding, Brendan. Remember?"

"*Oh*," he said. "Oh, yeah. Yeah."

"So can we meet up sometime?"

"*Yeah*," he said. "Yeah. Tomorrow?"

"Any day you like would be great," I said, careful not to let Jaxson and Judith hear the date of my appointment. "I'll text you."

"Yeah," he said again. "It was really nice to hear from you, Sonia. You can call anytime."

I hung up on him. Judith was fighting laughter.

"This is crazy," Jaxson said, putting his head in his great square-fingered hands. "You're both crazy."

"I'll just look around when I see him," I said. "See what opportunity awaits."

"So *altruistic*," Judith said. I could not help but admire the extent to which she was enjoying this. She could be in just as much trouble as Jaxson, for all she knew.

"I still can't believe she's gone," Jaxson said.

"She is, though, isn't she?" Judith said. "Thank you for meeting us, Sofia. You'll be in touch if you hear from the police again? And if you find anything out from Brendan?"

"Sure," I said, gathering Alison's bag, her laptop bumping gently against my thigh. "I'll let you get the check."

8.

Patricia Smith lived in a fairy-sized cottage on the Venice canals. A tidy white fence strung with bird feeders and Christmas lights surrounded a postage stamp of lawn and blooming clematis. Whoever she was, she was either very rich or had lived in Los Angeles for a very long time.

I rapped on the door, rocked back on my heels, and waited. A few minutes later, it opened to reveal a middle-aged white woman with a wild mass of black hair streaked with white, dressed in some improbable and wildly unflattering combination of a dashiki and a sarong.

"Who the hell are you?"

"I'm a friend of Jaxson's," I said.

She barked out a laugh. "What does *he* want?"

"Nothing. I just want to talk to you. Can I come in?"

She studied me for a moment. "You have two minutes," she said, opening the door wide enough to let me in.

Her house smelled heavily of tobacco and patchouli and weed. Sunlight filtered through webs of rawhide knotted with crystals and prism-strung mobiles; piles of books supported wax candles and geodes and viny green plants that climbed the walls in questing tangles. The makings of a joint were laid out on the coffee table amidst incense burners and overflowing ashtrays, coyote skulls and sun-bleached bits of driftwood and crumbling smudge sticks of sage. A black cat regarded me balefully from the couch. The whole effect was not the sanitized pastel macramé–dream catcher aesthetic of Abbot Kinney but something richer and more witchy, undercut with menace.

Patricia sat next to the cat and went back to rolling her joint.

"You're a writer," I guessed, stalling for time. She rolled her eyes. "Nonfiction?"

"Metaphysical," she said. "Luckily, divorce has been good to me. But you already knew that. Why are you here?"

Divorce, I thought. An astonishing possibility glimmered. "You were married to *Jaxson*?"

She narrowed her eyes. "Fifteen years. You didn't answer my question."

The cat yawned luxuriously. With a deft flick of her tongue, Patricia sealed the joint, leaned back against the couch cushions, and lit it with a turquoise-studded Zippo. She exhaled a long, satisfied plume of smoke. "You didn't know. Which really makes me wonder why you're in my house."

"It's kind of a long story," I said.

"I told you two minutes."

"Did you know Alison?"

"Who?"

"Keene. Alison Keene."

"Why?"

"She's dead."

"So?"

"So the cops have your name." I didn't think Patricia needed to know that, in all likelihood, the LAPD had no idea she existed. I wanted to know why Ray did. "That's why I'm here."

She coughed up a plume of smoke. "What cops?"

"I can't tell you the whole story in two minutes."

She narrowed her eyes and took a thoughtful drag.

"Fine," she said, pointing at an armchair upholstered in shabby velvet, currently occupied by another cat, which, although also black, was three times the size of the one that sat next to her. I nudged it with one finger; it yawned at me, showed its claws, and settled more deeply into the cushion. The chair was covered with cat hair anyway.

I sat on the floor and told her about Alison.

It took longer than I'd thought it would, and I'm sure part of the story made no sense to her whatsoever, but she let me run it out until I was done and did not comment when I brushed away tears with the back of one hand. When I stopped talking, she rolled another joint in silence; this one she offered to me, along with the lighter.

"I remember her, yes," Patricia said. "One of his students."

"She said he started a writing school."

Patricia laughed through her nose. "Writing school. Sure. If that's what she wanted to call it. That's certainly what *he* wanted to call it. Bunch of impressionable girls, handsome fellow telling 'em all how talented they were, the careers they had ahead of them…" She rolled her eyes.

"That's how you met him, too?"

"*I* met him at the beach. But it did work out for the best in the end," Patricia said. The cat nearest to me stirred in its sleep and emitted a dense, buzzing snore. Patricia's weed was good; my brain felt as though it had detached from my body and was hovering at some blissful point several feet over my head.

"You didn't leave him when you realized he was sleeping with Alison?"

"I loved him," she said without a trace of self-consciousness. "I was young. I didn't know a thing about anything. He's always been charismatic. I was off my head. The money came later. Luckily it didn't occur to me to divorce him until after he'd gotten the first advance and moved us out here. Community property." I was starting to like her. "He went to court kicking and screaming, but I cleaned him out. Only good thing I got out of that marriage. That's ancient history now; I don't know why the cops would want to talk to me. Or, for that matter, why you do." She looked at me. "They think he killed her?"

"Did you know Alison wrote *The Bone Girl*?"

"In New York he spent years working on the same novel. Years. His masterpiece, he called it. 'This is gonna make my name, Patricia, this is gonna make us a million dollars, I promise.' *I* waited tables, *I* bartended, *I* worked five odd jobs at a time to keep a roof over our heads and food on our table. It was supposed to be a trade: first his turn, and then, when he sold the book, he'd support me for a while. Which he did in the end, although I don't imagine that's how he planned it would go. I got into his computer one night when he was out drinking with his students, finally read the manuscript."

"And it was good?"

"No," she said. "It was awful. I finally realized what a mistake I'd made. I almost left him that night. But the rent was due, I had no savings left, I had nowhere to go. That was a dark night of the soul, let me tell you."

"And then he sold it?"

"He said it was his, but I knew better. *His* book was about a writing student who falls in love with her teacher."

"It was not."

"I'm afraid it was."

"Wow. The student was Alison?"

"Goodness, no. He started it years before he met her. That was…" She thought for a moment. "I can't remember her name. He'd been reading a lot of Jonathan Franzen."

"I don't know what that is."

"Doesn't matter. But suddenly Jaxson's finally done it, his agent's returning his emails, his book is going to auction, nine-house bidding war, yada yada." She waved a hand desultorily, and the cat on her couch mouthed a toothy protest. "When I read the galleys, I realized it was a completely different book. It was beautiful. Well, you've read it. All that mythology, poetry, redemption—really a remarkable novel. The movie isn't any good," she added, "but I bought this house with my half of the option." She smiled at her cats.

"You never said anything?"

"I filed for divorce the day after the first royalty check cleared."

"How did he get Alison to write it for him?"

"You a writer?" I nodded. "Well, if you're any good, don't let him send *your* book to *his* agent."

It took me a moment to catch on. "Oh my *god*," I said.

She gave me a Cheshire cat of a grin, all teeth and secrets. "Did I let that slip? How careless of me."

"He never said the book was hers?" I said.

"He didn't tell her until it'd sold," Patricia said. "By then..." She shook her head. "She still could have said something, I suppose. She never did."

He ruined my life.

"Do you think he could have killed her? Her suicide note..." I paused. "It looked like his handwriting to me," I said finally.

"It's hard to imagine." She tilted her head, considering the cat, which had rolled over on its back to expose its belly for petting.

"You never do know about people," I said.

"No," she said. "You never really do."

I passed the joint back to her. We finished it in a pleasant, lazy silence.

"What are you going to do?" she asked when she had ground it out in her ashtray and tucked her feet underneath her on the couch like a child. "Tell the police?"

"I don't know yet. I don't think it's the police looking into her death so much as this one detective. He seems kind of... obsessive." That was certainly not untrue.

"Being around that kind of money will do that to people."

In that case, I wondered, what had it done to me? "Did you know his other friends? Judith and Celia and all those people?"

"I met Celia when she came out here to flatter him after she bought the book. She took us to Hinoki & the Bird," Patricia said, a faint note of awe entering her voice. "Never eaten anything like that in my life. She's a piece of work."

"That's a charitable way of putting it. Do you talk to Jaxson anymore?"

"Would you?" She rolled another joint. I took the hint.

"Thanks," I said, brushing cat hair off my thighs. "I'm sorry to bother you."

"Don't worry about it," she said. "I hope you nail that bastard to the wall."

"I don't even know if he did it."

"Does it matter?"

"It matters to me," I said.

She smiled. "That's because you're young."

9.

Judith called me when I got back to my car. "Why don't you come over? I think we have some things to discuss."

"Is he there?"

"No," she said, amused.

"Sure," I said. "I think that's a great idea."

"You remember how to get here?"

"Of course."

I'd never seen Judith's house in full daylight. The bleak concrete planes and severe glass, unrelieved by a blanket of twilight, seemed even more austere. I hadn't noticed, either, that the front garden consisted of earth bristling with cacti and strewn about with razor-edged pieces of obsidian. *Nice touch*, I thought.

Judith opened the door to my knock. "Come in," she said and stood aside to let me in. She was alone in that vast house, from what I could tell; I wondered what she'd been doing before I got there. Surfaces gleamed; decorative pillows were poised at precise angles on the couches; expansive bouquets of flowers bulged out of vases staged prettily on end tables. Her house always looked as though no human actually inhabited it.

I followed her into the kitchen. More polish, but here

at least were small signs of life: chilled white wine sweating in a glass, a ring of condensation on the counter, an open laptop. She shut it with a click as we came into the room.

"Working?"

"Shopping," she said. "I'd like to talk to you for a moment about Alison."

"He wants the book," I said.

"Yes," she said. "*We* want the book."

"You want to finish it for him."

"I offered."

"He said no," I said.

She smiled at me sunnily. "Wine?"

"Sure."

The wine was crisp and cold. "Thanks."

"He thinks he can finish it himself," she said. "As long as he has the manuscript. You've read it, I assume?"

"Yes," I said.

"Ah," she said. "So you do have her computer. I thought so. Is it good?"

It's mine, I thought. *Obviously it's good.* "It's good."

She nodded. "Jaxson won't stop calling me. He's beside himself. The problem is that no one can write like her."

"I can," I said.

"*You?*" She laughed. "That's charming. If he gets the manuscript, he'll make a mess of it, realize he can't manage."

"And then he'll call you."

"And then he'll call me."

"Who else knows she wrote *The Bone Girl*? Celia?"

"Of course. She thought Alison hired you to help her write. Alison hadn't turned anything in for god knows how long. Celia's moved the pub date back for the second book four times already."

"What was the big deal about Alison being late?"

"Do you have any idea how much money *The Bone Girl* made? He's singlehandedly keeping his entire publisher afloat. If the second book doesn't happen…" She shrugged. "At some point the fans get tired of waiting. They move on."

"Celia didn't care Jaxson wasn't writing them?"

She laughed. "Half the people on the *Times* list don't write their own books. Jaxson looks like a writer. That's all that matters. They were both happy to let Alison do the heavy lifting."

"Is that how Alison had money?"

"Whatever gave you the impression that Alison had any money?"

For once, I was speechless. "Her house?" I said finally.

Judith made a face of absolute disdain. "That dreadful little shack? That's hardly *money*. Anyway, Jaxson bought it for her. I know Alison considered herself terribly bohemian and all, but not everyone can manage to live like that."

I swallowed.

"At any rate," Judith continued, "once Jaxson has the book, all that will be sorted out. Why don't you just name your price, and we can all go our separate ways."

"What if he killed her?"

She shrugged. "I can think of worse things."

"You had just as much reason as Jaxson to want her dead."

"You think *I* killed her? Please. That cop already put me through the wringer. 'Who saw you at ten p.m.? Who saw you at midnight? Where was Alison?' *Obviously* I didn't kill her. What possible reason would I have for killing Alison?"

I raised an eyebrow.

"Sure, I would've stepped in if Jaxson had finally fired her. But I wouldn't kill her."

"You didn't like her much."

She looked at me in surprise. "I liked her a lot."

"You had a funny way of showing it."

"I'm not a nice person," she said. "If you hadn't noticed. You haven't answered my question. Why are you *here*, Sofia, if you don't want money?"

"I want to know what she died for."

"She killed herself."

"That's not what the police think."

"What do you think, Sofia?"

"I think she was unhappy."

"Alison was complicated," she said. "As you know. She was difficult to get along with. Amoral, in a lot of ways. Like you."

"Like me?" I asked, startled.

"Sure." She gave me a sharp look. "Running around after Alison with your little notebook—what, you think I didn't notice? We all did. Jaxson and I talked about it all the time. Jaxson was terrified, I'm sure. He had no idea how much you knew or what use Alison could possibly have for an assistant. Why *did* she keep you around, Sofia? Were you holding something over her? Were you helping her write Jaxson's books, or are you just a grifter?"

"I never—"

"What do *you* get out of it now that she's dead?"

"I was her friend," I said. "A real friend. Not like you."

"You mean a friend she paid?" She ran one finger along her collarbone. I recognized the gesture; it was Alison's. "You're so much like her. You think you're better than all of us when you want exactly the same things."

"I know what you get out of being friends with Jaxson," I said. "What does he get out of being friends with you?" The look she gave me was full of haunted malice. "He's *afraid* of you."

"Please," she said.

Judith. Rattling around in this vast house like a lone penny in a plastic purse. She was cruel because she was lonely. Because she knew the only way she could make people come to her was to hold up a carrot or a stick. Her whole life hung on a fine chain of other people's secrets. I almost felt sorry for her.

"Can I smoke in here?" I asked.

She ran her hands through her long coppery hair. She'd dyed it again since the funeral. "You're really something, aren't you? Come this way."

She went back to the refrigerator and seized the wine bottle by its neck. I took up my glass and followed her across the Clorox-blasted plain of her kitchen, the obstacle course of the overstuffed living room, a maze of hallways. The house was enormous, even more so than it looked from outside, all cement and glass and harsh angles and ten-foot-tall abstract paintings and lumpen forms that were, I supposed, some sort of modern art, although they looked more like the victims of Pompeii. We emerged in a bedroom as vast as the living room, its floor polished black cement scattered with white shag rugs. An immense bed with a steel frame, posts like finials at each corner, dominated one end; the other sported a bleak ebony credenza; otherwise, there was no furniture. An expanse of windows opened onto a balcony overlooking the ocean.

She sauntered out onto the deck through an already-open sliding glass door and sank delicately into a chaise longue. I sat, less gracefully, on its twin and lit a cigarette.

"May I?" she asked, pointing.

"You smoke?"

"When the occasion calls for it."

I offered her the pack. She took one and leaned forward as I lit it for her. Her shirt dipped low, revealing small, hard breasts stuck like globs of wax onto her bony, freckle-dotted sternum. She was wearing a bikini under her shirt. "These are hers," she said. "Her brand."

"She didn't like people knowing she smoked."

"She was funny about a lot of things." She slid off her sandals and flexed her painted toes, blew smoke out her nostrils with satisfaction. "God, that's good. I miss it sometimes, but Kevin would divorce me if I took it up again."

Kevin must be the husband. A million-dollar nonevent. She refilled my glass then her own. We'd worked our way through most of the bottle.

"How did you meet Jaxson?" I asked.

"I was his student, too," Judith said. I laughed. So did she. "Believe it or not, Jaxson is rather a good teacher."

"You lived in New York?"

"For a little while."

"Did you sleep with him, too?"

"Ancient history," she said. She glanced over at me. "Jealous?"

"No," I said.

"His list of conquests is long," she said.

I ignored this. "Jaxson's how you got hooked up with Celia?"

"It's a tough business," she said. "You do what you need to." She laughed. "Technically, I *am* a better writer than he is."

"You threatened to out him to get a book deal?"

"*Threatened* is such a strong word," she said, smiling down at her wineglass. "The thing Alison never understood is that women don't get deals like Jaxson's. They let women make money writing about garbage. They don't let us be *artists*. If she'd tried to sell *The Bone Girl* as herself, they would've put a headless girl in a dress on the cover and relegated her to the midlist for the rest of her life."

"But it's the same book," I said.

"You think that matters?" Judith said. "You think what Barry writes is better than what I do? Barry gets awards and *Times* reviews, and I get shelved in fucking paranormal romance. But I just cash my checks and let it go. Alison was different."

"What would've happened if she'd gone public?"

"It would've been her word against his," she said.

"There was her computer."

She reached for the pack and lit another cigarette. "Writers send each other drafts of their manuscripts all the time. Jaxson isn't stupid; he knew not to put anything in writing that he'd regret. They did the whole deal under the table, and Celia looked the other way."

"It still would have looked bad," I said.

I watched her think; it was a remarkable thing. She should've been a general, not a writer. "You really do think he killed her," she said. I didn't answer. "Honey, she knew what she signed up for when she let him publish the book under his name. I'm sorry she's dead, but if it was that hard for her to watch him take credit, she's better off."

"Did you tell the detective she wrote the book?"

"Why are you so obsessed with this? You got what you wanted from her, didn't you? Why don't you just give me Alison's computer and leave all of us alone?"

"Because I cared about her," I said.

"Did you? Somehow I missed that." She poured out the rest of the wine. It was hot, and I felt dizzy, a little drunk. "She used to look for her book every time she went into a bookstore. The Medea book, I mean."

"Was it ever there?"

"Of course not. It's been out of print for years. But they always have *The Bone Girl*."

She ground out the cigarette and stood. I went into the bedroom after her. She whistled, and Princess Snowflake came trotting in, looking up at her expectantly. She liberated its rhinestone pendant from its collar, opened a tiny latch with one long nail, knocked a sizable bump of cocaine out onto the back of her hand, and snorted it with brisk efficiency.

"My husband goes through my things," she said matter-of-factly, licking the tip of one finger and rubbing the residue on her gums. "I had to promise I'd quit; he put me on the phone with his lawyer and everything." She absently rubbed her nose with the back of one hand. "It's *his* dog." She handed me the pendant and, once I had ingested my own portion, reattached it to the dog's collar. "You may go now," she said to the dog. It trotted away obediently.

"Something else to drink? I don't have anything more fun than this, sorry," she said, taking a bottle of vodka out of the credenza. *Who keeps liquor in their bedroom?* I thought. "Oh, come on," she added, misreading my expression. "I know what sort of thing *you* like, Debbie Downer. You're as bad as Alison."

Now it was my turn to shrug. She slid to the floor at the foot of the enormous bed, and I sat next to her. The skin on her legs was evenly tan and perfectly smooth. The cocaine fluoresced through my system with a lovely, sparkling glow. *I can do anything!* I thought with delight. *Anything at all!* She took a swig directly from the bottle and handed it to me, the length of her thigh deliberately moving against mine. *I know what you like.* I took a drink and put the bottle down.

"Good stuff, right?" She tilted her head back, rested it on the end of the bed.

"Where'd you get it?"

"Brendan."

"Ah, our local method actor."

She laughed. "You remember that cunt Anna?"

"Edward Catten?"

"Yeah, her. She was flying back with like a *gram*, and she got it onto the plane and then got it into her head that they'd catch her with it in Los Angeles—this was after she'd been through airport security, mind you—so she took it into the bathroom and snorted all of it at once and spent the rest of the flight losing her mind. Got a nosebleed all over her shirt on the descent."

I tried to picture Edward Catten's fragile parent enmeshed in this debacle.

"Gosh," I said. "That's a lot of cocaine. Where was Alison getting her pills? Brendan?"

"Why don't you ask him yourself? Be sure to wear a hazmat suit."

"Yeah?"

"He's given herpes to half the West Coast. Alison called him the Vector."

"Thanks for the advice."

"This thing with Jaxson," she said. "How far are you going to take it?"

"I don't think that cop is going to drop it."

"Maybe not, but you can." She shot me a sidelong look. "You had just as much opportunity to kill her as Jaxson did. I'd let this go, if I were you."

"Maybe I'm a better writer than you are, Judith."

"I doubt that," she said. "And I've known Jaxson a lot longer than you have."

"You really think you can finish the new book?"

"I don't need the computer," she said. "But I'd like it. And I don't think you'd like that cop's attention on you for too long." She laughed softly through her nose. "Alison might've bought your countess bullshit hook, line, and sinker. But don't ever make the mistake of thinking I'm that stupid."

I unfolded myself from her floor. "I should be going. Can I use your bathroom?"

The bathroom off her bedroom was as barren as the rest of the house, but Judith's medicine cabinet was a treasure trove. Unlike Alison, she went for speed, with a hefty backup of Ambien to chase her Adderall on restless nights. The amber plastic bottles were labeled with Judith's name and that of an L. T. Darthrop, MD, who had, apparently, a liberal hand.

Judith's bedroom was empty when I came out of the bathroom, the bottle of vodka tidied away; I found her in the kitchen, texting furiously. She put the phone down quickly when I came in.

"You should think about self-publishing," she said.

"I thought I might try your editor first."

"Well," she said bitchily. "Don't ask *me* if you need a blurb."

I had fourteen text messages from Jaxson when I got back into my car. I stared at Judith's vast, ugly house, thought of the sunburnt, barefoot little creature I'd been once, long ago, scab-kneed and free. There'd been a time when I was too young to understand how poor my family was, but that time hadn't lasted long. What hellhole had Judith crawled out of to get to the place she now stood?

I didn't like her, but I wasn't unlike her, either.

Anyway, she was the only honest person I knew.

10.

When I got back to the apartment, the door was hanging on its hinges. There was little to disarrange, but the bedspread had been dragged off the mattress and the mattress slit open. Alison's clothes were strewn about. He'd thrown open all the cupboards and ransacked the bathroom vanity. I knelt, felt under the mattress—the folded paper with Alison's pills was still there. My lucky charm. I tucked them in my pocket.

All right, I thought. *You call the play, Jaxson.*

I dug out Wendy's old duffel bag, stuffed it full of Alison's books and clothes and makeup, the few battered paperbacks of my own that I cared about, the bottle of whiskey. The rent was paid through until the end of the month, and the woman I'd sublet from didn't have the number of my burner phone. I looked around the apartment one last time. The occasion was almost ceremonial. Whatever happened next, I'd never come back here again. A cockroach crept out from under the kitchen cabinet and waved an interrogative antennae at me. I raised one hand to it in farewell, thinking only about how easy it is to leave everything you have when you have nothing left to lose, and then I went back downstairs.

Jaxson's motorcycle was nowhere in sight. I got into my car and called Ray.

"Just stay until I get there, baby," he said.

"Ray, I'm scared." I wept a little.

"I'll keep you safe," he said. "I promise. I'm on my way."

I rolled down the window and lit one of Alison's cigarettes and swallowed one of Alison's pills and waited for oblivion to find me. It didn't take long.

I told Ray I'd be happy with a Motel 6, but he insisted on the Chateau Marmont.

"You're my star witness," he said. Who was I to protest? He paid for three days in cash. I didn't ask where it came from. At first I'd seen Ray as a terrible danger, but I was beginning to realize my association with him was rather fortunate.

"I'll put a uniform across the street," he said. "You'll be completely safe here."

A uniform, I thought. *Right.*

The room was lovely: wood floors and raftered ceiling, soft rugs, broad-leaved emerald plants out the window, the kind of place Alison would have wandered around dreamily, trailing her fingers across the dustless hardwoods.

Ray fucked me, as I had expected he would. "I'll protect you," he said tenderly. "He can't find you here. I promise." I cried prettily into his chest while he stroked my hair. This aroused him so that he fucked me again.

When he finally left, I locked Alison's money and computer in the safe in my room and texted Brendan. I selected my outfit carefully, casual but with the possibility of sex on the table: a pair of Alison's hundred-dollar yoga pants, heels, a T-shirt cut low, my hair in a loose ponytail. A dab of Alison's lip gloss, a spritz of Alison's perfume. I looked for Ray when the valet brought around my car, but there was no sign of him, or of Jaxson, either.

The rooftop bar—dirty glass railing, Astroturf and beach umbrellas, a shallow fluorescent-blue pool—was all business types and tourists, already drunk beyond recall though the sun had not even dipped below the horizon. Brendan sat alone at a table by the near end of the pool, wearing a pink collared T-shirt and madras slacks—an attempt, I could only guess, at camouflage. He was watching a girl in a bikini shriek and giggle in the water as another girl splashed her vigorously, his mouth hanging slightly open.

"Hi, Brendan," I said. His head jerked around.

"Sofia. Wow. Hi. Hi, Sofia." He had about him rather a strong aroma of liquor already. He launched himself to his feet and pumped my hand with as much vigor as if we were at a leadership seminar. "You look really great. Sit, sit down." He pushed me into a chair and pulled his own closer. "Wow. You really look... You look great. What are you drinking?"

"I couldn't decide! You pick." I bit my lip like one of Judith's princesses.

He liked that. He came back from the bar with two plastic glasses of dishwater-colored liquid brimming over with olives. "Dirty martini," he said proudly. "With extra olives. Did you bring a bikini?"

"I forgot."

"That's too bad. You could've had your martini in the pool." He actually waggled his eyebrows at me.

"Next time."

"Yeah, next time." He ate an olive and looked at me

expectantly, waiting, I suppose, for me to take the conversation somewhere he might follow. When I made no move to do so, he drained his cup in one long swallow and sallied forth valiantly on his own.

"I'm working on something new," he offered.

"Oh?"

"A book."

"You don't say."

"It's like… Do you know who, like, Zelda Fitzgerald was?"

"No," I said with a straight face.

"She was married to F. Scott Fitzgerald?"

"That explains the last name."

"The writer? He wrote *The Great Gatsby*?"

"Never heard of it," I said.

"You should read it. It's my favorite book because it's really good. It's like…" He thought for a moment. "It's really good."

"Sounds good."

"Yeah, it's great. It changed my life."

"Wow."

"Yeah, definitely. But you know what the crazy thing is?"

"I don't, Brendan."

"*She* was a writer, too! Zelda, I mean."

"Wow," I said again.

"Yeah, right? I mean, like, who would've thought. I mean, obviously, he was better? And he helped her a lot with stuff. But she was still pretty talented. She was also, like, totally…" He circled one finger around his ear.

"Deaf?"

"No, crazy. She was really crazy. And drunk a lot."

"They do that, I hear."

"The Fitzgeralds?"

"Writers."

"Right." He looked at his empty cup as if it might supply him with the reason why.

"You're working on a book?" I prompted, relenting.

He brightened immediately. "I'm working on a book!"

I summoned a reserve of patience I had not known I possessed. "About Zelda?"

"Yeah! Well, no." He looked down at his glass again, and from there to the skyline, where the swollen orange sun was at last retreating below the horizon. "Nice sunset. It's so pink out here. The sunset, I mean. In New York the sunset isn't as pink. It's more like…"

"Zelda?"

"The sunset?"

"Your *book*, Brendan."

"Yeah, right! So it's not really about *her* exactly? I mean it *is* about her, but like if she was a teenager? And she has a lot of problems. Oh, and it's set in the eighties. She's like this *punk* Zelda. In my book she's a poet—you know that chick Sylvia Plath?"

"No," I said again, just to see what he would do.

"She was this poet." He hiccupped. "She, like, offed herself." He mimed opening a door. "Put her head in the… oven? I think? Her kids were like totally in the room. Super fucked up."

"Wow."

"Yeah, right? Wow. Wow. Wooooow."

"Are you okay, Brendan?"

"Totally. Great. I'm great. So, like, in my book, the chick is sort of like if you crossed Zelda with Sylvia Plath? So she's, like, really talented but *super* crazy. But then I was like, well, what if she had been crazy, but she found the right guy? Because, I mean, Fitzgerald was always going off to Europe and stuff."

"What does that have to do with Sylvia Plath?"

"*Nothing*," Brendan said impatiently. "He *tried* to take care of Zelda and help her with her writing, but then he was like—I think he was in France? Or something? Anyway she was all like institutionalized and drunk and way too nuts. But I kept thinking, what if she met the right guy and he could, like, save her." He looked thoughtful. "Like Alison," he said. "Like if she had just met the right guy? Somebody who could take care of her. She was pretty hot for someone so old."

I saw my opening. "You spent a lot of time with her?"

"Zelda?"

"With Alison, Brendan."

"Oh, her," he said. "Yeah. Lots."

"She bought drugs from you?"

He stared at me. "Who told you I sold drugs?"

God in heaven, I thought. "You did, Brendan."

"Right," he said. "Alison. I got—I got a really good story about Alison for you, Sonia. You won't believe this story. All true. Swear to god." He lurched abruptly to his feet. "I'm going to get another drink. I'll be right back. Don't go anywhere, Sylvia."

"I'll have the same thing, thanks."

He blinked. "Do you have any cash?"

Bemused, I dug around in Alison's bag and handed him a wrinkled twenty.

"Do you have any more? The drinks are kind of expensive here."

"That's all I've got, Brendan."

He looked sadly at the bill for a moment and then stumbled in the direction of the bar.

My second drink was stronger, suggesting that either Brendan had tipped or, more likely, that the bartender had taken pity on me.

"You were going to tell me a story," I said, although I had a good idea I already knew what it was.

"Jaxson Dace," he said. "Jacccc… Jaxs…" He hiccuped again. "*He*'s not what he seems. You think he's talented, huh? Everybody does. I had dinner with him," he added.

"Did you?"

"Big dinner. Editors. You know Celia?"

"No," I said.

"She's my editor. And Jaxson's editor. We have the same editor."

"Gosh."

"She's really good. Roof—roof—*ruthless*. She sent me a letter—they edit your book, they send you an edit letter? It has all the…" He paused, searching for language. "Edits. Some of 'em are *wrong*."

"I'm sure."

"They're editors, but they c'n be *wrong*."

"Certainly."

"But we had dinner. Me and Jaxson. Celia. The… *publicists*."

"How nice." I had heard about this dinner; Judith had been there, too, and had spent a gleeful afternoon at Dharma House recalling that Brendan had explained at great length to the entire table his poetics project of translating early aughts *Pitchfork* reviews of Arcade Fire albums into Latin.

"But the thing is—the thing with Jaxson—he *didn't write that book*," Brendan said, slurring. "That dinner, it was a lie. 'N he's a *liar*. Alson… Als… She wrote the whole thing. C'n you believe that?"

I did not like this turn of events at all. If Brendan let loose Jaxson's secret before I was done, my chance was shot. I considered my options. "I can't believe that," I said. "Want to go to your apartment or something?"

"No," he said. "I wanna be up here with *you*, Sylvia. Sofia."

"I meant both of us."

"Oh." He stared at me. "*Oh.* Yeah. Okay. Yeah. Great." He stood up so fast, he knocked his chair over. "It's just downstairs."

"You're living in the *hotel*?"

"Just until I find a place."

I righted his chair for him and steered him gently toward the elevator. "So nice," he said faintly. He slumped against the walls as we dinged our way to his floor, tripped over his feet as the doors disgorged us into a low-lit hallway that smelled distinctly of carpet cleaner, and fumbled in his pocket for his room card, which he dropped on the floor and stared at sadly.

"Let me," I murmured, bending over in front of him to pick it up and giving him a coy glance over my shoulder.

"Room number?"

"That one." He pointed; I swiped the key through its magnetized slot and slid into the room ahead of him.

It was a disaster. Bottles were scattered everywhere across the floor; magazines lay open on the bed; glasses sticky with whiskey crowded both nightstands. The carpet was strewn with crumpled socks and several pairs of Superman-print boxers. The bathroom wall was made of glass, for the purposes, I supposed, of shower displays. A curtain could be drawn if one did not wish one's morning bowel movements to be similarly performative.

"Wan' drink?" Brendan asked, unearthing a bottle of Old Grand-Dad from under the comforter. "'S good."

"No, thank you."

"Suit yourself." He snatched a dirty glass and filled it to the brim and then took a long pull directly from the bottle. I looked about me for a surface that did not suggest it might transfer a sexually transmitted infection to my person and settled for perching against the desk.

"You c'n sit—on the *bed*," he said. He undid the buttons of his shirt while looking at me in a significant way. "He's a fraud, y'know. Total… *phony*."

"Who, Brendan?"

He paused with his fingers on the last button, blinking at me and listing slightly.

"Jaxson," he said. "I should tell everyone. I should *tell*."

"I don't think you should, Brendan."

"But I do," he said petulantly. "It isn' right. He should have to make room for like… like, *real* authors. Like me." He went for the buttons again. "You must be really sad.

If I can do anything—I just want you to know—I'm *here*. For you."

"Thank you, Brendan," I said. "That's very nice. Are you sure you're going to tell people about the book? I'm sure Jaxson would pay you not to."

"Naw," he said. "I gotta." He stared into the void, his mouth open. "I never saw that much blood before," he said. "I never saw a dead person. It wasn't like it is on TV. I should put some of that stuff in the book."

"What stuff?"

"About the *blood*," he said.

"Does Zelda die?"

"Yeah," he said. "Slits her wrists in the—bathrub. Bathtub."

"Everybody loves a dead girl."

"That's what Barry said!" He goggled at me. "Can you—'scuse me a minute, Sofo—Sofer—Sofia?" He burrowed through a pile of papers on the nightstand, tossing loose sheets to the floor in a frenzy. He rose triumphantly from his nest of detritus clutching a tattered notebook. "Do you have a—pen?"

I did, in fact, still have the sad old Bic I'd used that first day at writer's group, what felt like years ago. Luckily for Brendan I am not a sentimental person. I handed it to him. He opened his notebook and scribbled furiously. "Okay," he said, breathing noisily. "S'okay. I'm—done. The thing is I should've told you—I'm kind of—out. Of product," he added helpfully. "My guy hasn' come through today. He's a *real guy*. Doing *real shit*. Tattoos n'everything. Do *you* have any Adderall, Sylvia?"

I smiled at him. What a lovely opportunity; he was doing my work for me.

"Actually, I do."

"You're a—a peach," he said, toppling backward onto the bed and making some effort toward removing his trousers. "C'mere. You're beautiful."

"Yes, thank you," I said again. I sat beside him on the bed and handed him enough of Judith's Ambiens to kill an elephant and his cup of whiskey. He propped himself up on his elbows, swallowed the pills, and spilled the rest of his drink on the bedspread.

"Can you—can you—take off your clothes, I gotta get—I gotta—" He tugged ineffectually at his pants leg.

"If you like," I said, pulling Alison's T-shirt over my head. He stared at my breasts with childlike fascination. I stood and slid Alison's tailored yoga pants down my hips. His mouth opened slightly, the tip of his tongue protruding. I stepped out of the leggings and stood before him.

"I have to tell you somethinnn'," he said suddenly, sitting up. "I don't—Sofo—Sylvia—I don't believe in love."

"Brendan, you'll break my heart," I said. He nodded vigorously and then put one hand to his head.

"Beautiful—girl—this Adderall is—is really—good—" he said, and then his eyes rolled back in his head, and he fell atop the pillows as though he had been shot.

"Beauty is terror, Brendan," I said.

I waited as his breathing slowed, wheezed to a halt. When I was sure he was dead, I searched his room.

Alas, Brendan's secrets were, for the most part, as uninteresting as he was: a small stack of pornographic magazines, more empty bottles, a baggie with a few desiccated nuggets of weed, and a glassine envelope full of cocaine tucked between the pages of an advance copy of his own book, along with a receipt for the previous week's hotel bill, which had been paid in full ($1,984.15) by a Laura L. Faylor, presumably his mother. Really, I was doing her a favor. And now no one else would have to read his books.

I put my clothes back on, tucked his notebook under my arm, retrieved my pen, and gave the room one last once-over. I left Judith's empty prescription bottle next to Brendan's stiffening hand. That ought to give her something fun to do for a while when they found him.

Brendan's penis, limp and turtled as a mushroom, was clearly visible through a rent in his boxer shorts.

I threw his notebook in the hotel lobby trash on my way out.

11.

Ray was waiting for me outside my room at the Chateau Marmont.

"Hi, Shari," he said. His eyes were dangerous.

I tilted my head at him flirtatiously. "Shari?"

"Don't you fuck with me," he said.

"Okay," I said. "I'd rather not have this conversation in the hallway."

"Suits me just fine," he said. I unlocked the door with steady hands and let him go in ahead of me. He sat heavily on the exquisitely upholstered armchair, stretched his long legs in front of him, crossing them at the ankles, and folded his arms behind his head. I locked the door behind me, careful not to turn my back on him, and sat on the bed facing him.

"You lied to me," he said.

"I left a few things out. None of them have anything to do with Alison's death. Do you want a drink?" I got up, poured myself a shot of whiskey and drank it in one gulp, poured another.

"Sure, Shari. What do they say? It's always happy hour somewhere?"

I poured him a glass and brought it to him, sat back on the bed, cradling my own drink in my hands. "Don't call me *Shari*."

"Sorry, Sofia. Or should I say *Wendy*?"

"She had nothing to do with this."

"Too bad for you she got pulled over for a broken taillight last month," he said. "Which is why when I ran her name, I thought, *How can Wendy Reyes be in two places at the same time?* So then, I had quite a conversation with county clerk Seamus Trotts in—" He looked at his notebook.

"Pine Oak," I said.

"That's it!" He tapped the page jauntily with his forefinger. "Pine Oak, Iowa. Very small town with a very big drug problem, as it turns out. I ask a couple of questions, and suddenly this clerk is telling me all about a sweet, young high school girl, name of Shari Ross, who gets herself a real bad guy for a boyfriend her junior year. Does the name Earl Sticklin ring a bell to you, Sofia?

"Well, this judge sure knew it. This Sticklin kid drops out of high school to help around the house—big Catholic family, not a lot of money, older brothers already in and out of trouble—sad old story, only this kid decides, in order to make his fortune, he's gonna start selling drugs. In a big way. And boy, does he. Whole town knows what's going on, only the kid's dad is a sheriff—convenient for him, since old Dad makes sure his son never gets busted for a thing. Soon enough, old Clerk Trotts tells me, Earl's got poor Shari wrapped around his little finger."

He leaned back in the chair, its forelegs coming up off the handsome hardwood floor. "So what does she do, Sofia? She drops out of school, too. Starts helping him out with the family business. And I don't mean law enforcement, here. Real waste, the clerk tells me."

I got up, poured another whiskey. This time I drank it with my back to him, my mind working fast. I handed him the bottle on the way back to my bed.

"But I guess our heroine got fed up with the edgy life," he said, taking a long draw from the bottle. "Few black eyes— fell down the stairs, she said, but her house didn't even have a second story, trailer trash herself—and the bloom wears off. Only Earl didn't want to let go of his girl, *Sofia*. Especially not when she knew so much about his occupation.

"And then one night, Sofia, Shari and Earl are out for a drive, maybe they've had a bit to drink, Shari's behind the wheel—and the girl runs her car smack into a tree. Kills Earl in an instant. Incident report says" —the notebook again— "he was practically decapitated. Terrible tragedy, right? But here's the weird thing: Shari Ross disappears. Earl's smeared all over the inside of the car, but somehow she walks away. By the time the ambulance shows up, she's gone. Clean as a whistle. Nobody's seen her since. She left her wallet, her ID, everything she owned. Clerk Trotts— big talker, this guy—tells me it's like this girl turned into a ghost. This story at all familiar to you?" He took another drink from the bottle. "Do you know, Sofia, there's a whole website dedicated to missing people? That you can put in just a few old facts—age, ethnicity, sex, and so on—and pull up every girl your age who's vanished in this country in the last decade? Do you think it's all a big coincidence that Shari Ross looks exactly like you?"

"That's all circumstantial," I said. I had in fact looked up my own profile a number of times. *Status: Missing. First name: Shari. Last name: Ross. Age last seen: 18 years old.* They'd posted an old yearbook photo; Mamie must've given it to them. I wondered if she'd made Earl's father coffee in the dirty kitchen, if she'd told him she was sorry her daughter killed his son. If Pops had stood over her shoulder in his old mechanic's jumpsuit, in case Sheriff Sticklin took to mischief.

Ray leaned forward, bringing the chair back down with a crash that made me jump. "Did Alison find out? Did you kill her to keep your secret safe?"

"No," I said, meeting his eyes. "She didn't know. Nobody out here did. Speaking of secrets, I called the station. What's the charge for impersonating a police officer? Misdemeanor? Felony?"

I had to hand it to him; he didn't even blink. "I never told you I was a police officer," he said. "I told you I was a detective."

"Does 'detecting' fall under secret shopper or escort services?"

"Freelance," he said with a winning smile. "Now that we know each other a little better, I have a proposition for you. I'm not too interested in spending the rest of my life following shoplifting teenage debutantes around the aisles of Mimi's Discount Slutwear, and I think your considerable talents are a bit wasted behind an espresso machine. Fleeing the scene of a suspicious accident isn't a good look, Shari."

"Neither is impersonating a police officer."

"*Tut, tut*," he said. "Like I said, I never told you I was."

"You've been going around questioning all of Alison's friends!"

"Where I also told them I was a detective, not a police officer."

"Semantics," I said. "How the hell did you get Alison's suicide note?"

"It wouldn't be entirely comfortable for me if you were to contact my employer," he conceded. "Which is why I think we should work together." He took another drink from the bottle.

"What do you want?"

"I want to be a writer," he said.

"Everyone wants to be a writer," I said automatically.

"But not everyone is dear friends with Jaxson Dace." He held up a hand over my protests. "I know there's more to this than what you're telling me, believe me. I also know Jaxson killed her. Because he was banging her, because she was going to go to the wife—only you can tell me that. But the why doesn't matter. What matters is that he did. And you're going to help me prove it."

"And then what?"

"You're a smart girl."

"You want to *blackmail* Jaxson into a writing career?"

"I think I have real promise," he said modestly. "I have a whole series."

"Let me guess. Starring a handsome private eye who's got a way with the ladies."

"Spy, actually." He winked at me.

Oh, Wendy, I thought. *What have I gotten myself into this time?* But I'd already seen the shimmer of a way out, gleaming on the horizon like the first star at twilight.

"You know these people," he said. "You know what makes them tick. You know Jaxson. You're a sharp dame, Shari. You think fast on your feet. And you have great tits.

When all this rolls out for me, I'll be sure to take care of you." He stood, walked over to me, and sat next to me on the bed, bringing the bottle along for the ride.

"And if I say no?"

"Earl's death is an open murder investigation."

"I told you it was an accident."

"Doesn't matter what you tell *me*, baby. You'll still have to go back there."

"Did you tell them you'd found me?"

"I said I had a lead." He traced the line of my jaw with a blunt, calloused forefinger. "You're like a girl out of Dashiell Hammett. Should I do a citizen's arrest right this minute? Slap some handcuffs on you and send you back to Iowa?"

I did not like this turn in the conversation at all. "Handcuffs sound like fun," I said in Alison's flirtatious voice. I took the whiskey bottle out of his hand and straddled him, pinning his arms to my mattress, let my hair fall across his chest. "But let's lock you up first." I could feel his cock stiffening against the flesh of my thigh. "Insatiable, Ray," I murmured low in my throat.

"Takes one to know one, Shari," he said.

I sighed inwardly and took off my shirt.

"Was it good while it lasted?" he asked later, winding a lock of my hair around one finger.

"You were great, baby."

"I meant being a drug kingpin."

"Oh." I considered this. "It was something to do."

"I always wanted to be a criminal," he said dreamily. "I think that's why I love writing so much."

"Mmmm," I said.

He propped himself up on one elbow. "So what is it?"

"What is what?"

"The thing you're not telling me. Who broke into your apartment?"

A plan, slotting itself neatly into place. I ran one finger along my collarbone, bit my lip, looked away.

"Come on, baby," he said. "Tell me. Was it Jaxson? It was Jaxson, wasn't it?"

I showed him the wall of text messages from Jaxson. "Wow," he said. "What the hell does he think you have?"

"He thinks I have Alison's computer."

"Why does he care about that?"

"Alison wrote *The Bone Girl*," I said. "And she was writing his next book when she died."

He gave a long, low whistle. "Holy shit. *Do* you have her computer?"

Alison had said something once about men being largely incompetent villains; she hadn't been kidding. "No," I said breathily. "But Alison was threatening to expose him, go public. He was looking for another ghostwriter."

"Who else knows this?"

"Judith. Celia. I saw Judith and Jaxson fight with Alison the night she died, Ray. I think he knows I was there." I let a single tear roll down my cheek. "I want to help you, Ray, but we have to be careful. I think he might be trying to kill me, too."

"You let me worry about that, baby," he said, tucking a lock of hair behind my ear and kissing my forehead. I could feel his erection.

"Oh, Ray," I moaned and pressed myself against him. "I'm so scared."

More whiskey, more sex, more purring and squeals, hamburgers and champagne from room service. He didn't even notice the Ambien I put in his drink. The moment he was out, I went into the bathroom and called Wendy.

"I'm in trouble," I said.

Silence. Then, "Sticklin found you."

"Not yet, but it won't take long. There's a detective here who knows about Earl. I have time, I think, but not much."

"Cop?"

"Not exactly. It's a long story."

"What are you going to do? Run?"

I was used to disappearing; I was, by then, rather good at it. I had Alison's cash, Alison's clothes, nothing to keep me here.

But I was tired of living like a poor person when I was a thousand times smarter than any of the rich people I knew.

"I'm not sure yet. But I'll come for you, Wen. No matter what happens, I swear I will. You and the baby."

"I don't care about the baby," she said. "Maybe the car crash isn't a big deal. All that was a long time ago."

"Not that long ago. Anyway, there's no statute of limitations on murder."

"You didn't murder anybody."

"Technically, I did."

"It's not like you *shot* him or something. I wish I could help you."

"You've already helped me so much, Wen. You've helped me more than I ever had a right to ask."

"It was nothing," she said.

"It was everything, and you know it."

"I just wish I'd gone with you."

My heart leapt. "You do?"

"Every goddamn day, Shar. Sometimes at night, after the baby's asleep, I'll drive away from town for an hour, trying to work up the guts to keep going. I hate this place. I hate it more and more with every second of my life it swallows whole. I hate being a *mother.* The baby wants me all the goddamn time. Just cries and cries. I hate Ste—"

She bit back the words like she was afraid of them.

"I don't have any money," she said instead. "There's no use pretending I'll ever be anything else."

"I'm going to get us both out of this," I said. "I'm done running. I have money now. I just have to take care of this detective."

"How?"

"I have an idea."

"I remember the last time you had an idea."

"That was your idea."

"It was a terrible idea."

"It worked, didn't it?"

She laughed. "I guess you could say that."

"Don't worry about me. I'll call you soon. I love you, Wen."

She was silent. Then: "Be careful."

"Always."

"More like never."

"Fuck off."

"I love you, too."

"I should go. I just wanted to tell you—I'm gonna come get you."

"I'll hold my breath, slut."

What Alison had written of the second book was messy, sprawling, in places almost incoherent, but I could see the structure underneath, the missing pieces, what it needed to become something closer to a whole, as if I were hovering above a vast plain with the roads marked in neon fire.

I knew Jaxson's book—Alison's book—*my* book—inside and out. I'd dreamed it. I'd inked it into my skin. I'd breathed whole passages. I'd grown up with it. I'd used it to survive. What if there was another Shariandwendy out there who needed a book like *The Bone Girl* as badly as we had? I knew that longing better than Jaxson ever could.

And now it was my turn to write it.

I poured myself another glass of whiskey, opened Alison's most recent FuckThis draft, and began to type.

12.

I wrote all night, the words coming out of me like a spring rising out of a desert. It didn't feel like work at all. It felt, as Jaxson had once said, like someone else moved through me—an ironic choice of words, in his case. It felt like a card trick. It felt like magic.

It felt like home.

The morning after I finished Jaxson's second book, I woke up to the sun pouring in through the open blinds. Ray was still out cold. I didn't remember falling asleep. The whiskey bottle was almost empty, but he'd done a lot of that work for me. The draft I'd finished the night before was rough; even I knew that.

But I also knew it was good.

I printed out the first fifty pages in the Chateau Marmont business center. Back in my room, I locked up the computer again. I made up an email account—*serendipitous666@gmail .com*—and emailed everything I'd done to myself as a backup.

Half Alison's cash was still in my car, the rest in Alison's bag. If I had to, I could run. I was hoping it wouldn't come to that.

Baby, I didn't want to wake you up. I have to confront him, I wrote in my notebook, sitting cross-legged on that glorious bed. *I'm so scared. But it's the only way I can get him to leave me alone. I know he killed her. He might kill me, too. I want to help. But I have to do this the only way I know how.*

I chewed on the end of Jaxson's pen.

I think I might be falling in love with you, I added. *You're like Philip Marlowe. The Bogart version. So strong.* I tucked the notebook next to his inert form and scheduled a wake-up call in fifteen minutes. "Call back until he comes around," I said. "Come bang on the door if you have to." Next to me on the bed, Ray twitched and groaned.

I tipped the valet twenty dollars I'd taken from Ray's wallet when he brought my car around. "Thank you *so* much," I said.

"Take care of yourself, miss," he said and tipped his hat.

Jaxson still hadn't changed the code on his gate. In the unkind light of day, the house was sadder and less monstrous, like an aging film star clinging desperately to better days. To my relief, the grounds were empty. I preferred not to run into Oliver, god bless him.

Jaxson himself answered the door. He stared at me for a long moment, as if he had forgotten who I was, and then he let me in.

"That's her dress," he said.

I ignored this. "Where's Minna?"

"She moved out," he said. "She's had a girlfriend this whole time. The other girl from the movie. She's leaving me. She said she only married me for—god, does it matter what Minna said to me? Did you hear about Brendan?"

"What about him?"

He ran a hand over his face. "He overdosed. Last night. He's dead."

"What a loss to literature," I said.

"I'm starting to think I'm cursed." His face was stripped bare, his expression desperate; all his bravado, his radiance, was gone, exposing the ravaged mess beneath. "You have her computer?"

I pulled the pages out of Alison's bag and handed them to him. "What's this?" he asked.

"I'll make myself a drink while you read," I said. I remembered the bottles in the library, the beveled rocks glasses. I sat in his chair and put my feet on his desk, sipping his whiskey. I pulled open the drawers, looked through his files until I found THE SCHOOLGIRL, took out the sheaf of envelopes, many still sealed. I selected the most recent and slit it open with his fine obsidian letter opener.

Jaxson,

Do you ever wonder what it would be like if I met you in California? Would we recognize each other? I feel your book has marked me through and through, like ink dropped into a glass of water, so that the color of my thoughts will never be separate from it again. I have to tell you something, something that you did for me. Something that you showed me how to do myself. I was in love with my own sorcerer, and he was cruel as Calliope's; I had my own Clio, and she was far too loyal to be any figment of my own mind.

Calliope and Clio, Jaxson. Poetry and history. The muse who sang the story and the muse who wrote it down. It was my

Clio's idea to use what you wrote in the book. Fire and metal and blood and glass. Like a spell. She was going to do it herself, that's how much she loved me. But I never would have let her take a risk like that for me.

He was my mistake, mine alone, and I was the one who'd have to set myself free.

He's dead now, Jaxson. I killed him; he will never hurt me, or anyone else, again. I can't tell you where I am now, or where I'm going. But I think we'll find each other. I think I'll see you soon. I have faith in fate, Jaxson. It's your book that taught me that.

I'm writing this leaning against the steering wheel of the car I bought with Clio's money. We're heading west. Me and all my ghosts. My sister will follow when I have a safe place to keep her.

I love you without even knowing you. I love you because of language alone.

Jaxson, I'll see you soon. I wonder if you'll know me. I know that I'll know you.

Calliope

I folded that one and put it in Alison's bag. The rest of the letters I took out onto the balcony and burned. I brushed the ashes out over the stones and sat on the edge of the balcony with my feet dangling into the abyss.

Half an hour or so later, Jaxson came out to join me, holding the pages.

"How much more is there?"

"It's done. It's just a draft, but it's a full one."

"She never told me she finished it," he said.

"She didn't."

"Then how—where did you get this? She hasn't done anything like this in years. Not since the very first—" I watched him work it out. "Oh my god," he said finally. "How did you do it?"

"I know *The Bone Girl* better than you do," I said. "My best friend and I used to tell it to each other in the dark. Whole passages from memory. I've been living in Alison's voice for years. I just thought that it was yours."

"You told me you'd never read it before you came here. You told me you didn't know who I was."

I looked him in the eye. "I didn't know it was *you*," I lied.

"Are you—what are you going to do? What do you want for this? You want money?"

"Money is a good place to start." I could feel fire singing down my veins; I could feel triumph flaring at the edges of my vision like a corona. This, this was the deal I'd been born to broker. This was the hard bargain beating through my heart. For Alison. For Wendy. For me. For all the girls, longing toward a different world. I was taking this man for everything he was worth.

And, when I was done, he'd get down on his knees in front of me and beg me to take more.

"You fought with her in here the night she died," I said.

"What are you talking about?"

"You were here alone with her," I said. "Judith saw you. I saw you. The gardener saw you; he told me later."

"The police—if that were true, the police would've—"

"He knows you fought. He knows she wrote the book. Her suicide note is in your handwriting, Jaxson. He has that, too."

"*What?*" Somewhere in the house, I heard a door creak open. I could see Jaxson's mind working down the path I'd laid for him. He took a step toward me, his face pleading. "Sofia, you don't think—"

"It doesn't matter what I think."

"Sofia," he said, taking another step toward me, reaching for my hand. "Sofia, sweetheart, this is crazy."

"Don't move," Ray said, stepping out onto the balcony. "Don't you touch her, you bastard." He had on the fedora and the trench coat. An unlit cigarette dangled from his mouth. The Ruger from his glove box was in his hand and pointed at Jaxson.

"What the *fuck*?" Jaxson said. "Is that a fucking *gun*?"

"And if I had a knife, I'd cut your throat just to see what kind of garbage came out," Ray snarled. "You all right, Sofia?"

"Ray," I said, wide-eyed as a rabbit. "You're here."

"What do you *want*?" Jaxson asked.

"Career advice," Ray said. "Where do you get your ideas, Jaxson Dace? Is that why you killed her?"

But Jaxson had forty pounds of muscle on Ray, and he was as fast as a cat. All that surfing. He hit Ray's wrist first, sending the gun flying. Ray roared in fury, landing a solid right hook that knocked Jaxson's head backward and diving for the gun. But I got to it first.

"Sofia!" Ray bellowed, anguished. Jaxson tackled him again, and they grappled mightily, locked in a terrible embrace. But Ray was no match for Jaxson's beach-honed strength, and Jaxson pushed him slowly, inexorably toward the balcony edge until he was bent backward. Jackson kicked his legs out from under him and let him fall. Ray cried out once, and there was a sickening crunch, and then silence.

Jaxson stared at the rocks below the balcony, breathing hard.

"Oh my god," he said. "What did I do? What did I just do?"

I wept prettily. "Oh my god!" I agreed. "What have you done, Jaxson?"

"Sofia—" He was at my side now, babbling, his face cycling through confusion and terror and confusion again. I put my arms around him, and he sobbed into my chest like a child.

"I didn't mean to—" he cried. "He just—I didn't kill Alison, Sofia. I would never—no matter what, I would never do something like that. You have to believe me."

I looked at him for a long time. He was so beautiful in the sunlight. That face, those eyes, those hands.

"I believe you," I said.

Well. Of course I did.

EPILOGUE

The Final Girl

Reading back over this, I feel as though I've done Jaxson an injustice. People really did love him. No one knew him very well; no one but Judith, and Alison, and now me. He was like a tarot card: the Artist. But *The Bone Girl* meant so much to so many people, and Jaxson looked exactly like the person who should have written it. He was larger-than-life, magnificent. He was made of muscle and gold. And he could be generous, and kind, and funny, and wise. He was, as Judith said, rather a good teacher.

He was everything you'd want a writer to be.

Jaxson sent me an email, actually, a few days after Alison's funeral.

sofia
he wrote

I know it's wrong but since that night I think of you constantly—at night, most often, but in the morning, too, running along the beach, I think of you beside me. You knew better than anyone how unhappy Alison was—in times like this, I know, the first impulse is for us to blame ourselves, but she would have found another way even if we'd stopped her then—I know she would. (She was so stubborn.)

At some point I realized that Alison was an extremely sad person. Not the kind of sadness that comes from a bad book review or one of Celia's ed letters (ha) but the kind of sadness that happens in an artist—that makes a home in her heart. The kind of sadness that doesn't leave. I don't think she ever would have found a way to live. It breaks my heart to think of you worrying. I know you must be. But none of this, not what she did, not the way I feel about you, is your fault. She would want you to be happy. You were such a good friend.

"The person in whom Its invisible agony reaches a certain unendurable level will kill herself the same way a trapped person will eventually jump from the window of a burning high-rise." (David Foster Wallace)

I know it sounds crazy but I already miss you.

—j

The quote isn't from any of Wallace's books. I know, because it was the first thing that came up when I googled "best suicide quotes," too.

The night before Alison died, we drove up the coast to a beach she knew about. "I want to feel the ocean on my skin," she said. We left our clothes on the sand. Child of the Midwest that I am, I was uneasy in the dark, depthless water. Alison swam like a shark, cutting away from me in a clean line until I lost sight of her. I let the next incoming wave spit me up onto the sand and sat for a long time letting the night air dry my skin, my hair wild with salt. When she came out of the water, we dressed in silence and did not touch. She drove me back to her house, and I fell asleep on her couch, in her clothes. The next day she took me to Jaxson's party.

I spoke to her before I left that room.

Surely you didn't believe me when I told you I didn't?

"Alison," I said from the open door, and she raised her head from the floor and looked at me. The lamplight shone on her dark hair.

"Sofia? What are you doing out there?"

I didn't answer. She got to her feet and poured herself a whiskey and came out on the balcony to stand next to me, her cheeks still glossy with tears. The air was cool and still. All around us was the great silvery mass of the Pacific, and the blood in my veins sang the way it had the night I got into the car with Earl for the last time. The sound of my future opening wide before me like a book.

"I can't do this anymore," she said. The glass slid from her hands and shattered on the balcony beneath us.

"I know," I said.

The world around us suspended, holding its breath. Waiting for the curtain to drop.

It took her so long to fall. In the wake of that arc, the scent of her perfume clung to my skin. And the suicide note—well, I told you in the beginning I had a talent for forgery.

That much, at least, was true.

Did she jump? Did I push her?

I don't know. You tell me.

I see her nearly as often now that she is dead as I did when she was alive. I see her in my dreams; I see her in the apartment Jaxson bought me in the Village, in the corner of my favorite café in Soho, in the row behind me at Carnegie Hall.

She likes to wander around my apartment in the early winter mornings in her stocking feet and an old sweater, rearranging the flowers. She never speaks to me, but I have grown used to her company. *My love for you was greater than my wisdom*, I say to her, but I am sure, wherever she is, she cannot hear. And I have Wendy now.

Wendy, the bright heart that beats through all the stories I tell.

You can think me selfish. But Wendy: I set her free. If there is a book where all our deeds are recorded, for good and for ill, I think there is a mark in my favor for that.

The funny thing? I dream of Alison, all the time. But I hardly think of Brendan and Ray at all. And I never dream about Earl anymore. I helped Jaxson put Ray's body back in his car, to drive it up the coast that night to a place where the only thing separating the highway from a perilous drop into the ocean was a fragile curve of guardrail. I told him to put the car in gear and push it over the edge.

The story told itself: Ray speeding around a hairpin turn, the loss of control, the wrecked ruin of his car saturated with saltwater and blood. It took a day or two for them to find him. The police had already ruled Alison's death a suicide, Brendan's an accident, although I'd heard Judith had an uncomfortable few hours at the station. There is no one left who'll tell.

Judith knows what side her bread is buttered on. I think, after everything, she's a bit afraid of me.

I kept the gun, just in case. And Alison's suicide note in Jaxson's hand.

You never know.

Alison brought me into her life because of what she thought she could steal from me, but in the end, she gave me what I chose to take. I believe that's justice. I believe she loves me. I believe she follows me now in a way that is not a haunting.

I believe, wherever she is, that she is proud.

I asked Jaxson and Celia if we could launch the new book in New York. He agreed. He lives here now; Minna got in the divorce, and sold immediately, the house in Los Angeles. She got quite a lot of his money, too. I told him not to fight her; she's earned it. And I knew the new book would more than make up for what he lost.

I was right. The book debuted at the top of the *Times* bestseller list; it was optioned for film the day I turned in the final draft. A National Book Award nomination, full profiles in major literary magazines, royalty checks with amounts I would never have dared even to dream of before I came to LA. The fans were ecstatic, the reviews lavish.

A master at the height of his powers.

An even more stunning achievement than The Bone Girl, *if that can be believed.*

Jaxson took Wendy and Judith and I to Bloomingdale's to buy us our book-party dresses. "Anything you want, ladies," he said, ever gallant.

Wendy and I had reserved seats in the front row. My dress was silver, sewn with a galaxy's worth of sequins. Hers was gold. Sun and starlight, heavenly creatures. I've never seen Wendy so happy as she was that night.

The girl who introduced Jaxson was so nervous, she squeaked. When he came onstage, she trembled like a reed in fast water. He paused and looked out at the breathless throng. He was wearing a suit I'd picked out for him, a cool, dark backdrop for his radiant hair. There are lines at the corners of his eyes now that weren't there before. He's self-conscious about them, but I think they make him look distinguished.

"There are two people to whom I owe an unrepayable debt," he said. "One of them is gone from us forever. But I am eternally grateful that one of them is in this room tonight. This book is for my dear friend Alison, who walks now with Calliope and Clio." He bent his golden head to look at me, shining in my star-sewn dress. "And for my wife, Sofia, the most brilliant woman I know."

Judith snorted behind me.

"I would be nothing without the women who have made me the man—the writer—that I am," Jaxson said.

A wave of sighs moved across the room like a summer breeze. He opened my book and began to read. Next to me, Wendy was crying.

Did I tell her? Of course not. Wendy deserves better than the truth.

I can tell you instead what I learned in Iowa. I can tell you about the cicadas humming in the long grass, the summer heat building over the prairie, the dense anvils of thunderheads massing in the sunset-blushed sky. I can tell you about my parents, with their dead eyes and empty hearts, the house that made Earl look like a good decision. I can tell you that Wendy is the only reason I'm still alive and not because of the night she saved me.

I can tell you, over and over and over again, about Alison. I think of a night, a week or two before I slept with her, where I stayed late at Alison's house and she put on a record by a band whose singer she'd known in New York. She had a thousand stories like that she'd drop like hard candy thrown from a parade. The music was hard, heady rock 'n' roll, the kind of music that made you want to drink yourself into oblivion, to draw blood. We danced around her living room like maenads, shrieking and whirling, our hair drenched with each other's sweat, howling. I think about the dilated moment before the car hit the tree I'd steered for, so much longer than you would expect. Earl's face white, his mouth forming an O of astonishment and rage—not fear, never fear, not Earl, not even in the final seconds. I think of the noise his body made as it crumpled into metal and glass.

I think of how no one should have been able to walk away from that crash, but I did. What do they say? *God willing*. It's the willing that does it, I think. Not so much the gods.

I think of how *murder* and *mercy* are words that come from the same place on the tongue. I think of Wendy, getting in the car for the last time, the money I sent her in her pocket, driving herself to the bus station and leaving Stephen's old station wagon—its seats splitting, vomiting up springs, the rear muffler dragging behind it, the tires worn bald—in the parking lot. Getting on the bus to New York with nothing but an envelope of cash in her purse.

You won't ever have to be yourself again, Wendy, I said on the phone.

It's Clio now, slut, she said. I could hear the smile in her voice.

The sun is coming up; I have been writing for a long time. It is the first week of December, and the sky is sooty with clouds. I'm working on an email to Jaxson about the next book. It has something in it of Arachne's story. Of what jealousy can do to love. Of what ambition can build out of silk.

My love—I've sent it to Celia already, I type. *I think you'll go wild. It's a story you might know.*

My notebook is close by. Lately I've been drafting long-hand. There's something more honest about it.

You might believe in the truth more than I do. But the truth is only one method with which to arrive at a purpose. The truth is a story, like any other. What matters most is how the story ends.

I met Celia for coffee in Midtown last week, after she'd read the book. She came down from her office in her fur coat and heels.

"This is good," she said, paging through what I'd sent her. "This is very, *very* good, Als—" She froze. "Jesus," she said.

"It's all right," I said. "I miss her, too."

"I don't," Celia said, going back to her pages. "You're much easier to work with."

"*Thank* you."

She set the pages down and leaned back in her chair. "Has he seen this?"

"Not yet. I wanted to show you first."

"He's not going to like it."

"He wrote it."

"People will think it's a confession."

"Maybe it is."

"You'll have to change the title. '*The Ghostwriter*'? Gives the whole game away."

"That's fine. Call it what you want."

"I'll have to check with Legal."

"Will there be a problem?"

"No," she said. "No, I don't think there will." She looked down at the pages again, back at me. "Is this—did he really—?"

I waited, but she left it hanging in the silence. "Would it matter?" I asked.

"Scandal's good for sales," she said, shrugging. "You can cash his royalty checks if he goes to jail."

Yes, I thought. *I certainly can.*

After my meeting with Celia, I went out into the New York winter: that vibrant and glamsy sky, snow-blown, the creamy glow of brownstone windows through the lowering storm like a picture out of a children's book. As it turns out, mine's a heart that needs cold to thrive. I walked to the bar Alison used to tell me about, the bar she'd loved. I'd found it a few months ago entirely by accident: an out-of-the-way door on the Lower East Side, a battered old signboard. I'd recognized the color of the light leaking out the window. *The only dive bar in New York with light like that.*

It was dark already, though not very late in the day, and the bar was empty. Inside it was tiny, vinyl-covered black stools at a silver counter like a fifties diner's, the bartender leaning into the rail in a way that suggested he was ready for a long night. I got a whiskey and sat in the window and looked out at the street that had been Alison's and was now mine, and I thought of the girls I'd been before and the girls I could still be someday, the girls nested endless within me, the stories I still had to tell.

How many times can you leave a life behind?

As many times as you want, as long as you're willing to do what it takes.

I finish my email to Jaxson, hit Send, light a cigarette. Perhaps today I'll visit the Met. I never get tired of Henri Rousseau. The lion in the desert, under a pale moon. The jungle full of animals, their eyes gleaming among the leaves. Do you know the most wonderful thing about Rousseau? In all his life, he never once set foot outside of France. Every jungle he painted was a jungle he'd never seen.

Inhale, exhale. The smoke rises. Books all around me. Cello suites, dark windowpanes.

And in the garden outside my window, snow begins to fall.

Fin.

Acknowledgments

Thank you: Jen Overstreet, designer extraordinaire; Manu Shadow Velasco, copyeditor par excellence; Meg Clark and Nathan Bransford, who have read more versions of this book than any human being should have to; and to you, dear reader, with love.

About the Author

SARAH MCCARRY is the author of the novels *All Our Pretty Songs*, *Dirty Wings*, and *About a Girl*, the editor and publisher of the chapbook series Guillotine, and the Executive Director of the Eve Kososfky Sedgwick Foundation. Her work has been shortlisted for the Lambda Award, the Norton Award, and the Tiptree Award, and she has received fellowships from the MacDowell Colony, the Joint Quantum Institute, and The Arctic Circle.

@sarahmccarry   sarahmccarry.net